Not Unkind and Not Unkind

JD Cameron

Published in 2008 by YouWriteOn.Com

Copyright Text JD Cameron 2008

First Edition

The author asserts the legal right of copyright

All rights reserved. No part of this publication may be reproduced, stored in a retrieval system, or transmitted in any form without the prior written consent of the author, nor be otherwise circulated in any form of binding or cover other than which it is published.

1.

Maxine is not my wife anymore but she appears to be. Everyone's happy that we've put our differences aside because apparently it'd be daft to throw away 20 years. There's food in the fridge and there's a line of herbs on the kitchen windowsill. She cooks every evening and if I'm not in she puts something to one side for me. She's on about sorting out the back garden because, she said,
- If I must live here, I want something beautiful to look at.

On a Monday she's out at yoga and on a Thursday she's out with her mate, Elaine. On a Saturday she does a big shop at *Sainsbury's* and every other Friday she's out with a bunch of mates I don't know doing things which don't concern me. Every other Saturday or so D and Linda come round or we go round to theirs. I don't know anymore if they're our friends or our co conspirators.

Maxine's moved herself and her cushions and pillows back into the bedroom. She said it looked like a grungy teenager had occupied it in her absence. She also said,
- Let's not fool ourselves, Simon, that this means anything.

In the morning we each get out of bed like we've had a regrettable one night stand which neither of us wants to discuss. We silently negotiate access to the bathroom and lock the door. She takes her clothes into the bathroom and gets dressed in there. If she's taking her time and I'm in a hurry, I'll knock quietly and politely on the door. If I take too long, she goes to the other bathroom. She never asks me how she looks and I never tell her. At night we go to bed and stake our claims to our respective sides of the bed. We don't read in bed these days because that'd involve one of us at some point having to ask the other to turn the light out. If, during the night, my foot touches her calf she flinches; if hers touches mine I move it. We do this every morning and every night.

I think it's probably fair to say that ours is not the sort of union that either of us envisaged ending up in. Things are not the best but they're at least predictable and it doesn't feel like anything's going to change anytime soon. I'm not so sure that I'm in a position to expect

much more with all that's gone off. I know she feels defeated by this but I can live with things the way they are; it doesn't hurt anymore and it barely touches me. There's things I could sort out: like understanding what it is that's led us both here and from time to time I've wondered – while we're laid out like corpses on the bed – what'd happen if I said summat to her, but I reckon it's too late for all that now. She'd say – and she'd be right – that I'm the one that's led us here, that I've made my choices and imposed them on her (in fact, she's said exactly that on more than one occasion). There's nothing more I want to know. The other night we found ourselves sat in front of the TV together and in a rare unguarded moment, she said,
- I can't forgive you, Simon.
I said,
- I don't expect you to, Maxine.

So that's where we're at. I don't expect Maxine to forgive me and I don't expect my Dad to issue some sort of posthumous statement of absolution. I've given up on all that. Elizabeth Jane Watson (19) may well be 20 by now and maybe she's put everything that's gone off behind her. Maybe she's one of these – unlike Maxine – who can forgive people for what they've done. If I knew she had, maybe it'd start a Mexican wave: I'd forgive myself then Maxine would forgive me and we'd truthfully reconcile. Maybe Eliz is somewhere in South East Asia – or wherever it is she's gone off travelling to - thinking that what once seemed so awesome is dwarfed by all these Buddhist temples she's staring at. Maybe Maxine'll grasp in time that there's no point holding on to the past and she'll become as pragmatic as I have about the future. She might realise that there are worse things in the world than this. Maybe pigs will fly.

You get all these groups that people can go to; they've survived this, that or the other and they get to talk to people in similar situations. It's all to do with realising you're not alone and sharing, apparently. I reckon they should have groups for people like me who've done something wrong but hardly anyone knows because we don't talk about it. Except, of course, people like me wouldn't go to a group.

I heard Maxine talking to Elaine the other night on the phone. I was busy pretending to be asleep because it's easier these days to feign sleep than to lie in bed obviously awake and silent with someone who clearly doesn't want to be there. She got out of bed quietly and continued the call from the landing. I strained not to hear but there were fragments that I caught,

- It's bloody awful, Elaine…I don't know what I'm doing here …I'm trapped. I can't move the kids again…It's a fucking mess, Elaine…I feel ashamed of him and of myself…

I don't know how I would've responded to that sort of call at that time of night but I hoped that Elaine would find some sort of positive or rousing spin to put on it. With all the self-help books she reads, you'd think that Elaine could locate some pearl of wisdom which would put Maxine's situation into perspective. She was out of the room for a good 20 minutes and when she crept back into the bed we reluctantly share I heard her sniffing and gulping as people do when they're trying not to cry out loud. It should've broken my heart.

People ask you, don't they, if you could change one thing in your life what it would be. I think about that sometimes but there's no single thing I can hold accountable for the way things've turned out. And, at the end of the day, things are not so bad. I look at the customers who come into my shop buying shit and thinking it's good enough or that it's all they can afford and I think, at least I'm not you. A woman came in the other day and she was pulling an ancient tartan shopping trolley behind her. She was getting on a bit and she was after something for her grandson but she couldn't remember exactly what it was. She'd the money in an envelope – to the penny - and I went through all the things that cost £49.99 with her. We eventually hit upon the shittiest MP3 player in the world. I imagined her grandson's face and his disappointment and I found her another, slightly less crap model at £69.99.

- There's an offer on. You can have this for the same price as that other one.

D – my mate and (unbelievably) business partner - said afterwards that I was a soft touch and that before we knew it, there'd be half a dozen coffin dodgers at the door wanting summat for nowt. So, the point is that being me is better than being her.

It's nearly Christmas and we've expanded our already diverse stock to include fibre optic Christmas trees and decorations. You can't move for baubles. The PA's been blasting out Christmas songs since the end of November; they're on a loop and I find myself whistling them even when I'm at home. We were putting up the tree the other day – a real one at Maxine's insistence – and she turned to me and said quietly,

- If you don't stop bloody whistling, I'm gonna strangle you with the Christmas lights.

The twins were there and they laughed in a way that struck me as cruel. It's come to something when your kids find the prospect of their mum killing their dad amusing. I've no idea what the kids are after for Christmas but there's a pile of wrapped presents in the bottom of my wardrobe and I expect they're from us to them. D's come upon a consignment of Indian gold that he informs me is top notch,

- If you're after summat for your lass, I think you'll find this'll meet with her approval.

I chose a bangle and declined his free engraving offer. I wrapped it in a sheet of gold paper and tried to imagine Maxine being the sort of person who could accept it without rancour. In the end I couldn't so I gave it him back and told him I wasn't sure it was her sort of thing. D and Linda have invited themselves round on the 23rd for dinner; Maxine said that since this festive fucking feast (her words, not mine) was going to happen anyway we might as well invite Tony and his missus from next door. Then she said,

- The more the fucking merrier.

She's written a list of things to buy. It's on the fridge and each day she ticks a few items off. I've to get a mixed case from *Oddbins*. What all this means is that she knows and I know I'm not going anywhere before Christmas, and then there's New Year and after that there's Maxine's parents' 40th anniversary. D's on about an excursion to Barcelona to celebrate the first birthday of our business venture in

June. We can fly from Leeds so, as Linda's pointed out, that's handy. D's put the money down on the flights and I've to sort him out nearer the time. Then there's the anniversary of my Dad's death and that'll doubtless involve something solemn and family – centred.

Last night – before we added new things to the list of things that have gone wrong between us - I went into the kitchen and Maxine was sat at the table as she often is these days. She was reading a book and in the background a CD played. Her hair was tied up in what they call a chignon. If I were someone who was allowed an opinion on these matters I would have told her it suited her. On the work surface there was a plate covered in clingfilm. It contained all your major food groups. Next to it, there was a bowl with a green salad in it and next to that a tiny jug that contained a dressing.

- Is that my dinner?

She nodded without looking up. I walked past her and put the plate in the fridge. I was hungry but I'd no time to eat. She said,

- There's poached figs and crème fraiche in the fridge as well.

I've never really been one for figs but I made a sound that, to the untrained ear, might sound approving. I stared into the fridge for longer than strictly necessary. Everything was perfect in there. I looked up and she was still looking down at her book.

- I'm off out, Maxine. Don't wait up.
- Like I would.

She turned to me and something rippled across her face which could have become a smile. I detected that I had a moment's grace. All I needed to do was to hold her gaze and then as I walked past her to the door I could pause. I could say something nice to her about how I appreciated the effort she'd gone to. Then she might say something like,

- Well, someone's got to be on top of making sure people eat properly in this house.

Then I could place both my hands on both her shoulders and if my touch was light she might not resist. I could ask her what she was reading and she wouldn't answer; she'd just lift the book up and show me the title and I'd say it looked interesting. Then I'd walk over to the

kettle and shake it and gesture towards her. She'd put a thumb up and say,
- All right then, if you're making one.

Then she'd go back to her book and she'd start whistling along to this Isley Brothers track she had on the CD player. I'd decide that whatever I had to do could wait so I'd leave my jacket on the back of the chair and sit down. And I'd say,
- What was that really good track of theirs?

And she'd say,
- *Harvest for the World.*

And I'd say,
- No, not that one. The other one.

It'd be *Love the One You're With* and I'd say,
- Why don't you put it on?

She'd go to the track and she'd say it reminded her of when we were young and daft and I was in my rare grooves phase and I'd drive round the place in the Golf Gti blasting out tunes and she used to say,
- Can't we just listen to Radio One, sweetheart?

I'd fetch over the tea and she'd be smiling and remembering, and everything that's happened between *Love the One You're With* and now would be forgotten for a while. I might suggest that we dance and she'd say, don't be bloody daft. But she'd let me drag her to her feet. She'd shuffle reluctantly for a few seconds then she'd relax and I'd say,
- When was the last time we danced together, Max?

She'd feel small and new and I'd trace her spine with my fingers. Maybe her forehead would find its way to my shoulder where it belongs. Maybe one of the kids'd walk in like they used to when we did things like this and one or the other of us'd tell them to piss off. When we'd finished dancing, I'd bring through a whole bunch of other CD's from the living room and while I was eating and we worked our way through a bottle of wine, she'd be laughing and carrying on about what this, that and the other track reminded her of. At some point, she'd look at the clock and say,

- Bloody hell. Where's the time gone?

She'd say she was tired and we'd go upstairs. If we'd got on top of all this at that moment, there was a bunch of other things I could have said to her. By the morning we would've been getting close to some sort of accommodation and I would've been spared everything that happened afterwards.

My phone vibrated. I glanced at it and it was a woman called Sarah who wouldn't stop texting me. I was supposed to be there half an hour ago and she reckoned that if I didn't get my arse into gear now she was off out. Maxine and her book became one again. The moment of grace had gone and with it whatever chance I had. It was all about timing and mine was off.

If I could change anything, it'd be everything mainly.

2.
If someone were to ask Maxine when it all went wrong, I reckon she'd pin it on the disaster that was my excursion into the IT business back in the 90's and on the events of Christmas 2003. She'd be wrong. It takes a lot more than a failed business, a traumatic festive season and a few poor decisions to produce the situation we now find ourselves in. I've been working towards this all my life. That said, the Christmas of 2003 is not one that either of us are likely to look back on with fondness.

      In 2003, I was out and about a fair bit. The weekends stretched from Thursday to Sunday till it got to the point where staying in was the new going out. To the dispassionate observer, my lifestyle probably looked a bit chaotic but there was a sort of order to it which was apparent to me if no one else. Fridays, for example, I'd knock off that bit early from the shop and leave the cashing up to Marcus. I liked to think of it as a professional development opportunity. I'd meet up with the lads in town and we'd go to the same bars we always went to then it'd be on to someone's house to round the night off. It'd get to that point where it was hard to say whether it was too early or too late. I remember one Saturday morning sitting at the bottom of someone's stairs in Headingley with some sad sap looking scared and carrying on like Chicken Licken: the sky's falling down and all that. He was on about,

      -    Where's our lass?

And I'd had to point out that the last time he saw our lass was Friday morning when he set off for work and it was now Saturday morning. And, no, she wasn't likely to want to come and fetch him right now on account of it being 6.30a.m. He was sat there; his face as still as stone except for the tears and I remember thinking thank God that I was on top of myself. There was an unlit cigarette hanging from the corner of his mouth and he was staring at the lighter in his hand as if he'd forgotten what it was for. I asked him what was wrong and he answered like he was a poet all of a sudden: I don't know what hurts anymore. Or Elvis Presley: I feel so lonely I could die. Whoever he'd come with had long gone and he was like the kid whose Mum hasn't turned up to collect him at the end of the party.

There was no reaching him but I tried, anyway, and it was like everything I said to make him feel better went through this contamination process before it reached him: all the positive stuff was filtered out and all he heard was stuff that made him feel worse. I said,

- Once you get home and get your head down, you'll feel better.

And he said summat like,
- I don't know what home is.

It was getting on for 7 by this time and I knew I had to get home and showered and off to the shop but he started making the sounds men make when they cry and I was drawn into this intimate thing where I had to hold him and let his shoulders judder beneath my hands and let his tears and snot soak into my shirt. And I wondered, what happened to my tie?

There were sounds coming from other parts of the house. Maybe a CD was stuck because all I heard was these same two bars coming at me over and over, and there were voices from down the tunnel in the kitchen where someone was making tea and someone else was asking if there was any bread in the house for toast. A woman with her hair all over the place squeezed past me on the stairs without saying excuse me. In another room, two people talked and talked at each other but neither heard nor cared what the other was saying. There's a word – atomised – that describes this.

In short, the night of 23 December 2003 was like any other night. When I got my act together and I got home I phoned Marcus and asked him to open up for me. I made some polite enquiry about how many staff we had on and told him I'd be in later when I'd sorted out the final few items on my Christmas shopping list. I didn't have a shopping list and I hadn't done any Christmas shopping.

I tried to sleep but then I remembered saying to some sad sap,
- I'm lonely too,

And I couldn't sleep. And I couldn't tell my head from my house because they were both sheds. Things wanted doing to the house to make it better. The bedding hadn't been changed in weeks but that was because I was barely ever in and if I was, chances were I'd crash downstairs. When I found myself alone at home and straight and awake, I was like a hotel guest: Where do they keep the sugar? What, no tea? This bathroom looks like it's not been cleaned in weeks. The neighbours hadn't said anything, but then I hadn't seen the neighbours. The tropical fish hadn't missed their tropical food – not once they'd died. The wheelie bins hadn't been wheeled out in a fair while on account of there being nothing to put in them and no one to wheel them out. The hallway was a sorting office. In short, Maxine had fucked off.

Back in the summer, just after she and the kids had gone, I'd looked out of the patio window and my garden was like *The Day of The Triffids* so - in a rare moment of lucidity - I got my brother in law to come round and concrete the back and front and he said,

- It's gonna look like a fucking car park.

And I said,

- Not if you don't paint white lines on it.

He must've alerted our lass because she came round and she was on about,

- What happened to the water feature?

So I said,

- What fucking happened to you?

I find that if you want to sleep and you can't sleep it can make you want to cry. Things come to the surface. If I'd had weed, I'd have been able to ride this one out and float down like a feather instead of plummeting right down to the bottom like a faulty lift but I'd checked all the debris in the bottom of the cigar box and it was just seeds and tobacco and crumpled *Rizla's*. There were other places – emergency places – I could check but I'd already checked those and it was like there'd been too many emergencies recently. It was time to use my one remaining lifeline. I texted D and I said,

- Sort my life out, fella.

I didn't want to make it sound too urgent. And I texted again and this time I said,

- If Charles is in the area, tell him he can drop by too.

Because it was Christmas and it was not the time to be knocking the Charlie on the head.

I found myself cursing that lad I'd comforted because he'd used me like a flannel to wipe up all his shit and now all his shit was my shit: I'm lonely too, for Chrissake. I went back upstairs to bed. I shook my head and hoped that all this stuff would trickle out of my ears like wax. I found myself thinking about what our lass used to say when things got on top like this. She'd say, just breathe. But thinking about our lass and breathing were not things I could do at the same time.

Outside, all the numb nuts and the winners and the losers were making all their noises. All the noises were directed at me through this mic that came straight into the bedroom and under the duvet to where my head was. If I closed my eyes I wouldn't see my hands clamped between my knees, but I might see worse things. All the worse things came, anyway, and it was like someone was squatting in my head and they were telling me all about myself and I couldn't stop them. They were extracting all the key points and summarising the issues of note by way of introduction, and I knew that soon they were going to be explicating and analysing and making links, and then they were gonna be concluding and recommending. So that by the end of it all, it would all make the worst sort of utterly coherent sense. If I tensed every muscle and made it into a wish, then someone might hear and take pity on me: please just let me sleep and then let me never wake up. I wish I'd never woken up.

3.

So, I was laid there thinking about how I was gonna properly get my head down and I was sweating like a good un by this time. I reached over and touched the radiator and told myself that was why I was so hot. I went downstairs to adjust the timer. Then I remembered that there was a half bottle of wine in the kitchen from that night I brought that lass back. She called herself Eliz; I've no idea why she shortened her name to Eliz when there's Liz and Lizzie and Beth to choose from, but I wasn't interested enough to ask because it wasn't like that was the point. She worked downstairs from my mate, Mick, as a PA to one of the Directors. She was leaving to go off travelling and I met her at her leaving do. She came back to mine because she lived in one of those places that ends in *ley* somewhere outside Leeds and there was no way she was getting a taxi back that close to Christmas. I drove her back to mine slowly and carefully in the full knowledge that my performance in the breathalyser stakes wouldn't stand close scrutiny. By the time I got her back she was looking less of a prospect. I suggested a glass of wine but she only liked white and I only had red so she mixed hers with orange juice: like Sangria, she said. She watched me build a spliff and when I asked her to select a CD, she'd not heard of anything I listen to. She said something about her younger brother who, I noted, was just a bit younger than my eldest. Which had got me thinking about how old I was and whether the number – 38 (or 35 if I was feeling lucky) – said anything about me at all. When I found an excuse to go to the bathroom for a line and a glance at myself in the mirror, I found that the man who stared back at me   looked older than I'd remembered; there were lines I hadn't anticipated and a weariness that told me I should be in bed alone. That pretty much killed the evening off but I persisted, anyway. Then I told her she was tired and directed her to a bedroom which was not my bedroom.

So, the one positive outcome of an otherwise wasted evening was that there was half a bottle of red wine in the kitchen. I poured it into a half-pint glass and downed it. I put the glass on the side with all the other glasses; it looked like someone had had a party but it wasn't me. The wine must've dislodged something because I managed finally not to be awake. No time later, there was a bomb exploding at the front door and then the mobile was ringing and then the bomb was going off again and then there was a car horn beeping. I leapt out of bed, all my senses alert like a full on commando, because it was D at the door.

- Now then, fella.

He let himself in and turned on the TV because he's lost without broadcast noise,

- All right, Si? Could do with a dust in here, mate.

He did the thing to the blinds that makes them let light in but there was no light because it was dusk suddenly and whatever the day was or could have been had gone. He put the TV on mute and pressed play on the CD remote; it was Bebel Gilberto. He pronounced it shit and wanted to know if I'd ditched my taste in music along with my pride in my surroundings. It was getting on and we could have been there all night talking rubbish. I told him I just needed enough for the holidays and maybe a bit more in case I was entertaining over the festive period.

- Like, fucking do drop by for drinks and all that?

If I hadn't known D since school and I wasn't so relieved to see him, I'd have smacked him. He carried on about what he'd got the kids and asked me what I'd got mine but I didn't know because getting the kids' stuff had been a matter of handing over a wad to our lass sometime in September. And then he was off on one about the size of the turkey and how it was full on *Cristal* with the scran this year. He'd got his missus two leather sofas; they'd only arrived that afternoon and he'd put a padlock on the living room door so as not to spoil the surprise. The way he was laughing at this cunning ruse, you'd think someone was tickling him.

- You're not after any leather sofas, are you?

Like they were the sort of thing you might run out of. I pointed at my two leather sofas - one of which he was sat on - and said,

- No, I've got plenty mate.

He shrugged, like I was missing out on a great deal and I was going to regret it sometime soon.

- Tyres? Full on *Michelin...Dunlop*? They're going like nobody's business. Winter and all that. Or there's your yoga DVD's. They're surprisingly fucking popular with the ladies. It means they can watch TV and exercise at the same time. Got one for our lass: stocking filler and all that. She'll love it. It's all your spiritual aspect and the fact that all the celebs are at it.

He put his hands together and wiggled his head round like he was straight out of *Bollywood*.

- Oh, and I've got gazebos, but to be honest they're enjoying limited appeal at this time of year. It's like I've said to people: in six months time, your missus is gonna be on at you about patios and outdoor heating solutions and barbecues and whatnot and all that'll be missing is your gazebo.

He squinted out at the concreted garden and let this particular offer drop. I strummed a tune on the arm of my leather sofa and looked at the clock. He was carrying on about Christmas cheer so I was forced to unearth the only remaining alcohol in the house which was a bottle of Absinthe that I'd bought for fuck all in Prague on a stag weekend. It was impossibly green. I combined it with sugar and water and he said,

- Heavy duty, man.

Being with D was like swimming through glue and I was trying to appear interested and engaged but all his carrying on was beginning to do my box in. I wondered how much more I needed to know about his various and predictable confrontations with staff in upmarket department stores:

- So I fucking said to her, listen, love… I think you'll find my money's as good as anyone else's so just hand over the fucking *Moschino* boxers and we'll say nothing more about it.

Eventually, he built a spliff and handed over the merchandise. The weed was seedy and the Charlie was lumpy but the Trades Descriptions Act didn't apply to this transaction. If I had the sense I was born with I'd take my custom elsewhere, but I've known D forever and I suppose he's what passes as a best mate. We know each other from school where we were both on the outside looking in: I had no mum and D had something in him which we now politely refer to as Asian. In a school like the one we went to, people like us sought each other out and formed ragged, cynical crews which prowled through the corridors trying to look menacing and unapproachable.

He told me he'd done me a good deal and added a little extra in. I took it that this was my Christmas present. I handed him a wad which he failed to check and I did the closest thing to relaxing that it's possible to do in D's company.

He got up to go finally, but he'd stuck around that long I was wondering whether he was expecting a Christmas bonus like you'd give the paperboy or the milkman. The visit needed winding up,

- Cheers, mate. See you at the do on Boxing Day.
- Will you be bringing your lass?

I pointed out that, things being as they were, I couldn't be certain that she'd be accompanying me on this occasion. I also alerted him to the inaccuracy of his description of her relationship to me.

- In case you hadn't noticed, our lass doesn't live here anymore. Neither do the kids. Taking these factors into account, I'm not so sure she is our lass anymore.

It was a tough thing to say and I didn't like the way the words tasted in my mouth. He shook his head and said things about the importance of family and how it was always possible to rescue things. I agreed because to disagree would prolong the conversation.

It was getting on. I sorted my life out a touch and planned my Christmas shopping. I drove up to the off licence for any expensive single malt for my Dad and half a dozen bottles of assorted spirits for assorted family members. *M&S* was still open so I swept the shelves for Belgian chocolates, biscuits, liqueurs and gift sets. I stood in the queue feeling alert and responsible and thinking I was like all the other men in there only that bit faster and that much less discerning. I could've wrapped up the house in the gift-wrap I bought.

There was a big bit of me that felt good and on top of things and that wondered how I'd let myself feel so shit that morning or the previous night or whenever it was. I told myself that I was lucky that I was the kind of man who could shake himself out of all that and get back on top of his game without having to leak into someone's shirt. The queues were long and staff in Santa hats walked up and down offering luxury assortment biscuits and mince pies. All around, I could sense some men getting a bit fraught, a bit anxious, but me – this new, improved Simon James Williams – I was on top of my game and so I exchanged these knowing looks with other men: raising our eyebrows and exhaling with a *sshhh* and shaking our heads at each other and I was thinking,

-D'you know summat: Christmas is not all that bad.

I was even thinking that I might pass by hers this evening on my way out and see the kids: Merry Christmas and all that. First, though, I needed to nip into the shop and cash up before the Christmas break. By the time I got there, my manager was pulling down the steel blinds. I tried to remember when I'd last been there.

- Wondered where you'd got to, Si. I tried you on your mobile earlier but there was no answer.

I let this little dig go because if I responded to all of Marcus's digs we'd never get any work done. I told him something about last minute shopping and asked him how we'd done. It had been manic apparently; there'd been a run on a budget *Yamaha* amplifier and he reckoned we should've have ordered more in.

- The minidisc players have not gone down so well. I reckon we're gonna have to discount them in the New Year. The *XTC* lighting effect's gone well and the *PV 2600's* done ok.

What he was saying basically was that all the stock he'd insisted we order in had gone well. He can be a bit anal, can Marcus, when it comes to matters audiovisual but then so are a lot of our customers. He lives alone and spends more time than is healthy contributing to online electronics forums. I made a routine query about his plans for the festive season and he told me why it was he was off to his auntie's this year rather than his Mum's. It was all to do with his Mum's new fella. I congratulated him on taking a stand. He plotted out for my benefit where everyone else in his extended family stood on what struck me as a needlessly complicated (and time – consuming) issue. I nodded and made the sounds you're supposed to make to indicate interest while I reconciled the till. I eventually persuaded him that he needed to be getting home and I finished off the cashing up.

By the time I pulled up outside my house I was running late. I shifted all my *M&S* bags into the boot, ran into the house and got shaved and showered and changed. I tilted my head back and all was looking safe in the nostril department. I examined myself in the full-length mirror on the way out and, to be honest, I wasn't looking so bad. Fair enough, my skin was a bit sallow and I wondered how much longer I could plausibly say I had black hair but at least it wasn't receding. Back when Maxine loved me, she'd tell me I had beautiful eyes and she'd try to find a way of describing their colour.

- Are they grey or are they hazel?

She'd stare right into them like a new word for their colour would reveal itself to her. It never did.

At my suggestion, we were keeping it local that night so I drove up to one of the many bars half a mile from my house which over the previous year or so had transformed the neighbourhood into a convenient destination for alcohol tourists from across North Leeds. I'd decided to leave the car there and walk home because I'm a responsible man.

Then, without warning, it was 7 o'clock on Christmas morning and I wondered where the time had gone and what I'd done with it or what it had done with me. On the positive side, I was at home. I find that sometimes I need visual cues to remind me of stuff and on this occasion the figure located at my left below served this function. Eliz was a lump in the bed next to me. The pillowslip was stained with her lipstick. She was sleeping - which I classified as a result on account of at least she wasn't whining anymore. She was there because she reckoned I'd told her the other night that I was going to be in this bar or that bar on Christmas Eve, and because her friends had made alternative arrangements (for reasons which became obvious as the evening ground on), she turned up. She clung on to me all night like she was some extra limb I'd sprouted. As the night ground relentlessly on, she told me things I didn't need to know and was under the impression that I was different – from whom, I don't know - but she gave me the clear impression that being different was a good thing. (Within a couple of days, I was to unburden her of this optimistic assessment of my character). She followed me back to Terry's and huddled in the kitchen with Terry's missus carrying on about love and how you know when it's right and I hoped she wasn't talking about me.

The kids next door screamed like they were frightened and I remembered that it was Christmas morning. Everything in me knew I had to get Eliz out of my bed and over to where she lived before I got on the road. Tea looked considerate so I made her a cup of tea and nudged her awake and told her that I'd give her a lift home. She wiggled over to the window and parted the curtains.

- I was hoping for a white Christmas.

She sounded genuinely disappointed. I commiserated with her over the absence of snow and told her we'd best be getting a move on. I told her it'd been fun because it probably had. I gave her my mobile number and took hers and stored it under "don't answer" so I'd know to reject her call if she rang. I wondered for a moment precisely why what had happened between us had happened but concluded that it probably didn't matter since it would never happen again. She sipped her tea slowly like we had all the time in the world.

I got showered and tried to remember where it was I'd left my car. My mouth tasted like a cocktail shaker and I brushed my teeth and tongue for several minutes. I disinfected my mouth with *Listerine* and downed a double dosage of extra strength *Alka Seltzer*. I practiced smiling at myself in the mirror and I looked like someone kids should be scared of. I told her to just wait there while I went to fetch the car. She asked me whether I didn't fancy just snuggling up for a couple of minutes. I didn't.

I wondered – as I drove her home – how long it takes for alcohol to leave the system. On the way, she told me how nice it had been and I was glad she didn't know my second name. She wondered aloud what she'd be getting for her Christmas and speculated that it'd all be travel related. I think she maybe wanted me to ask about her trip and to show some interest in South East Asia and Australia and wherever else it was she was going. But I was preoccupied and hungover and poor company. I dropped her off, kissed her cheek and said something about seeing her around. As she walked up the path, I wound down the window and wished her a merry Christmas. It felt like the right thing to do.

I drove back to Leeds and I knew the reason the roads looked all wrong and like I was driving through a film set was because I shouldn't be driving. I put a CD on but all the CD told me was that I was rubbish.

It was Mental o'clock and there was no way I was getting to where I needed to get to unless I did stupid things. There was shit in the boot that wanted wrapping but most of it was not going to get wrapped. On the way to my house, I dropped in at my Dad's and Maureen was there. She was there because she lives there. He got his whisky and she got a *Deluxe Pamper Set* and a bottle of brandy. I sat down for a little while and smelt the turkey and listened to them tell me that they were having a quiet one this year and told myself not to feel bad. I refused the *Bailey's* because I was driving. Yeah, right. I made a promise I knew I was going to break about Boxing Day. They walked me to the front gate and my Dad handed me a bunch of stuff I'd to give the kids.

- Tell them I've kept the receipts in case they want to change anything.

He started to tell me what it was he'd got each of them and how he and Maureen were in *Debenhams* for ages trying to decide on a perfume for our Stephanie. In the end, they went to *Harvey Nichols* because, as it turns out, there's no difference in price. I said,

- You'd never think it, would you?

But really I was thinking, please just let me go. Maureen lurched towards me in a way that suggested a hug might be in order. I allowed her to put her arms around me and over her shoulder I saw my Dad glance at me with a look which expressed either relief or despair. Sometimes it's difficult to distinguish between the two.

I got home. There was a landfill of random gifts that I'd shifted into the living room. I didn't know who they were for and I found I'd no sellotape but there was a *Pritt Stick* somewhere. I'd bought it when I was trying to make a good impression with Maxine. The idea was that I'd spend quality time with the twins making a scrap book which they'd take back to hers at the end of my contact visit. It'd be a tangible illustration of my engagement and commitment – qualities which I apparently lacked. In the end, I was running late and it was easier to go to the cinema. Which was me all over, according to Maxine.

It took me stupid time to find the *Pritt Stick*. The gifts stuck to me as I dropped them in the boot. I got back into the house and my head was in bits; I tried to avoid my own gaze as I bent over a CD and scratched it with my *Mastercard*. I was on top of what remained of my game again and it was only Mad Man o'clock. When I got to hers, I said,

- You all right, Maxine?

And she answered like I'd asked her a different question,
- So what happened to you last night?
And I said,
- What d'you mean?

And she said,

- You phoned and said you were coming round to wish the kids Merry Christmas and all that? You're a fucking waste of space. D'you know that? You're a fucking waste of space.

But there was still a window of opportunity on account of she was smiling at these flowers I must have got from *M&S* and they were in my arms like I knew what they were doing there and she said,

- Fucking orchids; you know what I'm like for orchids. You little bastard.

And I felt like shit, actually, because these flowers were just one of my many random purchases and I'd forgotten about how she loved orchids and I was having to carry on like I knew what I was doing: like there was some grand plan. She put her arms around me like she meant it - because she did - and I had to pretend to be decent and misunderstood when in fact I was some arsehole who'd ditched some girl in somewhere ending in *ley* because I didn't want her to think that I was an arsehole. And I'd left my dad marooned with this woman he was pretending to want to be with when really I knew – for all your whisky and cigars – he'd rather I'd stopped for more than 30 minutes. Which I would have, were I not so fucked up. But I was somewhere else now and I'd no other plans so maybe there was time to make amends to someone at least. At last. But first – because I was on a topping up vibe – I needed to go upstairs and find myself a flat surface and a door that locked.

From then on, it was gonna be weed all the way because she'd be all right with that once dinner was out of the way and our Stephanie'd sloped off to her boyfriend's house and our Ben was communing with the PC and the twins were buzzing off their selection boxes and games consoles. Then we might be able to sit down – the two of us – and peel back the years and I could become like I was or I hoped I was. We'd been through some major unnatural disaster - me and our lass - and it was hard to remember how things were. I had a mate once – he worked at YTV – and he told me about how much footage you have to shoot for a five-minute scene. It's all in the editing. You've got a story to tell and that means you've got to take most stuff out so the story flows. By the end of the day, the past nine months would be on the cutting room floor where they belonged.

It was the end of March when it had all kicked off. It came on the back of a rumbling discontent that'd become the soundtrack to our marriage. She'd been on at me for years about one thing or another: there was all the predictable stuff about loving me but not liking me and her being a valuable person whom I failed to value but those were only the words she put round feelings she'd had for years. They were words which told me what I already knew and which I felt about her too - as you would after so long. You don't go around saying them unless it's for effect, so that when all those words are said you can each make promises you won't keep about how you'll change and how things will get better. There was nothing specific, though - no one cataclysmic event or final straw (none that I was aware of at the time, anyway) which came close to explaining her next move.

She's always been one for kicking off, has Maxine, but when she told me to go she was calm and cold and she looked at me like I was someone she didn't want to know anymore. What she actually said was that we couldn't go on like this anymore, like it was an irrefutable fact. I told her that we couldn't just kick 18 years into touch; I said something about shared history and the kids (which was a mistake because then she went off on one about where I was at the twins' last birthday and where I was when our Stephanie's boyfriend was carrying on alarming and she'd had to call the police. I was in a bar with my mates, which was apparently where I always was when things got tricky).

- The truth is, Simon, you don't give a toss and you haven't given a toss for years. I'm like something you've got in the back of the wardrobe that you've not worn for years but you keep hold of just in case you find some use for it in the future.

To be honest, that hurt. She said it was because the truth always does. Then she said – and this threw me – that our marriage was like a public show of private grief. With everything that's gone off since, I've thought about that little phrase a fair bit. Obviously, I accused her of all sorts. I wanted to know who she'd traded me in for and I told her that he'd get as sick of her as I had. She, of course, said there wasn't anyone else then she made a generalisation about men and how we're all the fucking same in the end. I stacked up all the things I'd done for her and all our plans (though, as she pointed out, these were all plans she'd made to which I'd grunted assent). A guy she'd been seeing when I first met her insinuated himself into the conversation and I wanted to know where he lived now and when last she'd seen him. She pointed out that she was 18 at the time and that I had no say over what she did before I met her.

    I did and said all the stuff you say when you realise that a woman's serious: things you fob off as being to do with the heat of the moment and which don't bear close scrutiny afterwards. I wondered, but couldn't ask, whether she'd found summat out and I waited for her to hit me with some undeniable proof of some minor misdemeanour. But she didn't say anything about any of that and obviously I didn't press the point. I kept on telling her that she didn't mean it and she kept on telling me that she did and that could have gone on forever like some twisted pantomime if I hadn't have grabbed her shoulders and told her to shut the fuck up. I might have shaken her a bit – in the heat of the moment - and maybe (if you're a stickler about these things) that means that I got physical with her, but that wouldn't make any sense because I've always said that raising your hand to a woman is all wrong. When it became obvious that she wasn't going to be backing down anytime soon, I told her there was no fucking way I was going anywhere and that if she was so keen to terminate this thing then she could leave. Which was when it became apparent that she'd planned for just such an eventuality.

    By the time the leeches were involved with their negotiations and their shared equity and their contact orders, there was no time to think about the hows and whys of it all. Eighteen years became an unwanted gift that we each wanted a refund on.

    It was a Wednesday when she left. By the time I got home that evening, it was like a SWAT team had been in and obliterated every trace of her and the kids. I cried for two hours then I stopped crying then I started crying again. Then I called D and he came round and told me to be a man, which is what I've been ever since.

But all that was a long time ago and it was Christmas and all was good for the time being. I was stood with her in the kitchen – her with her hair (blonde; it suited her) and her smallness. Every time she's in the kitchen she shrinks because heels are a health and safety hazard. She was properly on top of the whole cooking malarkey on account of that's what she does day in, day out. *Epicure Consultancy* is what she calls her firm. She preps like she's in a restaurant kitchen and – years ago - I used to look at her from the doorway and think it was like watching one of those TV chefs only quieter. So, I was stood there and she was glazing and reducing and sautéing. The sprouts were sliced and done with almonds and she'd done things to make the turkey tender and succulent. The potatoes were par boiled then shaken then roasted and onions were baked with cream and something else. She'd done poached pears in wine and they'd be served with some sort of flavoured cream or crème fraiche. There was mash but it was sweet potato which tastes nothing like potato. The stuffing wasn't your *Paxo Sage and Onion*. She asked me to stir the gravy and taste it: Did it want more seasoning? The salad was as green as grass after summer rain and her forehead glistened. I offered to wipe her brow like I was a gentleman or a lackey and she said,

- I think I can manage that, sweetheart.

Suddenly, I knew what the word meant: it meant my heart was sweet. I could have said something poignant and what would it have taken – under those circumstances – to do that? Too much. The moment passed and she was handing me warmed plates and polished cutlery and napkin rings. I said,

- I've got champagne. It's been in the car all night, so it'll be cold.

And I fetched it. I was something like a man in a house which was not my house and on whose door I had to knock. But it was all good; the kids were bickering but not in a bad way and between us all there was some sort of choreography which allowed each of us to glide in and out of the kitchen with serving plates and gravy boats. I carved because I was the man and I piled up the plates and proposed a toast. It was to better times or to the past or to the future; I could have said more because I was feeling that way out. I could have gone on about how nothing matters but being around the people you love and who love you, but our Ben was squirming like he does and I thought, maybe later. At first the kids talked to me like I was a family friend they saw only occasionally; they asked about work and football and Auntie Jo and Auntie Sandra. Then they remembered who I was and the distance shrank and they were taking the piss out of me in a good way. They were looking at me and our lass like this was the way they wanted us to be together. They were full on remembering things that I'd forgotten about holidays and when I'd said or done this, that or the other. I was thinking, this is their history and they wanted me to confirm it so I did and I added in some stuff they'd forgotten and stuff they wouldn't know about from when they were tiny. I told Stephanie that we were her age – 18 - when we met and not much older when we had her. I was surprised at how much I remembered about Stephanie being born with her thumb in her mouth and Ben and his chickenpox and how Nina always spoke for Danny till they were three years old and then suddenly one day Danny said, shutup, Nina. And I was saying stuff to them about when I first met our lass and I thought I wasn't good enough for her and how it was much, much later that she said that she didn't feel good enough for me. And she said,

-Give up, you.

She cuffed me on my shoulder. And she was looking at me like she cared. And I was full on loving her at that moment with all the things we'd produced between us around us. There was a moment when we found ourselves glancing at each other and the years really did peel back; it was all in the eyes and in the way we knew that there was nothing unknown between us. I said,

-Been through the mill, babes.

And she said nothing but smiled straight at me.

I stared at my food and I knew I couldn't eat because every decision I'd made since D came round had made me ditch my appetite. She covered up for me and went on about how I'd eaten at my Dad's earlier.

In the kitchen afterwards she loaded the dishwasher,

-You're at it again, aren't you Si? It's fucking Christmas and you're bang at it.

She wasn't even shouting. I held my plate in my hand. The gravy and my sweet heart congealed.

4.
So she wasn't happy obviously – and understandably. I could have explained that there was a world – the one I lived in – where this all made sense: that I was on top of it all. I could've told her that she wasn't really in a position to be getting on her high horse and I could have carried on about stones and glass houses but all that would have been stoking the flames when what was needed right then was to just let the embers burn themselves out. So I said something which was not entirely untrue about being out with a bunch of mates and it being rude not to indulge.

  She took the plate out of my hand, scraped it and put it in the dishwasher.

  - When are you off, Simon?

  I didn't answer. What I wanted to talk about was that it'd worked, being sat there with her and the kids looking something like a normal family and feeling a bit like someone who I imagined I used to be: pulling crackers, reading jokes and trading trinkets. I wanted to know, but didn't ask, what'd made her bring all this up now on Christmas Day when I was doing my best to be a decent human being. There are men I know and she knows who'd need to be dragged - kicking and screaming - to spend time with their missus and kids. Except she wasn't really my missus anymore. I'd turned up in good faith and what did I get? Noise in my head. I let these small thoughts sit and linger for a few moments then I let them out like breath and they were gone. I stood and watched her wipe down the surfaces. I picked up a tea towel hoping she'd give me something ~~ but she just looked at me for too many seconds like she was expect~~ me to answer her question, so I said,

-Listen, babes, I'm sorry. Will you forgive me?

-What's the fucking point in being sorry? And what's the fucking point in forgiving you?

Our Ben loomed in the doorway, all angles and awkwardness, and said,

- Are we gonna open the presents or what?

The atmosphere was frozen and foggy like the worst driving weather but I was still hopeful that this could all be turned round. Maxine made her face into a smile and I followed her into the living room.

The kids liked whatever it was I'd got them. They gave me stuff they wanted me to like so I did. Our lass had got me an electronic organiser that did all sorts: e-mail, diary, full *qwerty* keyboard. She told me that I'd have no excuses from now on for not turning up or for turning up late. Fact was, it just gave me one more excuse because if there was one thing I'd have put money on it was that I'd lose this thing before New Year. I went out to the car and shook some boxes trying to remember what was inside them and this turned out to be harder than I'd imagined. I patted the breast pocket of my shirt and checked that the back up envelope and wad were there. It was an A5 envelope; it was crumpled and it didn't look too festive but I'd written something nice on it about love so it would have to do. I gave her that first. I honestly had not got a clue how much I'd put in there but she said it was too much so I said to her,

- Look, put it towards a flight to Canada.

One of her mates from school lives in Canada and she was always on about going to see her. She said,

- I'll be able to fly Business Class with this.

I said,

- You're worth every penny.

She smiled and leaned over and kissed me on the cheek. And I wondered where the fuck I'd got that sort of money from. And then I told her I'd got her one or two little bits and pieces as well and gingerly handed over half a dozen identical boxes each of which, miraculously, contained something different from the previous one. She looked at me with an expression I recognised. It said, why can't you be like this the whole time? From a big *M&S* bag, I took out unwrapped stuff which I said was for the family: there was a box of those tiny bottles of beer which our Ben'd work his way through; there were two bottles of whatever it is *M&S* pass off as *Bailey's*; there were biscuits and chocolates and a presentation cheese platter with chopping board and knife; there was a gift box of liqueurs and a gift box with two shot glasses and a tiny bottle of tequila which our Stephanie said ooh, that's cute to. With a flourish, I extracted a bottle of brandy and said to Stephanie,

- Give that to your chap.

I couldn't remember whether she'd ever told me his name, but in any case I didn't remember it. I threw the car keys to Ben and asked him to go fetch a couple more bottles of champagne from the boot. I was a full on Santa Claus but I was feeling a bit flat all of a sudden and I wished the kids'd piss off so I could build up and try and chill. There was shit all around me: piles and piles of paper; the sickly smell of chocolate and booze: just too much stuff, really. Because I looked like someone who was doing the right thing, though, the universe accommodated me. Stephanie stood up,

-I'd best go see Tom.

So I said,

- Are you sure you're all right walking, love?

Not that she'd any choice because I wasn't going to be driving anywhere anytime soon. She looked at me like I was daft.

- He's only three doors away, Dad.

She kissed me on the cheek before leaving. I should have framed that kiss. Our Ben mumbled something indecipherable which our lass translated as him being off to see his mates down the road. Nina and Danny were mashed on chocolate and E numbers and we carried them upstairs. I realised I didn't know where their bedrooms were so I followed our lass and found that they shared a room, which

made me feel bad because when we all lived toge_
bedroom each and it made me question what I was doing living in a
big house all on my own like fucking *Charles Foster Kane*.

I remembered that when she first moved out, she'd rung me and carried on about the heating.

- The heating's fucked.

I sighed because I was thinking about the places I needed to go to. But instead I said,

- What d'you mean it's fucked?

So she said,

- I turned it on and all the radiators are stone cold. They heat from the bottom up, don't they? Well, they're not.

I patiently instructed her to look in the small window in the boiler where the flame goes *whoosh*. But she reckoned there was no window even though there had to be. She went off and checked again and, returning, told me that there were lights called neons which flash to indicate a fault. The neon illustrated by a flame was not flashing and the boiler was making the sort of low humming noise a boiler might make if it were working. There were knobs as well, she told me. I remember thinking,

- Please make this the type of standard query that can be dealt with over the phone because I've got places to go where I should be already.

I told her not to touch the knobs. Emphatically - like I was giving someone telephone instructions on how to defuse a bomb. She went off and checked the radiators again and came back and told me that two of them were ok but the rest were lukewarm. I told her to bleed them and what to bleed them with.

- Turn it till you hear the gas start hissing. When it stops hissing and starts gurgling, turn it back.

I was on my way out and the phone rang again. I knew it was her so I got the sighing and cursing out of the way before I answered it.

- It's me again. Hissing and gurgling: which order?

I told her things hiss then gurgle and then the whole space is filled with water and everything is good. If the heat doesn't go all the way up, you might need to bleed again till all the space is full…

-To the top… does it sometimes take a while for the heat to rise right the way up?

So I told her she'd to wait till the whole radiator's full – to the very top – of hot water. Then all the hissing and gurgling stops and heat radiates everywhere. And I felt like I was talking her down like she'd talked me down so many times before, so though she irritated me to hell and I'd gone way beyond late, I felt like I'd been an all right person. I wished I was there and she could see how good I am at all this stuff, and I could see how much she needed me but it just wasn't a doable thing right then. And she said, before she put the phone down,

-I'm sorry to go on, Si. I need to get on top of all these things: bleeding and all that.

There was all sorts of stuff I could've said then like,

- Listen, I'm on my way, babes or shall I nip round or d'you want me to come round and have a look at the boiler if you're concerned?

I knew that any one of the above were what she wanted to hear because for all her carrying on about heating and bleeding, all she wanted was for me to be with her at that precise moment. But I said none of these things because there was a girl called Helen beeping her horn outside. So I just said,

- Stop apologising.

I lowered Nina into her narrow bed and I found myself wondering what had happened to Helen and whose hands her big tits were in now. I half considered renewing our acquaintance, it being Christmas and all that. There was just enough room for a small person to squeeze between the twins' beds, and the bedroom was a mess and wanted decorating. It was the sort of thing I could do or pay someone to do. I prised myself through the space and stood close to the door where I could breathe. And I properly needed a spliff on account of the way my head was trying to deal with Helen and with our lass and her bleeding. And the two things were spliced together in my head like that was how they were supposed to be, and one of them told me something I didn't need to know about the other. There was a time when I honestly felt that I couldn't live without our lass but the fact was I could and I had and I would. And being there was mainly about making me feel better about myself: less callous. I wondered, then, what it was I made of her and what she made of me. There was something like a full on bond which made neither of us happy but it was what we both knew and understood and (maybe, maybe, maybe) loved in each other. It was a secret we kept from each other.

I bent and kissed Nina on the forehead because it felt like the right thing to do and there was a moment when we stood in the doorway and the silence felt awkward, so I said,

- Make sure you only spend that money on yourself, Max.

And before the final syllable left my lips I remembered where it was I'd got that wad from: it was the fucking Christmas Eve cash takings. Looking back now – with what they call the benefit of hindsight – I wonder how differently things might've turned out if I hadn't remembered where the money was from or if I'd remembered a few hours or a couple of days later. But stuff happens when it happens and there's no changing it. I remembered putting the takings in the envelope and thinking to myself, remember to take £200 from this for our lass and deposit the rest when the banks open. The cash had to be there for the New Year bonuses that everyone had been promised and which would be hitting their accounts straight after Christmas. There were also direct debits and the VAT bill I'd just written a cheque for. And I'd given it all to our lass. I tried not to think about how much was in there but I knew it had to be a shed load because on Christmas Eve the shop's always full of bewildered mothers with lists of sound and light equipment for their sons and they invariably pay with the cash they've been putting by for months. Come January, their sons would be in wanting to swap whatever it was they'd been given for something more like what they were after in the first place. But that was a different story and one I couldn't even think about right then because then and January were separated by an envelope whose contents meant I might have no staff come the New Year. I carried on like someone whose only concern was the twins for a few seconds then said to her,

    - I'm just off for a slash. I'll see you downstairs.

In the mirror, I saw that I'd become someone whose face I vaguely recognised but couldn't put a name to. I splashed my face with cold water repeatedly and my nose was bleeding slightly. I let the cold water run for a long time and doused my face again, paying particular attention to the nasal area and it looked like it'd stopped but she had white towels and one of them had pink stains on it. I shoved it to the bottom of the laundry basket and replaced it with another. There was some sort of hair gel device on the glass shelf and I ran a slick of it through my bad hair then I splashed my face again and again till I began to feel sane.

When I got downstairs, my sister in law was there and she'd brought some cheap shit round for the kids. Mand's a year younger than our lass though you'd never know it to look at her. She's grown fat and married and there were mounds of flesh seeping out from her too small top but she's all right is Mand.

    - Now then, Si, long time, no see.

I said,

    - Not bloody long enough.

She wrapped me up in her blubbery embrace and she smelt of tobacco and talc. She told me I'd lost weight and launched into some anecdote about this man down the road whose missus had left him and how the weight just dropped off him; turned out it was all down to stress. Men are no good on their own, she told me, and looked at me meaningfully. Our lass raised her eyebrows like she'd heard this story before and if I didn't intervene, she'd be off on one and there'd be no stopping her. I asked her where David was and she told me he was slumped in front of the TV watching any fucking crap, rat arsed and full of turkey and stuffing. He'd said that was where he was stopping till he went back to work. She told me he was a waste of fucking space but I could tell she didn't mean it. She wasn't stopping, she said, which counted as a result in my book. I told her to wait one minute while I went out and found something which felt like a bottle and presented it to her. I told her she could top David up with it if he started looking restive. She laughed and said,

- I could do with him being a bit more restive. Know what I mean, Max?

I didn't need to tell our lass I was stopping. She'd softened with the champagne and the weed, and she'd had a cheeky snort herself as it goes. The bits of herself she didn't normally reveal to me came to the surface like a rash. It turned out, she didn't know how to love anyone but me and I was thinking, this is all good, but...and then she was on about stuff I didn't remember; about stuff we'd said to each other fucking aeons ago. Truth is, it wasn't touching the sides. I liked her better when she was carrying on at me about how fucking shit I was because that at least had a ring of authenticity about it. The only reason she was telling me all this shit was because I'd brought her down to my level. I wanted her to be better than I was because that was what I thought I could never live without. I said,

- Be who you are, Max. Tell me to chill or to breathe or tell me about a book you're reading that I'm not interested in.

That person would listen and would do herself what she said I should do. She might even be someone I could discuss my predicament with and who would call me a daft bugger as she handed me back the envelope. Then she'd have had a go at me and she'd have told me I needed to get on top of myself; that the way I was carrying on was not going to get me anywhere. She might have told me to leave at that point and that we'd talk about all this in the morning. Which would've been a good idea, looking back.

If she were still that person, she'd not have been sat with me snorting shit and being something she thought was honest but wasn't. Her hair was all over the place and her face was dripping down her skull. She fired words at me and they mainly missed their target but they were for her benefit and not mine. And the whole time I was sat there nodding I was wondering how I might introduce the subject of the cash and my future solvency. But she must've drawn me in because in no time we were talking on top of each other and there was a pile of words in between us that wanted sifting and putting in some sort of order but nobody was going to be putting them into order anytime soon. I knew suddenly that she loved me so much and so foolishly that she'd rather lose herself than lose me. And I wondered whether the way she was being was all down to me and whether anything that'd happened that day meant anything at all.

I was having a hard time understanding why it was she wanted me back when she was the one who'd told me it was all over. We were nine months on and it was like every true thing she'd said to me turned out not to have been true after all. Or - as she explained quietly - it was true at the time but no longer. Feelings – she told me – changed. And I was left wondering how, in that case, I was supposed to hold on to anything. If she'd just shut the fuck up and let me process all this in my own time, chances were we'd have slipped back naturally and effortlessly into something which worked but which left me room for manoeuvre round the edges but she was on at me like she was trying to make amends for something and I didn't know what that could be. All of which got me wondering what it was she'd done that she was so sorry for.

Finally, I didn't have to think because there was stuff I'd introduced my brain cells to which was doing the thinking for me.

We went to bed and it was shit mainly.

5.

We were laid in her bed with just the bedside lamp on. I'd managed to excavate a small space which was free of all the cushions and pillows she'd artfully strewn everywhere. She'd lost weight and her body felt like it belonged to someone else. My stomach turned. I tried to track back to where things got so fucked, to identify one decision I'd made whose consequences might come close to explaining why I was there in bed with a woman who should hate me and whose love was sucking the marrow out of me. She talked and talked at me, saying the same thing over and over like she was one of those dolls where you pull the string in the back and it says stuff but not stuff like,

- I think I'd die, Simon, if I didn't have you.

And I had to say things like,

- But you haven't got me.

It was clearly the wrong thing to say even though it was true. I told her she shouldn't settle for someone like me but the truth was, we were both trapped and we were neither of us trying to escape. It was a bit like what D told me about this lad he'd met in prison one time who said that he found it easier being inside than outside.

- This is like one of those open prisons where you get to go out to work during the day but you're banged up at night. It's like a pre release scheme.

Once I'd made this astute observation, I was struck by my own brilliance but she looked at me like I'd lost it so I took it back and told her to ignore me. And she said that I'd been ignoring her for the past God knows how long so she just needed to learn from my example. I let that one go.

I was still trying to track back, trying to retrieve the footage I'd edited out over the years but her words licked at me like flames and it was difficult to follow any one thought through to its conclusion. All these pictures formed themselves behind my closed eyes and they were like those flash cards she used when the twins were little. I held them up in my mind and told myself what they were. I settled on one image and it was a photograph from the *Yorkshire Evening Post*, taken a good eight or nine years previously, of Joe and me when they did a profile of our IT business. This was after I'd ditched the procurement job and before I'd moved into sound and light equipment. Mine has been a varied career. At the time, Leeds was just about beginning to believe its own publicity: we were the fastest growing city in the country; the biggest legal centre outside London. The Council told us we were world class and visionary and enterprising. Leeds was big and broad, macho and brash and it didn't suffer fools. Me and Joe – my business partner - liked to think of ourselves as the epitome of all that stuff. We'd worked together at a utilities company: I was an aspiring procurement manager and he was something in IT. One Friday evening, at the ritual after work session, he'd told me that there was a lot more to be made out of setting up on our own. He'd a few good contacts and with my managerial skills we'd make a killing. I talked to D about it, naturally, and he said,

- It's what I've always said to you, Simon, mate: it's your entrepreneurial spirit. That's the only way you're gonna make it in this country.

It was all surprisingly easy. We got in at the right time and in no time we'd a city centre office, an expensive coffee machine and a receptionist called Angela who preferred to be called Angelique. We'd a tab at a couple of nice bars on the river and were guaranteed decent tables at a few restaurants which were meant to be good, though to be honest we weren't that interested in the food. What we liked were the private dining rooms and the fact that the staff closed the door behind them and knocked before they entered. We liked to think that everyone knew us and that if they didn't, they weren't worth knowing. If I bumped into the guy I used to be back then, I'd smack him.

In the photograph, I'm stood looking smug and self satisfied outside the *Something Tech* offices. I'm wearing a pin stripe suit (or it's wearing me). My cufflinks are deliberately exposed: one says *dot* and the other says *com*. I squirmed at the memory. To my left, Joe laughs like something funny's just happened. D was absent from the photograph; he had what he referred to as an interest in the business like he was some sort of venture capitalist. Truth was, he knew fuck all about IT and the only times he'd accompanied us on sales meetings he'd proved a liability. Anyway, he can't stand not being in on things, can't D, so he managed to insinuate himself into the whole enterprise and had cards printed up emblazoned with his name and directorial status.

This was back when IT was still new and exciting and if you could convincingly say words like consumables and peripherals and RAM, chances were you'd make a killing. In the article I'd gone on about grasping the nettle and sailing on the crest of a wave. I'd recently given a well-received talk at the Chamber of Commerce and I can only guess that I was pretty taken with my imagined status as a motivational speaker. It was all bullshit, of course. Fact is, we were up to our ears in dodgy deals requiring trips to the States and Ireland, massive cash transactions and dealing with people who might as well have had *CROOK* tattooed across their foreheads. I remember when it all came on top and my Dad asked me how it was I'd got myself caught up in all that stuff and I'd said to him that I'd never thought we were doing anything wrong as such; ours was a legitimate business and we couldn't be held accountable for the calibre of our clientele. And he'd said something about how being a man was about being on top of all that stuff and not letting things spiral out of control. He put it down to greed and wilful ignorance. Which was my dad all over. At the time, I don't recall anyone turning down the free meals and I don't recall my Dad refusing to stay in the apartment in Tenerife. It's very easy, I find, to be wise after the event.

I found myself laughing out loud when I remembered carrying on like *De Niro* with my dark suits and shades and exchanging briefcases with men we called intermediaries. We were so fucking arrogant – all four of us: me, Joe, D and our lass – carrying on about elevating ourselves above the predictable lifestyles that our mates had lowered themselves into. Our lass'd carry on from time to time about being worried but she was never worried enough and she enjoyed the benefits as much as the rest of us. She adopted what she later referred to as an approach of pragmatic accommodation. She'd go on about why me and Joe had to spend so much time together and why didn't the pair of us just get a place together and leave her and the kids in peace. For effect, she'd sometimes suggest a prison cell and I'd say don't even joke about it. Towards the end, me and Joe spent no time together at all. It was part of his bail conditions.

I asked myself what all that was about? It was more than the risk, the excitement and the prodigious amounts of cash we were shifting: it was something to do with feeling better than everyone else. Lying there between all her cushions and pillows I tried hard to pinpoint why it might be have been that I felt good about myself when I was looking down on everyone else and I knew that this was not an appealing character trait. I thought back to when I was working in procurement for a utilities company and about all the protocols and how seriously I took it all; how I prided myself on doing things by the book and how much I disapproved of anyone who tried to cut corners. I was finding it hard reconciling that Si to the Si I'd become. I was seriously considering the idea that they were not the same person and I was properly worried because what all this meant was that there was maybe nothing reliable and true about myself. I tried to think about something else but I was off on one by that time and there was no way back.

And then I remembered something I thought I'd forgotten and I looked at our lass who, by this time, was staring at the ceiling smoking a cigarette. It struck me that I could ask her what I'd never asked her. If I asked her she'd give me an answer that would sound true but it would be a lie and that was why it wasn't worth asking (unless, of course, you're fucked and you're looking for things which might get close to making you feel marginally better about yourself). I practiced the question in my head first then I said,

- Remember when we had the business…

She turned towards me and nodded.

- Well, were you fucking Joe?

And she just turned away and said no - politely - like I'd asked her if she wanted a cup of tea. And then, I was the sad sap at the bottom of the stairs fretting over stuff that happened years ago and asking stupid questions I didn't want the answers to. I asked her if she was absolutely positive like there was some chance it might have slipped her mind and without looking at me, she said,

- Of course I'm sure.

She was lying and I was wondering why this bothered me after all this time when I was at it the whole time, and it wasn't even like I'd cared until I'd asked the question.

It wasn't like we were conducting an ethical business at the time and maybe it stood to reason that if you carry on in that way, it's going to leak into other bits of your life. It's like the whole notion of a bottom line goes out of the window, so it's not like I could really take the fucking high ground all those years later. I tried hard not to lose it and I told myself it didn't matter except it did and I remembered that this was what it felt like at the time: knowing something was very wrong (between the two of us: me and her) and not daring to approach it in case it blew everything out of the water. And that was why I never asked at the time. The truth would have required an appropriate response and I'd never known quite what that would be. She said,

- I didn't even like Joe.

And I could tell she was telling the truth this time. But you can fuck people you don't like if you're bored enough. And if it's just about boredom – or what they call ennui – you don't feel guilty and maybe years after you can say stuff like I didn't even like Joe and mean it. I remembered – it had only been a few weeks before – bumping into some woman in the bank and she looked at me like she knew me really well. She finally said,

43

- Long time no see, Si.

I mumbled something while I struggled to fit her face into my life and I finally remembered that I'd dabbled a couple of years ago. She twigged that this was obviously a less than memorable encounter and looked embarrassed. I tried to rescue things a bit with some mild enquiry about how things were going but the conversation was an engine that had stalled and there was no turning it over.

I wondered if Maxine and Joe had talked about me and if they'd laughed. Maybe I compared unfavourably to him in the only way that matters to men. We had a code at the time - me and Joe and D – it was the closest we got to a mission statement and it was: *what happens on the road stays on the road*. Maybe he breached that code and told her things about me and my extra curriculars. Maybe for her it was one of those what's good for the goose scenarios. In my head I was like Elvis Costello and *I Want You* and I was full on wondering whether she'd called his name out as he held her down and whether he'd undressed her and where and when and how. Precisely. But I was also not wanting to know anything. Being beside her was making my flesh crawl. Her smoke was like mushroom clouds above my head. And then there was the photograph again and Joe was grinning like the cat that got the cream and it was no fucking wonder looking back. I wondered whether it was true what they say about black men. But I didn't ask because it always turns out that what you think you want to know you don't want to know at all.

So, I'd got my story and all I needed to do was to make the facts fit it: I remembered when Joe got out of prison and we all met up for a reunion meal. It was an awkward situation which we tried and failed to make light of. When we'd got through the business of the financial settlement and onto the matter of pretending everything was fine between us, I detected something I can only describe as a psychic grimace between Joe and our lass and I recognised it at the time as the same way that I've looked at women I've fucked and wished I hadn't. It's something called regret or shame.

So it was like suddenly everything made sense and I was properly on the road to Damascus. I knew how they'd got away with it: it was because at the time I suspected something, the rapid, catastrophic and frightening decline of *Something Tech's* fortunes served to concentrate my mind on other things. And it was bloody weird that it should all come back to me now, with her lying next to me having just done something which they call making love but should more accurately be called making believe.

- D'you see owt of him?

I tried to sound casual and she tried to pretend she hadn't heard me.

He was still in Leeds as far as I knew and he'd reinvented himself as some sort of marketing and promotions consultant. If you ever find yourself doing a *Google* search for *marketing + Leeds,* his company'll pop up somewhere near the top of the list. The site's supposed to be funny and quirky and self-deprecating. If you click on *punters* you'll find that he's wheeled out all his most prestigious clients and got them to say how remarkable his company is. He's probably rolling in it. Did he do the marketing for her company? Did he design and optimise her website and take payment in kind? Had all this stuck with her like a hangover for the past God knows how many years and was that why she'd left me? D had said at the time,

- You want to watch out for him – he's slippery.

But then we all were back then and, in fairness, I was chasing anything with a pulse. We were neither of us blameless; we were both corrupt. It was your bog standard Pandora's Box scenario. Once you accept - without even discussing it - that anything goes, you can forget your *Queensbury Rules* and your marriage oaths and all the things that are supposed to hold two people together. We both devalued the currency and maybe that's where things started to get fucked.

She said, and I recognised that this was the nearest I was ever going to get to a confession,

- You have no right, Si, to carry on at me about anything. You must know that I know what you were up to that whole time and before and since and I've never fucking asked you once about all that because it's only gonna hurt me. So don't fucking interrogate me now.

She had a point, of course, but I wasn't really in the mood for her points. I was more in the mood for righteous indignation on account of it's not often I get to feel righteously indignant in her company. I was thinking - and it was making the world of sense – that if she hadn't fucked Joe, then maybe I wouldn't have turned out like I had. Maybe we'd still be in my big house (which used to be our house) where the kids had a bedroom each and maybe we'd be doing the normal things that couples do when the kids are getting that bit older and you've time on your hands. She was upset and I didn't care because, frankly, she deserved to be upset. She reached over to me and I carefully removed her hand like it was contaminated. Yet even then, when I was full on acting out this role like it was the best part I'd ever been offered, there was a small bit of me that was thinking: why am I doing this? It wasn't like at the time I was bothered enough to confront her or him. Maybe it's that whole thing about editing; maybe this was the previously unseen director's cut where I got to play the tragic hero and she got what was coming to her. She said,

- I love you, Si. I always have.

Like love was some sort of panacea. There were tears in her eyes and her mascara was like rivulets of muddy water. Her face was contorted as if she was expecting someone to hit her.

- I'm sorry for anything I've done that's hurt you.

But she didn't specify what exactly it was that she might have done, which is telling I think. You can't just give a blanket apology without saying what it is you're sorry for. Maybe she thought an apology was just like a standard pro forma that you print out and change the date and name. Her eyes were the same colour blue as the blue of the stone in the ring I bought her years ago and her hair was like honey. The ring went down the back of a kitchen unit and was never retrieved. Her left hand was a gag covering her mouth and with the right she reached over for another cigarette. I lit her cigarette and I could see in her face that she was stupidly grateful – like this small gesture meant something it didn't mean.

- Can we be friends?

And this is where I should have let it drop, really. There was no point in this shit anymore and if I carried on feeding this thing, I was likely to find myself remembering things that didn't place me in such a good light, like all the stuff about how it was that Joe ended up taking the rap for the whole *Something Tech* thing and the gentlemen's agreement that we struck which worked out fine for me and D but not so well for him. I never visited him once when he was inside and he was only up the road. There were all these places in my head that I didn't need to be going to; it was like avoiding landmines. So I did the right thing and murmured something conciliatory. She wrapped herself round my back like a blanket and it became obvious that she wanted to turn the light out so that we could each pretend to be asleep.

I was on the verge of acquiescing to this unspoken request when there was another flash card in my head and it was Christmas Eve. There was a huge wad of cash and I'd reconciled the till and then I'd stuffed it into an A5 envelope and put it in my top pocket. I'd said to myself, take all but £200 of this and bank it. As soon as the banks open, I've to deposit this cash because there's bonuses and VAT coming out. But I'd handed over that whole wad to our lass and she'd found places to go with it and how to get there.

She mumbled something into my back and stroked my shoulder, and if she could've seen my face she would've seen that I was frowning. I was in bits and I was having trouble deciding which of my many problems to concentrate my efforts on. There was the money thing and there was the new historical drama I'd invented and they both required fairly urgent attention. I put the reconciling with Maxine item on my to do list for the time being. She, meanwhile, was still on about putting stuff behind us and being friends again and I was listening to her but not really because there was this other narrative running at the same time and it was all beginning to feel like I was in some poorly dubbed foreign film. Ideally, I was after a way of dealing with both my priority tasks at the same time. Then I had a brainwave which – experience should've told me – was a bad sign.

- Is it true what they say about black men?

I had to stop myself shuddering when I said it because I knew how cold and pitiless this was. I got up before I got a chance to properly take in the bits of her that were falling apart. I got dressed without looking at her and went downstairs. The envelope was on the coffee table. I picked it up and put it in my pocket so quickly it was like I could pretend it had never happened. I told myself I'd replace it and that I'd phone her in the morning and explain something – as yet unspecified. In the car I thumped the steering wheel and said fuck, fuck, fuck. I caught my eyes in the rear-view mirror and they were glassy. A bit of me that was humane told me I should be crying or going back inside and making amends or both. Every other bit of me was floating off in different directions. There was nothing in me that I could trust to do the right thing. I looked into the world outside my car and it was all monochrome except for the grass on the verge which was a splash of emerald green where the streetlight illuminated it.

I knew that I shouldn't be driving but I was in my car; I knew that I should be at home or somewhere else where I could do no one any harm but I wasn't really up for being on my own. So, it ended up standing to reason that I had to drive to a place where I wasn't going to be alone.

6.
When I rang Eliz, she was young and alone enough to be flattered by a call at 3 a.m. She was at home and of course I could come round.

- You know the way, don't you?

Like this was some sort of illicit tryst. The road was empty on the way to the place that ends in *ley*, and though I tried to distance myself from what'd just gone off, Maxine's horrified face kept looming up at me.

I got there and she wanted to talk and to show me her presents and ask me what it was I'd got but everything I'd got was where I'd left it and I couldn't be bothered sifting through my head to remember what it all was and who it was all from and how much I liked it. She was wearing a silky slip device and heels, which struck me as odd and contrived. I suppose she looked nice and I suppose she was expecting me to say something nice about how nice she looked. A tiny artificial tree sat in the corner of her living room and its throbbing lights grated. By the chair where she'd been sat – waiting for me I assume – there was a glass of *Bailey's* and on the coffee table there was the bottle and another glass. I didn't wait for her to ask if I wanted a drink and poured myself a generous measure.

- You got a mirror handy?

She pointed at the mirror above her fireplace. I told her that wasn't quite what I was thinking of and found a CD instead. The smile she'd fixed to her face began to peel a bit. I felt her watching me as I

49

sorted out a line. It seemed pretty clear that she wouldn't be joining me, which pissed me off somewhat because the last thing I needed was to have some girl sit in judgment of me. The weaknesses in my carelessly constructed scenario were already becoming apparent and I couldn't really see things being rescued. It was going to be a matter of making the best of a deteriorating situation. I unfurled my note and placed it back in my wallet; one edge was pink and distressed. Eliz crossed and uncrossed her legs and glanced at me like I was the nutter on the bus that people try to ignore. There were far too many seconds of saying nothing; we both stared at the same spot on the polished wooden floor like there was something there that was important and beyond words. Finally, she offered me a light and another drink, both of which – to her obvious relief – I accepted. She seemed to take this as a good sign and slithered towards me, smiling. She started to say something which I reckoned I was probably not in the mood to hear so I headed her off at the pass by saying something coarse and probably unforgivable about us both knowing why I was there and why didn't we just cut the crap and get on with it.

    - I'm not really in the mood just now. Can't we just chat for a bit?

    I poured her a large glass of *Bailey's* and when she'd finished that I poured her another one. I listened to her talk, increasingly incoherently, about stuff I had no interest in: where she was travelling to and when. Talk of travel reminded me of Canada and of Maxine. It was getting to the point where it was either too late or too early to leave so I stood in front of her and pulled her up from her chair; her silky dress slipped beneath my fingers. She looked at me like maybe this was some sort of game that she'd best go along with and led me to her little bedroom. As we walked up the stairs I noticed a photograph of her dad or some other male relative. I really was not in the mood for family sagas.

    I told her to get undressed but she was taking her time, like this was some sort of dance of the seven veils. I hurried her along a bit and she stumbled over her tights like they were manacles. She persisted in her refusal to leave the set of the romantic comedy she'd concocted;

she giggled and sidled towards the bed. She said something (that's not worth dwelling on) about just wanting to get her head down and get to sleep, which made me wonder what she was doing there in the bedroom with me. I helped her down and made it clear that I wasn't really in the mod for pre orgasmic noises or any noises at all. I knew that this was going to be as tiresome as sex gets so we'd best get it over with so that we could get on with forgetting it ever happened. Since I wasn't up for some transcendental experience, I undressed to my boxers and t-shirt. Getting beneath the duvet was a courtesy I afforded her and which worked for me too; it was the not seeing and being unseen. I asked her what was with the candles and told her they were a fire hazard. She said something about creating an ambience. I blew them out and the room filled with the stench of blown out candles for a few seconds. I issued some unambiguous instructions to her and she went along with them in a manner best described as perfunctory and while I was directing her I was thinking, is this who I am now? Is this what I do? It felt like I'd discovered a new and unusual aspect of my character, but not in a good way.

    Maxine lurked somewhere in the background of all this and all of the things I'd thought about on this Christmas day crossed my mind again and again. Afterwards, I noticed that on her ceiling there were luminous stars and planets and they reminded me of the stars we stuck to the twins' ceiling and how we had to remove them because Danny got frightened and, crying, said,

- Take the sky down.

    The adhesive from the stars left torn, ragged shapes in the blue paint like something big had been clawing at the ceiling. We meant to touch up the paintwork at some point, but it became one of those small but important things that we never got round to.

    Eliz made a noise which was something like a small animal and I noted that within a couple of hours or so I'd managed to reduce two women to tears, which had got to be the kind of record I was never going to be in a hurry to boast about. I wondered if there was any way I could realistically expect to be allowed to turn over and go to sleep or whether I needed to be getting up and getting off. Which would be more in character with whatever new character it was I'd become? In the meantime, I had to inject some small element of humanity into all of this so I placed my arm carefully around the shoulder that only a few minutes ago I'd shoved southwards in a less than humane manner. Her shoulder tensed and she turned to me and looked like she was properly scared which was not really what I was after. On a satisfaction scale of 1 – 10, I rated this encounter at around zero. I was pretty confident that she'd concur.

7.
I sat on the edge of her bed and retrieved my crumpled clothes. Leaving our lass's I'd thought it wasn't possible to feel worse. Whatever bit of me that being with Eliz was supposed to fix was still broken and there were new fractures which were going to want sorting. Her squealing stopped and that brought some sort of relief but then she started sobbing dramatically like she'd stepped out of some 50's melodrama. I was at a loss as to what to do with her crying and shaking and decided to give it a couple of minutes to subside but a couple of minutes passed and there were no obvious signs of it letting up. I became uncomfortably aware that there was absolutely nothing I could do to make the situation any better and that if I fucked off, chances were, things would at least get no worse. Which just goes to show how wrong you can be.

    I mumbled something to her about how I'd best be getting off (as if I'd been carefully weighing up the pros and cons and had lucidly decided that this was the better option) and crept out of the place; it was all I could do to stop myself from wiping my prints like I was some kind of intruder. I looked forward to being outside where there was cold air and a car outside her gate which was going to get me out of her world and back into mine. The past few hours had been poor quite frankly and I really wanted to be putting them behind me. The bulb was bare on her landing and I thought to myself how sad it appeared; she'd only need a ladder or a tall man on a kitchen chair and she could get that sorted in no time. The stairs were uncarpeted so even though I was carrying my shoes in my hand, there was a lot of creaking going on. I got to the door and it was locked and the key wasn't in the door which meant I was going to have to visit the scene of the crime again and ask politely if she could kindly give me the key so's I could get out of this place and back to Leeds.

I became aware of a mumbling thrum as I approached her door. It was the sound of half a conversation and I wasn't sure whether I should knock or wait or what. I put my head round the door and she was talking quietly into her mobile so I looked at the ceiling and the walls like I was pricing up a decorating job. Awkward doesn't begin to describe how I felt. She ended the call and pulled the duvet up over her shoulders so she was just a head in a bed.

- The door's locked. D'you think you could give me the key and I'll put it back through the letterbox.

I even mimed what putting a key through a letterbox might look like. She reached over on to the floor and fumbled around till she found the keys. Her hand narrowly missed a used condom – which made me feel both sordid and like a responsible human being. She put the keys on the side of the bed where I could've been sleeping if I hadn't fucked things up, and I picked them up thinking that this had become a much more complicated transaction than it needed to be. She made a point of not meeting my eyes. I opened my mouth to say something appropriate – some sort of closing statement which might neaten this all up a bit and make it possible for her to pass me in the street without wanting to kill me - but nothing came to mind, so for a moment I stood there gasping like a fish out of water. She looked at me and I was mildly taken aback to recognise her expression as one of contempt. She spat some words at me which don't need to be repeated here and they crashed round my skull as I turned and left her shabby room. So I was on my way down again for the second time and this time I'd put my shoes on because we seemed to have gone beyond the point where small considerations matter. There was a bolt and chain and a Yale and a mortice lock on her door so the place had either belonged to an old lady before or she'd had her dad round to make the place secure. Either way, it was over the top. There was nothing there worth stealing.

The roads were so quiet it was like cars had only just been invented. I pressed play on the CD and it was one of *Massive Attack's* darker offerings. I put the radio on because I needed something to take my mind off things but there was only shitty commercial radio; I didn't really want to hear stuff I hated five years ago and I already knew where to buy tiles from. I found a station where someone was talking to me; it was a woman and she told me that it was nearly ten years since the Rwandan genocide. They reckoned that it was literally a decimation because that means that a tenth of the population were offed. It felt to me like this wasn't really suitable programming for the festive period but it got me musing on what it would be like if one in ten of the people I know were murdered and what if they were murdered by their friends and neighbours. There were people, apparently, who would pay their assassins to kill them quickly: that's your market economy for you. I felt properly scandalised by all this and I was halfway to plotting some sort of awareness raising campaign. I told myself that first thing the following morning I was off into town and I'd be buying the book they'd mentioned. But it was already tomorrow and it was nine and a half years too late.

Driving towards home, there were a lot of things I decided I didn't need to think about so, inspired by the woman on the radio, I tried to remember what I'd been up to ten years ago and whether I was aware at the time of what was going on in the world outside my world. I concluded quickly that I wasn't and this time I felt scandalised by my own ignorance. I knew that there must have been other important things that were going off at the same time because the world doesn't wait for one catastrophe to be over before kicking off with another. It was before Blair got in so the Tories must have been doing something which my Dad disagreed with. At some point they released Nelson Mandela and I went round to a mate's house and watched him being interviewed; we both said it was an unforgettable day, which is always a daft thing to say when you're pissed. Was it 1993…1994? There will have been floods and earthquakes and other natural disasters but I couldn't tell you what or where they were or how much our lass told me I had to donate. I did know, though, that sometime in the mid nineties I got her an African orphan as a Christmas present. I suppose I'm still paying for it now, though it's likely to be an adult. I wondered how long you could legitimately refer to yourself as an orphan.

8.

Ten years before I was at the dog end of my twenties so I will have been thinking I was getting old and pointless; our Stephanie and our Ben will have been whatever age they were. I struggle, sometimes, with reconciling their ages to mine because I can't believe I've been their Dad for so long. Maxine wanted babies; she wanted them young so that by the time they were off our hands we'd still be young enough to do what we wanted to do. The assumption was that we'd be doing those things together. I remember once telling Maxine that having our Stephanie had ruined my university experience – like doing a shitty degree in my home town would have been an intellectually transforming experience under other circumstances. The twins came along much later and I couldn't tell you precisely what they were for – it just happens and it doesn't cross your mind that they're going to be yours forever and that there's something indefinable that you owe them. Something like a duty of care which, in my case, amounts to money mainly. Our lass told me once that our Ben and our Stephanie refer to me as *The Bank of Dad*. Neither of us laughed.

Ten years before that night I was living where I live now, I was married to Maxine and I was doing as well in procurement as was possible for a man with moderate ability and limited enthusiasm. It'd only been three or four years since the company had been privatised so the place was littered with bewildered former public servants trying to come to terms with share offers and productivity incentives. Those of us that were new to the game couldn't get our heads round the notion that Yorkshire's water had ever belonged to anyone other than its shareholders. Around that time, I was promoted to a junior managerial post. When I was appointed my boss told me that he wished he was my age again, what with all the opportunities and professional development opportunities open to me. He told me that we were about to move into a new era in procurement; we were going to be developing strategic approaches, benchmarking our performance against other utilities and promoting positive supplier relationships. He told me that we were teetering on the precipice of excellence and I properly didn't understand what he was on about. What I did know was that once I was in management chances were I'd start getting invited to some of the freebie events that suppliers put on for us; I imagined myself at York Races or clay pigeon shooting at country hotels in the Dales. When he'd finished carrying on, he waved me out of his office like I was going on a long journey and told me that I was a good lad who'd prove an asset to the company.

He was one of these that read books about performance improvement and listened to management cassettes in his car. When he wasn't on about management and empowerment, he was busy being married to a spherical woman who smiled and tutted and picked him up from work on a Friday in a Volvo estate stuffed with three ugly dogs. Sometimes she'd wait for him in reception and if I bumped into her, she'd ask after the kids and our lass like she knew them. She'd a problem with her breathing – it'd be to do with all that excess baggage she was carrying, I imagined – so there were too many full stops in her queries and anecdotes and I'd have to wait a couple of seconds for what she said to make any sort of sense. Sometimes she'd pat the seat next to her and I'd be forced to join her while Malcolm faffed and fiddled before making his way downstairs. All the flowers on all the flowery blouses that she wore stretched and strained around her midriff as she hauled herself onto her feet when he entered reception, and he'd say,

- Now then, Maisie, girl. I've kept you waiting again, haven't I?

She'd look at the receptionist and raise her eyebrows. All her chins would quiver and her lipstick would splinter as she smiled at him and said,

- What are you like, Malcolm?

Then he'd touch her face and kiss her on the lips and there'd be a bit more banter about what he was like and what she was like. Sometimes, watching them walk slowly out to the car, I'd speculate on the nature of their sex life and sometimes I'd speculate on how they got to remain so fascinated with each other after so many years. They spent every weekend at a static caravan somewhere near Knaresborough. They had special caravan cutlery and crockery that they took with them and she'd sewn tiny curtains for the tiny windows. On a Monday morning he'd come into the office and say, fancy a brew, then he'd tell us stories about who'd been there and who'd not and which of their kids had popped up on the Saturday for a pub lunch. His face'd be all round and animated like he'd stepped out of an advert for toffees or life insurance for the over 50's and he'd announce the end of his stories by saying,

- Right then, lads, noses to the grindstone.

He'd walk out of the office on his short legs in his saggy suit, shaking his head and chuckling like there were more and better stories that he hadn't told us. You can laugh at people like that – and we did, all of us young guns with our hair products and metal briefcases and small, lithe wives – but to be honest, him and Maisie are two of the happiest and least harmful people I've ever met.

Someone told me that Maisie died a few years ago. Her obesity was a symptom of something other than gluttony and whatever this chronic condition was had felled her in the end. I bought Malcolm a card with a picture of a lily on it. I carried it in my briefcase for days but never got round to sending it which just goes to show that I'm not as nice a lad as he thought I was.

I drove hesitantly round the Armley gyratory; it seemed bigger and more treacherous at night. I breathed slowly and deliberately and it was like a triumph when I found the exit on my second circuit. I opened the window a touch and the wind sliced in. I tried to think of a significant event that had happened ten years ago but nothing came to mind. I was about to abandon this train of thought when it occurred to me that it had to be getting on for ten years ago that me and our lass had the run in with the car. Normally, I'd just let this random thought trickle away, but over the past couple of days my head had become a place where small thoughts settled and took shape.

When I met our lass I was 18, and the thing I first noticed about her was that she whistled like a man; I'd go into the shop she worked at for a sandwich and a can of coke and there'd be this tuneful whistling that accompanied whatever was on the radio. The first few times I'd looked round for any old giffer who knew how to make whistling sound orchestral. There was nothing of her, but she whistled like the men my dad spent his time with in the bookie's. It was something that set her apart and over the years it became the soundtrack to our lives: it was how I knew she'd walked in the door and how I knew to put the kettle on and to clear the table and to prepare myself for whatever it was she wanted to tell me about her day. Then she'd say,

- And what's your day been like, sweetheart?

And I'd witter on about tenders and proposals while she sorted out the dinner, laid the table and got me a beer, opened it and put it in front of me. We were straight out of *Coronation Street* back then. This was before the twins, so she'd have picked up our Stephanie and our Ben from the after school club and all the time she was fussing over me, she'd be fussing over them as well and I'd be thinking but not saying, let's get back to talking about me. In the gaps between fussing and issuing instructions and appearing interested in my day, she'd whistle. At the time, and at my insistence, she'd started a Catering Management course and she was combining that with working at some corporate hospitality firm so, on reflection, she was probably a bit frazzled most of the time but she never let it show. She'd come in and she'd be in her whites with her non-slip soles and a baseball cap with the name of the firm across the brim and she'd get on with the cooking. I told her once that anyone walking in to the house and seeing her in her uniform would think she worked there rather than lived there. She said,

- Well I do bloody work here, don't I?

Anyway, one night we'd had dinner and the kids had gone to bed. She'd washed the pots and I'd wiped down the surfaces because that was how we allocated tasks back then. We were sat in the kitchen because there was nothing on TV and it just seemed easier to be there than to be anywhere else. I flicked through *The Mirror* and our lass had a go at the *YEP* crossword. We didn't speak to each other and it struck me that this wasn't the comfortable, companionable silence that people talk about couples settling into. It was just that after we'd done the things we were required to do - the work, the kids, the food – it felt like we struggled to find anything to talk about. I remember wondering about what it was that we used to talk about and when it was that we stopped; whether there was a clear line that separated then from now and whether there might be something worse than silence that we might descend into next. I felt suddenly both embarrassed and worried at having become the sort of man who reads the paper in silence while his wife does the crossword. So I said to her,

- Max, when did we stop talking to each other?

She just looked a bit distracted and shook her head as if I'd asked a question which required a yes or no answer. I persisted because the more I thought about it, the more important it was that we got to the bottom of it,

- Is this just something that happens, Max, after you've been with someone for a few years? Do you just run out of things to say?

This time she shrugged and filled in a clue, which struck me as unnecessarily rude and dismissive. She was beginning to get on my nerves by this time and I tugged the crossword out of her hands so that I could see her face and she could see mine. I can only assume, looking back, that I'd had whatever a hard day in procurement might comprise. Maybe a supplier had failed to complete some quality assurance pro forma or there'd been some minor dispute over costings and value for money. I really don't know now but I do know that at the time I wasn't the sort of person who'd routinely tug a crossword out of someone's hand just because they'd failed to provide a satisfactory answer to a question. She looked at me as if I was one of the kids and got up to put the kettle on, whistling the whole time of course. I must have raised my voice because when she finally deigned to say something, it was,

    - There's no need to shout, Si. You'll wake the kids.

I said fuck the kids or something equally tasteless. Whatever it was, it became the subject of what had turned into an argument. She walked towards the door that led into the hallway; she still had the spoon in her hand that she'd been stirring the tea with. I think I may have grabbed her arm to make her stay. I don't think that constitutes a violent act but doubtless she would disagree. She tried to free herself from me, her baseball cap fell off and her hair tumbled over her face as if it had been caught in a sudden gust of wind. Her face looked like a photograph of a beautiful person as it always does when she's angry. Not waking the kids was suddenly de prioritised because she started going off on one.

My behaviour, she said, was graceless and tasteless and – worse – embarrassing and humiliating. The adjectival onslaught ended with references to my self-absorption and utter selfishness. That, she said, was why we didn't talk anymore. She said that my interpretation of talking was to come into the house and broadcast my news without showing the slightest interest in what anyone else had to say. When, she wanted to know, was the last time I'd asked her how she was feeling, but she didn't wait for an answer.

    - You either bark at the kids or ignore them and I'm so sick of it I can't even be bothered to complain anymore. It's a relief when you just shut the fuck up.

I took a moment to process this gush of information and to compose a fitting response and in that moment she must have fled the kitchen because the next thing I knew she was at the front door with the car keys in her hand. I followed her out on to the drive and she got in the car and turned the ignition on. I stood in front of the car and told her she wasn't fucking going anywhere. The lights came on in the porch next door and Mr Neighbourhood Watch poked his turtle - like head out of the front door. I pre empted whatever it was he was going to say by telling him to mind his own fucking business. I tried the passenger door, not really knowing what I'd do if I got in but the situation had developed its own momentum by that time and all I knew was that neither she nor the car were going anywhere.

What happened next doesn't sound so good but at the time it felt like the only thing to do. We'd obviously gone way past the point of having a reasonable discussion and I knew - because I was very familiar with the contours of our arguments – that this was going to get much worse before it got better. The rough outlines of my recollection don't place me in the best possible light but in my defence, I was younger then and maybe I believed that men needed to take control of situations before situations took control of them; I don't bloody know. I can only speculate as to where my head was at because I went on to do more things which were completely out of character. There was a shovel lying by one of the flowerbeds; at the time she'd got bang into gardening and she'd spend every weekend pruning and planting. So with the shovel, I smashed the headlights and the rear windscreen. She screamed –as I suppose is natural under those circumstances – and shrank into the driver's seat. Mr and Mrs Neighbourhood Watch stood, petrified, in their front garden till I told them – like I was a police officer attending an incident – that there was nothing to see and to get back indoors. The engine continued to rev for a while, and for a moment I worried that she might stay in the car and that another dramatic gesture might be required of me to bring this thing to a conclusion. I raised the shovel again but I found that I didn't know what to do with it anymore and threw it back in the flowerbed. It cracked a plant holder neatly in two and it seemed to be this – finally – that got her out of the car. In some sort of inverted version of triage, she crouched down by the pot to attend to the least serious casualty of the evening.

We went back inside and she was shivering though it wasn't cold. She was sniffing and looking at the floor like a frightened kid who's just been told off. There were bits of glass in her hair and they shone when they caught the light. Dragging her into the living room, I caught sight of our Ben and our Stephanie sat at the turn in the stairs looking terrified, quite frankly. They, too, seemed to be shivering and it was like our house had suddenly acquired its own microclimate. It was only then that I knew I'd lost it because it took me straight back to being their age and to sitting with my sisters at the turn in the stairs while my Dad boomed around the house bating my Mum till finally there'd be the sort of scream that could shatter glass and we'd scurry back up the stairs like rats and hide, sobbing, in one bed. I said to myself then – but not to our lass – that this was the last time I'd ever do anything like this. I made it a promise I'd never break but I broke it.

It was all sorted in the end; we archived it under the carpet where all the regrettable things go. I called D up the following day; chances were he'd know someone who could fix the car cheaply. He stood in the drive like a caricature of a dodgy mechanic shaking his head and stroking his chin. He asked me to tell him again exactly what had happened – as if in some way that might assist in his diagnosis of the car's evident problems – so I told him, but in the merciless light of day none of it made as much sense as it had in the dark. That's often the way, I find. My story unravelled messily and he said,

- I worry about you sometimes, kid.

I told him he was there to worry about the car.

I think it was after then that she stopped whistling or when I stopped hearing her whistle. This mate of mine told me a while ago that he'd said to his missus,

- I've not seen you smile in ages.

And she'd said to him,

- I have smiled but not in your presence.

I approached Clay Pit Lane, wondering why this had come back to me now when I hadn't thought about it for years. I wasn't feeling so good about Malcolm and Maisie either, though it was a bit late to start being worried about a fat dead lady and I didn't think they did belated sympathy cards. I was beginning to scare myself and I was worried about what new thought was gonna drift and settle into my head like snow. I needed to know whether our lass remembered that night happening the way I remembered it and why it seemed so pivotal. It felt like the most important thing in the world to ring her and to apologise for what happened all those years back, just to prove to her that I wasn't a heartless bastard and that though I'd still not quite worked out why I'd wrecked the car, I knew now that it was a bit of an over reaction to whatever she'd done or said to upset me. I wanted to tell her that I thought that I was exercising control over a situation which felt like it was getting out of hand but then I was left wondering what situation it was I was referring to: was it her whistling and doing the crossword while I was trying to talk to her or was it those things she said to me about how shit I was? In any case, she needed to know that I'd realised how much I missed her whistling and that it's absence made me feel like I'd taken something away from her. Mainly I wanted to hear her voice. I pulled over and rehearsed what precisely it was I was gonna say to her.

    I couldn't properly concentrate because the woman on the radio was busy comparing and contrasting the differing ways in which societies manage in the wake of catastrophic events and she was on about the bulging prisons in Rwanda immediately after the genocide and the Truth and Reconciliation approach in South Africa. She asked some professor about the healing properties of forgiveness, which was where I began to lose interest because it all became a bit speculative and technical. What I wanted to know – and this guy was clearly not going to be of much help to me in this endeavour – was whether an apology to Maxine for what I did all those years ago, would be of any use to her. Was there a statute of limitations when it comes to apologies? Would it help her do that thing they call moving on which is what we're all supposed to do these days? Surprisingly, the professor seemed finally to grasp the gist of my enquiry and started on about the British Government apologising for the Irish Potato Famine and some black group wanting an apology for slavery. I seriously doubted what possible good an apology could do so late in the day but, again, he came to my rescue and told me that for victims an apology can be helpful because it's an acknowledgement that what happened actually happened. So I called her on the landline and the mobile. There was no answer but I got to hear her voice and to end the call before recording my message. I repeated this ritual four times.

When I got in, the house was cold and it felt like someone had left in a hurry. That'd be me, I suppose. The remnants of my hastily improvised Christmas were all over the living room floor and it felt like a good idea to clear up the mess and to put the festive season to bed. I knew that sleep was going to come – if it came at all - in its own sweet time so I built a spliff and waited for it like it was a date that'd probably stand me up. I wasn't remotely surprised – and only slightly disappointed – that the several hours of sleep I'd hoped I might be entitled to turned out to be an unfulfilled promise.

8.
Christmas TV is shit. People say that every year, and every year it gets worse. If Christmas TV wasn't shit, we'd have pretty much nothing to talk about over Christmas. The schedule's designed to remind its viewers that they're sad saps with nowhere to go. It was 7 in the morning again and I paced the living room flicking through the 90 odd channels at my fingertips trying to find one which might send me back to sleep. It wasn't what you'd think of as peak viewing time but there was all sorts on which I could've found myself getting engaged in: people were still selling stuff on shopping channels; gangly men were engaged in some sport whose rules I didn't know but which involved running and jumping and lobbing things; on the porn channels people continued to be pornographic. My Rwanda experience had taught me that the radio was likely to prove far too stimulating an option so I turned everything off, looked at nothing and heard nothing.

It was that bit too early to ring our lass again, not that I knew quite what I'd say if I did. My over riding concern with explaining something I did ten or so years ago had been replaced with much more pressing concerns, not least of which was how I was going to go about explaining my behaviour of the previous night. I wondered whether flowers might help but I'd already done flowers. I decided to stack our lass on the *To Do* pile while I got on with other stuff. I found a pen and paper and tried to look like someone who might be project planning the next couple of days. I wrote the date at the top and underlined it. I wondered if the banks would open with it not officially being a bank holiday, but it's like banks can open when and if they want to these days. There's a bank at the top of the road that opens at 10.30 and closes at 2.30 three days a week. What's all that about? They're always on at me to go for internet banking but, like I've said to them repeatedly,

- How d'you deposit cash over the internet? Do I, like, stuff a wad in the CD drive?

Chances were, the bank was not going to be open, but that was cool because the salaries weren't due out till the Wednesday so if I banked the cash on Tuesday, I'd be sorted. I created columns on the sheet of paper and dated them but the paper wasn't big enough to accommodate anything after Wednesday. I tried to relax a bit; telling myself that today was a new day and that things were bound to get better. I made a number of pre emptive New Year's resolutions about the things I would and wouldn't do that would make things go smoothly the following year. I got another sheet of paper and split it into two columns; in one I wrote *To do today* and in the other *Future plans*. The *Future Plans* column looked a bit like it'd been written by someone who'd fucked up big time; *Reduce drug use* and *Try to see the kids more* were at the top of the list. Amongst the things I'd do immediately, I reprioritised ringing our lass and explaining the black male enquiry stroke envelope incident. The explanation would involve an unreserved apology for the thing I'd said. The good thing about an unreserved apology is that it's a stand-alone package. There are no compatibility problems with other applications; it doesn't require lengthy explanations and justifications. All you have to say is,

- Listen, what I said was totally out of order and I apologise unreservedly.

She could, of course, ask why I'd said what I'd said but in your unreserved apology scenario you can normally get away with not knowing. Ignorance, under these special circumstances, is not an excuse but it can help make actions appear aberrant and totally out of character. If she'd realised the envelope had gone I'd explain, fully and frankly, why it was I'd borrowed it and when precisely I'd give it her back, though I didn't myself know yet when this would be. I'd say that I'd left her a note explaining what'd happened and when she said she hadn't see any note I'd tell her she needed to look harder to find it. I'd ask her if she still wanted to go to D's Boxing Day do and if she did – which was probably unlikely under the circumstances – I'd call round and pick her up around 2ish. It was a bit of a slapdash plan and it assumed that she was going to be prepared to talk to me but the sleeplessness and the Charlie had combined to dull my strategic skills. I was operating in Safe Mode.

The house where I live was empty and still cold. The project plan was not going so well because I couldn't work out where one task ended and the next began; I considered and rejected a Gantt chart. It also seemed like I was coming down with a spot of Columbian flu so I went to find some kitchen towel. The cups on the open shelves in the kitchen were dusty and when I tried to lift one it stuck like it was happy being where it was. The work surface by the kitchen sink was a glass landscape and the sink itself was full of other things that wanted washing days ago. There were bottles of water in the fridge which harked back to a short-lived attempt at a healthy lifestyle. There was also an extensive sample of *M&S* ready meals for one which I must have pillaged on my invade and conquer mission the other day; their best by dates were all the same and it looked like I was going to have to be eating half a dozen of them a day for the next four days. I wedged the bulk of them into the freezer. I put a roast dinner for one in the microwave. On the fridge there was a shopping list secured with a magnet that told me that I loved New York – which I don't, as it goes. I've only been there the once, years ago, on a make up or break up mission with our lass. There was too much to do and too little common ground between us; on our final night we went to a comedy club and that was the only time we laughed in the whole five days. The shopping list was faded and the edges were curling in on themselves. It was full of things I was meant to pick up on my way home sometime in Summer 2002; things which I no longer needed like capers, anchovies, gnocchi and fresh coriander. A black bin bag, full of bottles that were not going to get recycled anytime soon, sat at the back door. I picked it up and put it in the cupboard under the stairs with the other bags. Behind the bags there were boxes but I didn't need to know what was in the boxes. The cupboard smelt like a tap room. I fleetingly considered that I might be becoming the sort of person you read about in the *Yorkshire Evening Post*:

Mr Williams lived alone, his wife and children having left the family home some months previously. Described by neighbours as a man who kept irregular hours, Mr Williams' body was discovered this morning by his estranged wife. Police describe the house as being in a state of neglect. It is believed that he had been dead for some time. No one else is being sought in connection with the incident.

I pushed a pile of newspapers and unopened mail to one side and sat down to eat at the kitchen table. My breakfast looked poor and unorthodox but was surprisingly tasty. The beef was tender and, though I'd had my doubts about the advisability of microwaving Yorkshires, they survived the ordeal remarkably well. I threw the container in the bin and washed the fork carefully before drying it and placing it in the cutlery drawer. I did the washing up and put all the pots and pans in the places they were supposed to be. I wiped down the work surfaces with some sort of disinfectant and swept the floor. I got out the *Dyson*, emptied it and hoovered the living room and hallway. With a clean tea towel and some spray polish, I dusted everything made of wood then I had to hoover again because dust and debris had gone everywhere. I replaced CD's in their cases and placed them in the CD rack and I removed a couple of cups from the mantelpiece and two glasses from the floor. These I washed carefully, dried and placed in the cupboards. In the washing machine there were some clothes that smelt like they were turning into something else; I bagged them up and put them in the brown bin outside.

9.

Across the drive, my neighbour waved at me and asked me if I'd had a good one. I grinned broadly and lied,

- Great… it's all about the kids, innit?

He nodded like I'd said something profound and approached the wall. I honestly did not have a clue what he was doing prowling round his garden at that time on a Boxing Day morning; maybe that was what people did when they were let out of work for Christmas. I could've done without a protracted discussion about the festive season and though I was likely to accept an invitation to pop round for a drink or whatever other bland offer he was going to want to extend my way, there was no way that I was actually going to turn up.

- I'm glad I've seen you. It's just that your Ben and Stephanie were round last night…

He cleared his throat. I was about to say they couldn't have been because I'd been with them last night.

- …Well, it were more the early hours of this morning to be honest. Anyway, they were braying on the door for ages and then they were shouting and carrying on… obscenities and all that through the letter box; summat about…

He cleared his throat again and lowered his voice before continuing,

- …you being a thieving bastard and what've you done with the money.

I found myself feeling a bit like I'd been punched in the gut. At the same time, I was really feeling it for Tony who's an all right lad, really, and definitely not the type who was going to be taking any pleasure from this particular exchange. He had evidently been sent on this mission by his missus who lurked in the doorway with her dressing gown pulled tightly around her. Tony had a leather jacket on over his pyjamas; he looked ridiculous.

- Thing is, mate, I wouldn't normally say owt but it just got a bit out of hand; the kids woke up and them lot on the other side came out...

He gestured towards Mr and Mrs Neighbourhood Watch's house,

-... and they were on about calling the police and all sorts like we had some major fucking civil insurrection on our hands. Then your Ben and Stephanie started carrying on about calling the police to investigate this theft and they're wanting me to give them the spare key so they can go in and find you. Obviously I told them I didn't have a spare key anymore – which I have, by the way, in case you're wanting it back.

He looked at me like he really wanted me to want to have it back.

- Anyway, I managed to convince Ben and Stephanie that you weren't in which took some bloody doing to be honest. In the end I told them that you'd said you were off to some party, though fuck knows who has parties on Christmas night. It might be worth remembering that if they ask. Anyway, top and bottom of it is...

And he glanced at his missus,

- ...you know me; I couldn't give a toss what's going on with your domestics and this, that and the other but you don't wanna be making an enemy of your kids, mate. I'm sure it's all some sort of misunderstanding and it can be sorted in no time. I mean, it all sounded a bit confused and weird; summat about an envelope and Canada. I couldn't follow it all to be honest but I reckon it can all be sorted if you maybe just go round and talk to them and your lass...your ex lass or whatever.

I listened to all this and while I listened, I tried to prepare a response for when he eventually petered out and I was also thinking, why is my business everyone else's business all of a sudden? And the answer was, because I'd made it everyone's business. What I wanted to do was to invite Tony into my house for half an hour and unburden myself, maybe get him to open up too about his toxic missus and his truculent kids who, on the rare occasions I was around on an evening, seemed to spend most of their time sat with their mates on my wall pretending not to smoke. Maybe he could give me some full on advice which might actually work and resolve all this. He struck me as a decent guy who could maybe impose some much needed sanity on a situation which seemed to be getting way out of hand. On the other hand, I wasn't that keen on anyone seeing a man leave my house in his pyjamas. So instead, I said,

- Listen Tony, mate, I can only apologise. I don't know what was going off there. The kids haven't taken this whole separation thing that well. You do your best, don't you? I spent all day yesterday round at theirs: presents, champagne, the full Monty. Last I saw of 'em was around 10ish when they were off out to their mates'. You wonder, don't you, whether they'd maybe had a bit to drink and got themselves whipped up into a frenzy? I don't bloody know. But, like I said, I'm really sorry - and apologise to your missus on my behalf. I appreciate you sorting it out and all that and I'll get right on top of it today. The whole envelope thing: that's just a massive misunderstanding as you rightly pointed out...

I started to concoct a version of what had happened - I thought it best to omit any reference to the removal of the money - and found myself beginning to believe the story I was telling (which at the time felt promising because it'd make it that much easier when it came to repeating it to our lass). I could tell, though, that he really wasn't that interested in all this so I left the story unresolved whilst making it clear that I was as confused as he was by what we'd now both decided to refer to as the situation. I managed a rueful smile and reached across to shake his hand. In my peripheral vision, I saw his missus disappear back into the house.

There was a body slumped in the hallway of my clean and tidy house and it was mine. It was only 8.30 and I was already run ragged. A tasteful black and white portrait of the kids – procured at considerable (though apparently justifiable) expense from *Dorchester Ledbetter* - stared down at me from the turn in the stairs. I considered turning their faces to the wall or turning my own face to the wall. It was becoming clear that my previous ringing and explaining strategy might require some tweaking under the current changed circumstances. As for apologising about summat that happened ten years ago, the professor turned out to be wrong on that one. It'd be a bit like apologising for burning the chips when you've actually burnt the house down. Knitting together the edges of my frayed nerves, I tried to imagine what an innocent man might do: ring indignantly and tell the kids about themselves; go on at Maxine about why she was letting the kids come down here and carry on alarming in front of the neighbours. By the time I'd processed these options, I was failing to feel stirred by them. This was largely on account of the fact that I was not – strictly speaking – an entirely innocent man. There was one remaining option and that was to go round to the house, apologise for my crude speculations about black men's tackle (there was no way round that one) and slip the envelope under a cushion or under the mattress or anywhere. I'd say that I saw that she'd left it downstairs so I picked it up and put it somewhere safe. On the one hand, I'd be left with the unpaid VAT and bonuses problem but on the other I'd redeem at least one small bit of myself. Basically, I would be back where I started but where I started was better than where I was. As I settled myself into this course of action and imagined her reaction and the kids' reactions and the furtive replacement of the envelope, it began to feel more and more difficult. I looked at myself in the hall mirror and the man who stared back at me looked terrified. My forehead was a screwed up sheet of paper, my eyes looked like they'd been drawn on by a 5 year old and my jaw looked like it had been dipped in iron filings. I went up to the bathroom and clawed at my eyeballs until I managed to remove the lenses that had to have been in for a good 24 hours.

I couldn't go out and I couldn't stop in so I sat on the bottom stair with my car keys in my hand. Finally I hit upon the thing I should've first considered.

- Hiya, Lind. It's Si. Yeah, I know it's early but I thought you'd be up, what with the do and everything.

She told me she'd been up since six, defrosting vol au vents and quiches and that I'd no idea how much goes into organising what she referred to as a function. I didn't really have a lot of time for discussing canapés and Cava but I went along with it for a couple of minutes before asking for D. She bellowed D's full name. D's full name is something Indian because his Dad was Indian but no one uses it except for Linda.

- Now then, Season's Greetings and all that.

In the background, I heard Linda shouting,

- Tiff, what did your dad tell you about messing about on that bloody sofa?

D, clearly alarmed, abandoned our conversation to tell Tiff exactly what he'd do to her if she didn't get her arse out of the room.

- It's a bit early for you, mate. Is there summat up?
- I've got a bit of a problem, D, and I thought you might be able to give me a bit of advice.

I went on to summarise the nature of my difficulty. It didn't feel great to have to have to say all this stuff out loud but it wasn't like I'd much of a choice. D is not really your ideal man for advice on this sort of issue, involving as it does inter personals which might require a lighter touch than that he normally applies. Evidently glad of an excuse to get out of his house, he was beeping his horn outside my house in ten minutes.

- Is there a particular reason why you have to announce yourself by beeping the horn, D? I've just had the neighbours on at me about bringing the area into disrepute.

D waved at Tony's missus who'd found a reason to be staring out of the front room window as he arrived. He turned the TV on and paced round the living room, picking things up and putting them down as he always does. His leather jacket squeaked expensively.

- That new?

He glanced at his jacket as if he'd only just realised he was wearing it,

- Off our lass… she got it from *Accent*. A mate of hers works there. 20% discount and all that.

He tried not to smile but I could tell he was pleased with himself and with Linda.

- Distinct absence of festive cheer in here, mate.

Like he was expecting me to have transformed the place into a full on Santa's Grotto since the last time he'd been there. He pointed at a space where a tree might go.

- D'you remember, I had a batch of fibre optic trees back in June? You should've grabbed one then.

Sitting down finally, he asked me to describe in detail what the problem seemed to be. I skirted round the outer edges of my predicament furnishing D with additional details as and when he asked for them until in the end he had what came close to the full, unexpurgated story. D shook his head intermittently and tut tutted under his breath like a teacher. When I'd finished, he removed his head from his hands and stared at me.

- What were you thinking of, fella?

He told me that it went without saying that I'd made some fairly crucial errors but this didn't stop him telling me what they were. He counted them out on his fingers.

- Firstly, you want to be saying no to drugs on Christmas Day - at least till the scran's out of the way. Secondly, you should've admitted your mistake about the money soon as you realised what'd happened; at that stage you were getting on all right with your lass so you could've mentioned it after the kids'd gone out. To be honest, a gift of money is to my mind a bit of a Christmas cop out but at the end of the day, if that's the best you can do that's between you and your conscience.

- D, can you get to the fucking point?

The fucking point was clearly some way off. He continued,

- Thirdly, you should've dealt with the Joe business years ago like I told you at the time. Of course he was shagging her but you can't be bringing all that up years later. When you do that, you're just opening yourself up to counter allegations and before you know it, you're locked in what they call bitter legal wranglings. Fourthly, I'm properly struggling to understand why you compounded an already grave situation by going round to that Eliz one's in the middle of the night. Don't even try and tell me why you did that cause it's never gonna make any sense to me. What've I said to you?

He told me what he's said to me a thousand times, which is that you should never let your dick lead your brain. I felt like he was expecting me to take notes when really I'd have liked to be raising some rather serious objections to his summary of my situation.

- Fifthly, you've now managed to expose your personal life to the glare of publicity. You're in the undignified position of having your neighbours know stuff about you that you wouldn't tell a priest. There's a reason why the suburbs are called the suburbs, Si; it's because people who live here live substandard lives. They get over excited when a dog shits on the pavement or someone forgets to put their wheelie bin out. You've performed what could be viewed as a valuable public service because this little incident is gonna have them talking for months. It'll make their shitty little lives seem a bit more bearable. There's no way you can be trusted to go round there and replace the money. There's just no way you're gonna be able to carry it off. Look at the state of you – you look exactly like the sort of guy who's just stolen a wad of cash. You're gonna have to give me a minute to sort this one out, mate. I'm gonna need to go through my database of remedies for self inflicted injuries.

Having exhausted the fingers of his left hand, he said nothing for a while and slowly built a spliff. I'd just had my character assassinated and, to be honest, I was on the ropes. As harsh as D's verdict was, I struggled to come up with much in the way of a defensive strategy. He passed me the spliff and outlined his proposed solution.

- Ok, this is what we're gonna do: you're gonna give me the envelope and I'm gonna go round to Maxine's. I'm gonna ask her if I can borrow some serving plates or summat for the do this afternoon. She's not likely to refuse, is she?

I shook my head though I'd no idea whether she'd refuse or not.

- Right then, while she's sorting that out, I'll wait in the living room and slip the envelope under a cushion or down the side of a sofa or summat. I think that could work. Obviously, I'll let you know where the envelope is when I leave the house. What happens then is that you go round later to pick her up for the do, carrying on like everything's fine obviously. For the purposes of this exercise, you've not spoken to your neighbour so you've no idea what went off last night. I'd strongly suggest that you get a shower and a shave before you go anywhere, by the way. Obviously she won't want to come to the do and she'll go off on one about the money and all that. You tell her that there's no way you took it and tell her that you'll look for it with her. Make sure she's with you while you're looking and, if anything, suggest to her that she looks down the side of the sofa so it's her that finds it and not you. OK?

I nodded. This was beginning to sound like a plan that could work. I became aware that my breathing was becoming less shallow and I started making a concerted attempt to draw breaths into my lungs and to expand my chest with my inhalations. I glanced at D and I realised that for all his madnesses he was the closest thing I had to someone who just cared for me, as rubbish as I am, and wanted nothing back. It's a bit like having a mum, I imagine, but it's that long since I've had one I can't be sure. What I did know, though, was that all the parts of myself I kept from myself, he knew. He translated me to the world and made me appear better than I was. I was emotionally depleted and he'd made me believe that there was a plausible solution to the unfeasibly complicated situation I'd managed to create. I said something like, thanks mate, quietly and I asked him the question I'd been thinking of asking my suburban neighbour,

- What's gone wrong with me, mate?

- There's nowt that can't be put right, Si. It's just that you've failed to exercise your critical faculties. You're all at sea, as they say.

Then he told me about a dream he'd had where he was in the boathouse on Roundhay Park Lake and he was sat in this rowing boat with the sun glinting through the cracks in the door. Next thing he knows, he's in the middle of an ocean – oarless – and it's pitch black. He reckoned he'd had this dream when he was banged up overnight years ago. It wasn't a story guaranteed to make me feel much better but I had to concede that it was apt. He stood and told me he was going to have to be getting off if he was going fit all this stuff in. He'd phone me and let me know how the land lay as soon as he'd deposited the envelope. He shook his head and ran his hand through his short black, ungreying hair.

- Are you gonna give me the envelope then, or what?

I went upstairs to get the envelope from my jacket. It wasn't there but that wasn't a problem because there were plenty of other pockets to check. I checked all the other pockets and it still wasn't there. There was a whole bunch of other places where it wasn't either: like under the bed; in the bed; under the sofa; in the kitchen bin; in the washing machine; on top of the wardrobe; underneath the wardrobe; in the cutlery drawer; in the fridge. I wheeled both the brown and green bins in from outside, covered the kitchen floor with newspaper, tipped them both out and stirred through the contents with a wooden spoon. I scooped up the rubbish and went over the floor with a mop but not before checking to see if I'd dropped the envelope in the mop bucket. I was either hyperventilating or about to have a heart attack as I tumbled round the house. D whistled as he pulled the drawers out of my desk. I told him to please give up whistling, that it was doing my fucking box in. I tried that thing where you stand really still and rub your temples as if that might summon up the lost thing. The two of us went through the house room by room untidying everything I'd previously tidied then I looked outside on the drive, in the car, on the pavement. I didn't talk because that would have diverted the effort I needed to exert on this task. My life had shrunk to the dimensions of an A5 envelope which was out there somewhere waiting for me.

Tony's missus did her reappearing act again and asked me if I'd lost summat. I wanted to strangle her at that point but instead I replied under my breath,
- What does it fucking look like?
And she said,
- Pardon me for asking.
D told me to chill the fuck out and asked me all the stupid questions people ask under these circumstances: where d'you last remember seeing it? Can you remember putting it down somewhere? Retrace your steps. I told him, through clenched teeth, that if I could remember where I last saw it, it wouldn't be fucking lost. Then I remembered where I'd last seen it.
- Fuck. Fucking hell.
He put his hand on my shoulder.
- It's at fucking Eliz's.

10.
I could see that D was struggling with this one; that I'd really stretched him this time. I became aware of my shoulder trembling beneath his hand and of him leaning towards me and telling me that we were off back inside. He was wearing an aftershave I recognised as expensive and it stuck in my throat. I would've thrown up but there was nothing in me. He enunciated his words as if he were talking to a small child or to someone whose first language was not English. I felt nauseous and light headed and all I really wanted to do was sleep because I was feeling properly tired at this point. After I'd slept I could die. My heart was busy palpitating or it was the return of the heart attack I'd been expecting earlier. A heart attack would have been a relief. As he opened the door, D said,
    -We need to think this thing through, Si.
    He guided me into the kitchen as if I might have forgotten where it was. He put the kettle on and stared at it as it boiled. Losing patience, he looked in the cupboard for the coffee and found only beans.
    - Haven't you got any proper stuff?
    He was referring to instant. I shook my head.
    - So, what the fuck am I supposed to do with this?
    He shook the packet. I found the coffee grinder which had last been used several months previously and noisily pulverised some beans. I found the thing you make coffee in. It's metal and you've to put it on the stove. If your luck's in you get a thimble full of muddy

residue at the end of a very lengthy process – which is what D got. He grimaced at it.

- Sugar?

I found some brown sugar but I'd have needed an ice pick to dislodge it from its packet. The coffee trickled down my shiny sink. I followed him into the living room.

- How much money are we talking here, Si?
- To be honest, I don't know exactly, D. I was in a hurry so I didn't do a full reconciliation. But we're probably talking a couple of thou, maybe more. Well, pretty much definitely more.
- Can't you get a cash advance on your credit cards?
- Maxed, mate: Christmas and cashflow and all that. It'll all be sorted in the New Year - we rake it in during the sales.

I wanted to cry.

- No situation is the worst situation in the world, Si. Whatever you're going through, someone else has been through the same or worse.

I didn't know how this was supposed to make me feel better and I was uncomfortably unaware, because I know him so well, that in going into motivational speaker mode, D was playing for time. He was going to start talking about options soon and how many I had.

- You've two choices, mate: you can find a way of getting into hers and getting the envelope or you can write it off to experience and find some other way of making good your loss. I'd lend you some cash myself but what with Christmas and all that, I'm a bit stony myself. I know Linda's got a bit stashed by. She reckons she read in one of her magazines that women should always have a nest egg in case their fella pisses them off big time. I think it's supposed to keep me on my toes…you know what she's like.

I watched his face begin to smile as he thought of her. They got together just after me and Max and every now and again they'll have these controlled explosions which make a loud bang but cause little damage. They're up there with Malcolm and Maisie in your happily married stakes.

- I can't take Linda's money, D.

Looking back, that's one of the few decent decision I can remember making in the past year.

- Remind me again what sort of timescales we're working to here.

I felt pathetically grateful that he seemed to have decided that *we* was the appropriate personal pronoun in this context. I told him that our time frame extended to the end of the day – and that that was pushing it.

- There's no saying what Eliz'll do with the money if she finds it. If I was her, I'd spend it. At least there's pretty much nowhere open today.

I explained that we were working to a number of imperatives: there was our lass and the kids who needed to be placated; then there were the bonuses and the VAT that had to be paid. Neither of the above could be accomplished without retrieving the cash. The cash, I reminded him, was currently in somewhere ending in *ley,* a place where I was not welcome. The option of putting it down to experience was not even worth contemplating, I explained.

- What d'you know about Eliz? Is she gonna full on refuse to let you into the house if you call round? Is there anything at all left in the charm bank or are you already in unauthorised overdraft territory?

I didn't know what I knew about Eliz. She wasn't someone I'd been planning on getting to know much about. I pretty much knew what had happened though, so I reluctantly recalled, then even more reluctantly recounted, the events of the previous night and in particular drew attention to her palpable fear and told him that she wasn't likely to be welcoming me with open arms. I managed to augment the version I'd given him earlier on in my first - apparently unexpurgated - version of events. It was weird, but as I said it all out loud and put words to the things that I'd done and to her reactions, I felt slightly more peaceful. I was constructing a narrative, of course, but I was trying really hard to make it clean and truthful. It was like my voice was on a delay because every word resonated in the air and came back to me so I got to properly hear what it was I was saying and what it meant. As I processed my story, I became astonished at how poor my instincts had been over the past couple of days.

By way of context and background, I found myself introducing supporting characters like the professor on the radio and Malcolm and Maisie and the woman I'd banged that I'd bumped into in the bank.

- Who the fuck is Maisie?
- Malcolm's dead wife.

I could see that D was having trouble suppressing his impatience but I didn't care because, telling him this story, I found everything knitting together and I needed things to knit together. I would've got on to my Mum and my Dad and all the shit that happened all those years ago but something which must have been a tear hung warmly in the inner corner of my left eye; it lost its purchase and made its way down the side of my nose. When it reached my lip, another one formed on the other side. I wondered whether what I was doing was crying or whether these two tears were just a slow leak, what with me being so full. I noticed D staring at his fingers and I said quietly,

- I was cold, and that's no way to be with a human being. I'd got it into my head that seeing her would wipe out the shit with Max…neutralise things. I was in bits, mate. I was not what you'd call a gentleman. If I was her, I'd never want to see me again. And the worst thing is, I'm not even like that – or I never used to be. I don't know if it was the gear or what but I just didn't give a toss. I wanted to be on top of summat and I ended up on top of her. She was fucking scared. Of me. And the daft thing was, I was scared too, but you cross a line and there's no stepping back, is there? I put whatever bits of me are decent in standby mode. I didn't matter and she didn't matter.

I stopped talking because I was pretty certain that D's impatience was about to turn into irritation and if that happened he'd be off and I'd be on my own. He fidgeted - but then he always fidgets. The difference was that this time, I could see that he was ill at ease with all this. He wanted to solve a problem, not to hear a confession. There was even more I could have told him – details – but I knew that, as close as we were, there are things we don't talk about. We both learned a long time ago that to be a man amongst men you need to abbreviate your problems - to make them into practical, soluble puzzles. So I said something to him which indicated that I'd been talking crap; I blamed the Charlie and the sleeplessness and the stress. I dragged my hands down my face and the teary residue was absorbed into my dehydrated skin. D stretched and yawned like he'd just woken up which was good because it meant that we could each pretend that I hadn't said and he hadn't heard what I'd just said.

- For one thing, Si, you've not to panic. If you look at the past 48 hours, you've frankly not been on top of your game and that's how you've got yourself in this fucked up situation. You've got a tricky one here – there's no doubt about that – but the only way you've got any chance of crawling your way out of this hole is first and foremost to clean up your act a bit. You look like a fucking *Big Issue* vendor; you need a shave and a shower and maybe then we might have a fighting chance of making you look like someone who people might take seriously. How much have you done, by the way?

I didn't answer because I couldn't remember how much I'd bought off him or where I'd stashed the rest of it. I considered gloomily that I might have left that at Eliz's too. My spirits lifted slightly when I remembered that I'd come across it when I was wrecking the house looking for the envelope. It was just a matter of remembering where I'd come across it and what I'd done with it, but that could wait.

- Si, how long have I known you? Forever, mate. And I'm telling you this as a friend: you need to take control. You can't be fucking swept along by stuff.

- Yes, dad.

He chose to ignore that one and I chose to ignore it. He's got a lot of time for my dad, has D.

- If you want to get back with Max – which, by the way, I think would be no bad thing – then you're gonna have to stop doing things which make it more and more likely that you're not gonna get back with her. As you know, I'm not one of your moral majority types, but I do try and exercise some sort of judgment. It was fucking obvious from the moment you met Eliz, that she fucking liked you. How old is she, by the way? Too fucking young is how old she is, mate. For those reasons alone, you should've left well alone; you're not in any position to handle any unrequited love malarkey. You can fuck anyone you want, mate, but you can't be ending up in situations where someone's scared of you for Chrissake. All this shit boils down to you not taking care of your inter personals. You've always got to be on top of your inter personals, mate. But it's too late to be going over all that; you're in the situation you're in and we need to get you out of it. Just make sure that you think on in future cause this, frankly, is one of the more challenging situations that I've come across.

    D rubbed his temples and his smooth skin crumpled. I remembered when it was me that was getting him out of scrapes the whole time. Back when I was responsible and before he acquired things he didn't want to lose. D's been hustling his whole life and he's accepted the risks which are a part of his vocation. He did a couple of stretches years back for daft stuff and he's grateful not to have been caught for the bigger jobs. When I've been able to, I've sorted him out; I've guaranteed his loans and appeared as a character witness but I've never felt compromised by what he's done. Looking back, the tables turned when our lass fucked off and what I did stopped mattering to me. I could've sat and pursued this thread for hours but there was no time to be philosophising over all that. I made a point of not looking at my watch because all it was going to tell me was that time was running out and one thing I didn't need to be doing was panicking. I'd handed my fate over to D and I needed to be doing what I was told, but before that I needed to check – for the second time – that I'd locked both doors. As I came back into the living room, he asked,

    - What're you doing?

    - Checking the doors, mate, I don't want the kids coming over and carrying on.

    D shook his head and it was like that'd become his default response to everything I said.

- See what I mean, Si? Don't you think it's a bit fucked up that you're scared of your own kids?

I didn't even bother acknowledging what he said on account of the fact that Tony'd just said pretty much the same thing to me no time ago; I just wished that he'd stop summarising and analysing and get on with the job in hand which was to sort my life out. I wondered whether it wasn't possible that this task could be accomplished without my input. Might it be possible for me just to go to bed, defrag and wake up sometime tomorrow when he'd sorted it all out? I didn't ask because even in my addled state, I knew it wasn't possible. One part of my head told the other to think straight - to be focussed - but it was a futile exercise because I couldn't control the thoughts which seeped in and nudged other thoughts out of the way. What if the kids have called the police about the money? Is what I've done technically theft? What if Mr and Mrs Neighbourhood Watch decide independently to call the police? Would they come now, all this time after, and what would I say if they did? I left D to mull over Step Two of our Grand Plan, Step One being transforming myself into the kind of guy who looked like he might be capable of sorting this shit out.

I showered and scrubbed myself clean. I washed my hair and conditioned it. I was surprised it didn't fall out in clumps. I shaved and I wished my hand would slip and cut my throat. The towel smelt of mould or maybe I did. I masked the rot with something that promised citrus scents. I wiped a space in the mirror and looked at my face; it looked scared and weary. In the bedroom, my clothes were the tail end of a jumble sale after my untidying up session. I forced myself to breathe slowly and I carefully replaced them in the wardrobe. In the bottom of the wardrobe was a bag of clothes I'd failed to unpack since my last shopping spree. I unpacked them and found myself baffled at how anyone could justify spending getting on for £200 on a pair of jeans and a T shirt which made me look like a middle aged escapee from a boy band.

I heard a car draw up outside and it was all I could do to stop myself from going to check on the doors again. I was really not feeling so good and I knew that in this state there was no way I was going to be able to handle the next couple of hours so I had no choice but to top myself up again. This involved standing still – naked from the waist down - in my bedroom and trying to remember where it was I last saw the stuff. Miraculously – and I took this to be a good omen – I remembered. I sorted myself out and placed the rest – which was not quite as much as I'd imagined – in my jacket pocket. My nostrils felt congested and my throat was dry but I was pretty sure that in a few minutes I was going to be feeling marginally better. Now, I told myself, was not the time for coming down. That evening, when all this was a distant memory, I'd knock it on the head for a few weeks, get all this shit out of my system. By tomorrow morning, I told myself, all this would have assumed the proportions of a cautionary tale to which we might refer in future: that was a close one, mate, D would say and I'd nod and say, tell me about it. Maybe we'd laugh. I tried to smile but rigor mortis had set into my face.

Downstairs, D was on his mobile.

- I'm on my way. I've just nipped into Si's. Everything's fine - he's picking up Max and they'll be over later. No, I've not got the ice yet; I'm gonna pick it up on my way over. You're gonna have to brazen it out, mate. You've no fucking choice. Go over to Eliz's, throw yourself on her mercy and hope she'll let you in. Contrite…that's a word, innit? Well, that's how you're gonna have to appear.

I was momentarily confused until I realised that D was no longer on the phone and that much of what he'd said had been directed at me. I'd kind of hoped that he might have another solution; one that didn't involve me doing very much at all and I was disappointed, frankly, that this was the best that he'd been able to come up with. He continued,

- I'll pretend to be her and you pretend to be you.

He stood and faced me, frowning, with one hand on his hip like some sort of method actor.

- Go on, then.

I was by this time entirely unconvinced of the efficacy of this approach but I'd no choice but to go along with it.

- Hi Eliz. Listen, I've just come round to apologise for last night. I know I was really insensitive and I'm really sorry. I think it was the stress of Christmas and all that. Thing is, I think I might have left an envelope here and it's really important that I get it back. D'you think I could come in and look for it? Soon's I've got it I'll leave you alone…what d'you think?

D was unimpressed by my performance; he told me I looked shifty and dangerous. He said I looked like the last person any sane woman would let into her house to look for fucking envelopes, which was rich coming from a guy who looks like your archetypal villain. It's a standing joke that he resembles every *Crimewatch* photofit you've ever seen. I was off on one about all this but he wasn't having any of it. He reckoned I was missing the point, wasting time and doing myself no favours.

- And you'd better change out of that fucking T-shirt. You look like a twat.

He told me we'd to switch places so that I was her and he was me and he'd show me how it was supposed to be done. We rehearsed a couple more times and by the end I had to admit that I was beginning to believe that this might work.

- So, d'you think we should make a move now, D?
- Of course we should make a fucking move now.

He looked at his watch. He was clearly imagining Linda waiting at home with her canapés and vol au vents, iceless and fuming. He went into the kitchen and gulped down a glass of water. I told myself that this unfeasible course of action was doable and would yield positive results, and this was only partly because there were no other options available. I repeated in my head D's script and inwardly rehearsed the postures he'd suggested I adopt. Apparently I'd to combine contrition, humility and shame. I didn't anticipate having much of a problem with any of these. What I'd not to do was to appear too demanding in respect of the envelope,

- Possession's nine tenths of the law, mate. At the end of the day, Si, you don't exactly have a right to go into her house. The idea is to get her to invite you in. D'you understand?

I understood. When we were about 12 or so, D introduced me to shoplifting. He'd been at it for months and he thought it was time I learned this most basic of life skills. He talked me through it at the end of our road: what to do and what not to do. I listened intently and ran through the manoeuvre over and over in my head on our way to the shop. Preparing for this grown up exercise was a bit similar to that, but not very.

- Are you sure you shouldn't come to the door with me, D?
- You mean for backative and all that?

I nodded, glad that he understood the obvious benefits of having him there with me.

- Simon, by your own admission, this woman's scared of you. To her, you're some sort of male predator. It is not gonna be helpful to approach her again today mob handed.

By this time, D was on his feet and he wasn't looking like a man who was keen to enter into any further discussion on the ins and outs of the operation. He was a man who needed to go sort his function out. He suggested we go in his car on account of he wasn't so sure he could trust me to drive, which again was rich coming from a man with nine points on his licence; it would've been 12 and a ban had I not generously taken the rap for 3 of them. I pointed this out to him and he said,

- Just get in the fucking car, Si.

11.

We headed out towards the place ending in *ley*. The roads were quiet and I began to think that they must clear the roads when I was heading out there. We got there in no time flat. D dropped me at the end of a row of terraced houses and told me he expected me back in no more than 15 minutes tops. The Yorkshire stone had been cleaned up and the houses looked like a street scene in the type of Dales drama series they show on Sunday night TV. It briefly crossed my mind that if you transported this street to north Leeds, the houses'd go for a fortune. Christmas tree lights pulsated behind the net curtains and in some of the small front gardens, kids played with their new toys in their new clothes.

Eliz's front room curtains were drawn and they didn't quite meet in the middle. I was a bit concerned that she might not be up. I really did not want to have to be braying on her door to rouse her; that would not give the right impression at all. The short path that led to her door was cracked and her windows could have done with a lick of paint. For the first time, I noticed a To Let sign and remembered that she was meant to be off travelling. She'd been on about it the previous night: Bali, Malaysia, Vietnam, Australia. I wondered what sort of person would want to rent this place with the state it was in. My mouth was dry and my heart was racing but that was nothing new. I reached for the knocker. She answered in no time which I took to be either a very good or a very bad sign. I was struck by how young she had become; I didn't remember her being this unformed. Her short blonde hair was unkempt and her lips were chapped. On her forehead, there was a spot which looked likely to erupt sometime soon. She was in a lilac towelling bathrobe which was too big for her and beneath that were pink flannel pyjamas with white clouds on them. On her feet she was wearing fluffy slippers. The cigarette in her right hand seemed incongruous. Something like disgust rose in my stomach as I realised that she was probably barely older than our Stephanie. I didn't want to know what this said about me.

She hugged herself and shuddered as if a breeze had passed through her.

- What do you want?
- I came to apologise unreservedly for last night. The way I behaved was unforgivable and I feel totally ashamed of myself…

I regurgitated the prepared speech for about 30 seconds as she stared at me impassively. The thing was, that even though the whole thing could be viewed as a bit of a cynical exercise to enable me to get in the house and retrieve my wad, I did actually mean what I said and frankly I was a bit disappointed that she appeared not to be touched by my contrition, shame and humility. I was about to get to the bit where I asked to come in for a moment when she said,

- So, what is it that you want exactly?

Which put me off my stride a bit because there were a couple more things I was supposed to say before getting to that bit: things about regret and my total acceptance of responsibility for what had gone off. On reflection, it's probably as well that her enquiry meant that the script was out of the window and that I was forced to improvise,

- What it is, Eliz, is this: when I came round last night, I had an envelope with me which contained a quantity of cash…

Before I could finish, she'd reached into her dressing gown pocket and she'd handed me my envelope. It was folded but the words – *To Maxine, with love always* – were visible. For the first time she smiled, but not in a good way.

- D'you think I was born yesterday? I knew you'd be back for this. Now, fuck off.

Granted, I'd been less than chivalrous in my behaviour towards her but I felt mildly affronted by her language. I was left staring at a slammed door with an envelope in my hand wondering whether I was now entitled to have a go at her. Ideally, I would have preferred to check that she hadn't pilfered any of the cash (D had told me not to leave till I'd done that) but it just didn't feel appropriate. At the end of the path as I turned to close the gate I saw her pale face staring out at me between the closed curtains of her front room window. I raised a finger at her and even as I made the gesture, I felt a bit pathetic and past it. Someone - a neighbour I assume - walked past me and stared for a moment too long. I expect that he was thinking, what's that guy doing coming out of Eliz's house? At best, he was gonna be thinking I was an uncle on a festive greetings mission but I didn't get the impression that he was thinking the best. I nodded at him and he nodded back tersely. I felt him watching me as I walked towards the corner where D's car was parked. I waited for some feeling of triumph or relief as I folded the envelope and placed it in my inside pocket, but it didn't come. I just remembered her chewing her bottom lip and leaning against the door jamb like it was holding her up and I felt like going back and putting the money through her letterbox.

On the corner, D was leant against his car. He was in an animated discussion with some young lad who was admiring his alloys. Naturally, D was telling him he could get hold of a set for him for a good price. As I approached the passenger door, they were busy banging each other's digits into their mobiles. Through the tinted windows, I observed D showing off his full body kit; he offered the lad a cigarette and I wondered how much longer I was going to be marooned in this shitty little West Yorkshire town. I glanced inside the envelope – it was full of 20's and 10's and the odd 50. It didn't seem like she'd had the wherewithal to take any; maybe she was a decent person. Finally, I saw D answering his phone and he reluctantly took his leave of his new best mate.

- Yeah, yeah, yeah...I told you I was on my way. No, I've not picked up the ice yet. Yeah, of course I know what time it is...20 minutes, tops...

He asked me how it'd gone and congratulated me on what must apparently have been a bravura performance. The envelope had become a baton in a relay so I passed it to him and he slipped into his inside pocket.

- You've checked it?

I made a gesture that was somewhere between a nod and a shrug. 30 minutes later, and after a fruitless search for ice, D dropped me outside my house while he went off to complete the next important stage of the mission. In his absence, I traced every step he took and hoped that his improvisational skills were on top form. D's always had what at best could be described as a spiky relationship with our lass. She's often said that he's a prime example of a man who's failed to grow up and that he's a bad influence, all of which is true but no truer of him than of most men. I was more than a bit concerned that with all the other things he had on his mind, he might be lacking in the deftness of touch department. I didn't even allow myself to contemplate what might be the consequences of his failure to perform what – in my own mind – had become a simple task.

15 minutes later he returned, laden down with four large *Pyrex* dishes and two serving platters.

- What d'you wanna do with these?

Party tableware was not my primary concern right then. What I needed to know - but didn't dare ask - was what had happened to the envelope. He dumped the dishes on my kitchen table.

- Piece o'piss, fella. She's not happy - as you'd expect - but on the positive side, the kids are not in. They're at her sister's and they're not due back till this evening. You won't be surprised to learn that Max is not in the mood for coming to the do. She reckons she's got a headache so she's not planning on going anywhere. Provided you handle your end of the operation ok I reckon there's every chance her headache'll disappear and you might be able to persuade her to change her mind. Don't go in there all guns blazing; remember, the reason you're there is to apologise for how you carried on last night. I strongly suggest that you use whatever persuasive skills you've got at your disposal to make sure that she comes with you cause that'll distract her from thinking through this cunning sleight of hand. You might want to subtly persuade her to scrub up a bit, by the way. She looks like shit.

Under normal circumstances I'd have had a go about his summary of Max's appearance, but the circumstances were far from normal so I let it go.

- The envelope's stuffed right down the side of the sofa… the left hand side. Go sort it out, and I'll see you back at mine in an hour or so…yeah? Did you find those ice cubes, by the way?

I nodded and began to feel my face lose its pained expression. My chest felt clearer and my breaths deepened. I presented D with four small trays of ice cubes; they were heart shaped. We both laughed.

12.

Our lass seemed less than pleased to see me but by then I'd become used to evoking this reaction in women so it was a water and ducks' backs scenario. I started in on the unreserved apology for the way I'd carried on the night before and told her I didn't know what I'd been thinking of accusing her of this, that and the other. She had one hand on her hip and she blocked the doorway. There were creases in her face that I'd not seen before and a certain blotchiness that was not the best look in the world. For an instant I wondered what it was that I was doing there. Then she reminded me.

- I'm sick of your apologies, Simon. They're boring.

I wasn't expecting my apology to cut much ice with her but, like D had said, it was probably not a bad idea to get it out of the way at the outset; it showed that my primary concern was not for myself. It was about making amends, he'd said. Remembering the professor on the radio, I continued,

- I want to acknowledge that what happened last night really happened. I don't want to gloss over stuff, and I want you to know that I know that I was completely out of order.

- I've heard it all before, Simon.

I couldn't argue with that one. I began to get the impression that she had heard enough from me and that she might be seriously considering closing the door and going back into the house alone – in much the same way that Eliz had less than an hour previously. I knew that I owed someone something and it could have been D or her or myself so I shifted my weight and put one foot over the threshold. I asked if the kids were in and she told me they were all out at her sister's – what with everything that had gone off it had seemed like a good idea. I tried to look like someone who didn't have a clue what she was on about. I asked her why she'd not gone and she told me she wasn't feeling up to it with all the shit that I'd caused over the past few hours. She started on about how I've got this knack of fucking things up just at the point when things are going well and put it down to an impulse for self-destruction. She was upset, and who could blame her? I could tell that she was about to illustrate her self-destruction theory with examples going back years but I'd heard it all before and anyway it wasn't in the script. I managed to manoeuvre my way into the house and lurked around in the hallway like I wasn't welcome there – which I wasn't.

- Simon, what the fuck've you done with that money you gave me yesterday?

She looked at me and then looked away. And that's when I knew: I knew she knew what had happened to the money but I also knew that she was open to a story which might make some sort of sense. She didn't quite hate me yet. I told her I'd no idea what she was talking about. As she told me what had gone off, I shook my head. The truth was, I could barely believe it myself. When she finished, I said,

- Is this some sort of sick joke? Have you any idea what it feels like to know that your family thinks you're capable of summat like this?

She listened, apparently unmoved, then asked,

- So what was this party you were at last night last, anyway, when the kids came round?

- I wasn't at a fucking party, Max. I was driving around, Max. My head was in bits.

Which was both true and untrue. To be honest, I was struggling to keep on message because she was stood in front of me with her arms crossed, trying to look ok while tears coursed down her cheeks. My voice cracked a little when I told her that I knew for a fact that the envelope was in the house somewhere. She, of course, said that she and the kids had turned the place over.

- I'm not saying you've stolen it but it's a bit bloody funny that it was there before you left and then it suddenly disappears when you do.

- What kind of sick fucker steals from his own…?

I couldn't finish the question partly because I didn't know how to refer to her and partly because I knew exactly what sort of sick fucker did what I had done. She sniffed and wiped her cheeks with a tissue. If I had my time over, I'd have told her something which approached the truth: that I wasn't thinking and that I'd dug myself into a hole. I don't know how much difference it would have made to her. And it was probably too late by then to avoid everything that came later.

- And that's to say nothing off the way you carried on last night, accusing me of all sorts when you're in no fucking position to be hurling accusations left, right and centre. I take it you've conveniently forgotten about your own misdemeanours.

She was off on one about some bird I allegedly shafted back in the year dot.

- Since when have you been some sort of paragon of fucking virtue?

I could've look at her seething face all day but I wasn't there to look at her face. I guided her inside and told her I'd look in the kitchen and she could look in the living room. She told me there was no point since she'd turned the place upside down twice already. I knew, though, that if there really was no point I wouldn't be there. I told her that it must be in there somewhere and that I wasn't leaving till we found it. There must have been some small piece of her that believed me because she reluctantly agreed to have one last look,

- Five minutes, Simon, and that's it.

I was honestly not feeling so good about this little stunt but I'd not much in the way of choice. I asked her if she could remember where she'd last seen it. I noisily opened and closed cupboards and drawers, mumbling from time to time about how I could've sworn I'd seen it here, there or somewhere else entirely.

Everything was neat and in its place. On the pin board there was a Christmas card the twins had made and inside it said, *Merry Christmas Mummy*. Presumably mine got lost in the post. I called and asked her if she was sure she'd looked in the bedroom.

- There's no fucking point since it's not fucking there.
- Have another good look in the living room, then.

I tried to sound exasperated and confused. As I announced my intention to join her in the living room she appeared sheepishly at the kitchen door, an A5 envelope dangling from her fingers.

- Where was it?
- Down the side of the settee.

She suppressed a smile and I suppressed the urge to punch the air. Instead, I stood close to her and I told her that finding the envelope was great but it didn't make up for the fact that I'd treated her like shit last night. I told her that I was gonna sort my life out and the words flowed freely and effortlessly either because I meant them or because I'd said them that many times before. For the second time in no time I told a woman that what I'd done was bang out of order and completely out of character and for the second time in no time I failed to believe myself.

- This has really done me in, Max. I know that I've gotta change; I can't go through this again.

All of which was entirely true. I didn't know exactly what it was that our lass was thinking but there was relief in there somewhere. At the end of the day, I suppose, none of us want to believe that the person we remember having loved is a complete bastard. I was finally unburdened.

The guy next door was complaining about someone – me, as it turned out - who'd parked in front of his drive. I told him to chill out, that it wasn't the end of the world and I felt my face crease into a genuine smile. Everything in me was light and clean and it was obvious that he could see that in me because he said it was all right, mate, and no big deal.

I read this article once about these researchers who'd tried to analyse what it was that made some people lucky and others unlucky; in the end they isolated it to having a positive, optimistic outlook. Maybe that was what I'd done; even in the depths of despair, I reckoned, I'd retained some hope that things could get better. I'd gathered around me the limited resources at my disposal and used them to best effect.

Maxine was wearing high heels as she always did when we went out together and she held on to my elbow as we approached the car.

- Do I look all right? I've not gone over the top, have I, with my hair and all that?

I told her she looked bloody marvellous because she did.

13.

Driving the short distance to D's party everything started to become clear. It was something to do with all the constituent parts of my fragmented life colliding and what ensues when that happens. Over the past couple of days I'd been bombarded with challenges and obstacles and it was like every new thing that'd happened to me had happened for me. There had been some higher purpose to all this and I was quite convinced that if I just let this small thought settle at the back of my head, and if I stopped worrying it like a scab, its purpose would reveal itself to me in its own time and when this happened, the issue of the shop and the VAT and the bonuses would resolve itself.

Our lass was sat next to me and she was as glowing and gorgeous as she'd ever been. She was even laughing in anticipation of the story she was gonna be able to tell the kids that night and she earnestly told me that first thing the following day she was going to get them round to mine to apologise both to me and to the neighbours. I told her that there was no need because even in my unnaturally elated state, I realised that this would be taking things that bit too far. At one point, she touched my knee in a way that struck me as uncontrived and entirely natural and it was then that I knew that I'd finally peeled back the years and that there was every chance that I'd be able to make good all my deficits and become the person that I was supposed to be. If I did that, then she'd become the person she was supposed to be. I touched her shoulder and she didn't wince and she didn't appear ridiculously grateful. She just accepted my hand being there as if that was where it was supposed to be at that moment.

We discussed inconsequential trivia and nothing was forced or laden with meaning. Maybe, I thought, this was the answer to the question I'd asked her all those years ago about when we stopped talking and why. Maybe it wasn't that there was nothing to talk about but just that we'd forgotten how to be this easy in each other's company. We got into an internal edit mode and maybe we just slipped into a defensive way of being which in the end fucked the pair of us.

A new thought came into my head like summer and I wondered whether I should tell her about it.

I'd ask her if she could remember not so long after we first moved in together when we'd no money and we'd sit in the flat with the rings on the hob providing the heat on account of not daring to put the central heating on. We'd buy 10 cigarettes and they'd last and a can of something to share or (if we were flush) a bottle of the sort of wine we'd both turn our noses up at now. We'd curl up on the sofa and watch any shit that was on and then maybe we'd go out with just enough money for a couple of cheap drinks. She'd stamp her feet against the cold because it seemed always to be cold then and I'd put my arm around her even though public shows of affection were frowned upon at the time. Sometimes – if she wasn't working and I had no early lectures – we'd get on the first bus in the morning and go as far as it would take us then we'd walk back home. We'd be cold and then we'd be warm suddenly. And I didn't need to be told then about how to breathe and I didn't need to take stuff to make me feel on top of my game, but we both breathed and we were both on top of our games. All that was true, and it's only ever been true with her.

I stored the story and told myself I'd ask her about it later when we were alone at hers or at mine. Maybe, I thought, I'd had to go through this terrible time and to drag her along behind me for us to get back to where we should always have been. It had maybe all been a matter of restoring our internal settings. All the cleaning of the house and the sorting out of the shit that morning began to make sense.

Someone - it might have been a priest or a mate or a greeting in a *Hallmark* card - said something to me once about suffering being the road to peace and I thought that they maybe had a point.

We arrived at the do to find D squaring up to the elderly gentleman who has the misfortune to live next door. The dispute seemed largely to concern D's failure to observe a protocol regarding the proximity of wheelie bins to the kerb. Apparently he had scant regard for pedestrians whose thoroughfare he routinely obstructed with his bins and his bin bags and his dumping of sundry items in front of his neighbour's driveway. D pointed out that his neighbour's driveway was no more than an obsolete decorative feature on account of the fact that he didn't have a car. D's always struggled with the notion of walking and, visibly perplexed, has asked me on several occasions,

- If God had meant us to walk, why would he have invented cars?

Obviously I've mentioned that it was some French bloke behind the internal combustion engine but as far as he's concerned that's just me missing the point. His is a simple faith; though he has no truck with God under normal circumstances, he retains a touching belief that if He did exist, he must have invented everything.

The elderly gentleman felt compelled to expose to D his torso and invited D to just fucking try it on. I got the impression that he'd probably overdone it on the sherry. It transpired that he'd served in the Merchant Navy for 20 years and thereafter worked on building sites as a steel erector. He'd eaten people like D for breakfast. It has to be said that his torso looked alarmingly and bizarrely impressive on one so apparently past it and D declined his offer opting instead to befuddle and bewilder by staking a counter claim which involved what he referred to as a near fatal accident to Linda caused by his neighbour's failure to prune back his privet.

- It nearly had our lass's eye out. She was that fucking close to being blinded. I've got photos, medical reports, the lot.

He sent one of his mesmerised kids to call Linda out to validate his story. Awaiting the appearance of his star witness, D summarised the case. He reckoned that it was gross negligence and that someone had to pay. I'd seen the photographs and, to be honest, Linda looked fine if a little hung over. He informed his neighbour that he would be pursuing a claim in respect of injury to feelings and that he was investigating some other spurious damages. She was scared to leave the house, it seemed, and therefore the economic sustainability of the family unit had been seriously compromised. He failed to mention that Linda hadn't worked since about 1993 (largely at his insistence) but this, I'm sure, was an understandable oversight on his part brought on, doubtless, by the trauma this incident had caused him.

Our lass nudged me and wordlessly told me to tell him to get a grip. But he was off on one by then and I knew, because I've known him that long, that there was no stopping him and that he was enjoying all this. The old giffer from next door was a worthy opponent and he was also clearly getting something out of the exchange. His wife appeared at the front door and she told him to stop carrying on daft and he told her to get herself back inside and that this had nowt to do with her. To be honest, it was all about the pair of them getting to role-play at being men. I was enjoying the spectacle and I, too, told our lass to chill and to let it run its course. She turned to the neighbour's missus and each shook their heads in the way that women do. It's like a code, isn't it, between them? By the time Linda emerged, the neighbour had come up with a counter counter claim concerning D's dog,

- There's all sorts you can pick up from dog shit. I'm gonna get straight onto the Council as soon as they can be bothered to go back to work.

This was an inspired move on his part because suddenly he and D found some common ground around Council Tax and what the fuck it actually is that you get for your money. It seemed that it was all about bleeding the common man dry. D regaled his neighbour with an anecdote about his extension and planning permission. It was like they didn't want your common, decent, working man – amongst whose number he generously included his neighbour - to make good. D pointed at the rubble in his front garden and at the foundations of his conservatory. Thwarted was what he'd been.

- I've had full on plans for this place: improving the neighbourhood and all that. And they're on about permissions and building regulations and it's like I'm not allowed to employ your local craftsmen because they don't meet your regulations bollocks.

D's neighbour, it turned out, had paid taxes all his working life and what'd he got for it: sweet fuck all was what he'd got. He'd been on at the Council about those lads that congregate outside the off licence and what response had he got? Well, none, actually. D told him that he'd more than happy to go down the road and sort them out; he wasn't fucking having his neighbours intimidated by a bunch of cunts (he excused his language but his neighbour seemed encouraged by it) who have no respect for an older generation which fought a war on our behalf. The neighbour pointed out that he was a kid during the war.

Linda appeared at D's shoulder, clearly ready to fight whatever war it was that D has conscripted her into. Both D and his neighbour seemed perplexed and irritated by her sudden intrusion on account of it disrupting their flow. The neighbour's wife appeared again at the front door and called him. His name, it turned out, was Henry. But he wasn't listening. Linda asked,

- So, what is it you're after?

Our lass tugged at my shoulder like she wanted me to intervene in some decisive way. D turned to Linda and made it clear that her presence was no longer required and she and our lass ended up going back into the house whilst D and his new best mate mulled over the various trials they'd overcome at the hands of bureaucrats. Finally and tentatively, the neighbour's wife reappeared to be informed by her husband that the two of them were nipping round to D's for a festive drink.

The population of the house reflected the diversity of D's social circle: there were lads we'd been at school with; distant and close relatives and friends; neighbours and a discreet spattering of women with whom I knew he'd enjoyed more than a passing acquaintance. Ignored by the front door was a clump of middle aged men dressed in Christmas casual; they turned out to be the fathers of some of the lads his eldest played football with on a Sunday. They mumbled ruefully about cups and league positions and I nodded along with them on my way to the kitchen. I liked to think that I occupied an honoured place in this annual gathering. It wasn't just because I'd known him so long; it was something to do with the fact that we've held on to each other despite all the changes that we'd been through. It was a bit like a strong marriage, but as I processed this thought I made a mental note not to mention it to D on account of the fact that he'd start speculating loudly about my sexuality.

In the kitchen, a bunch of women tried to help Linda with her canapés but it was pretty clear to me that they were just getting in her way. They dug and poked and grabbed at miniature pastries like refugees at a feeding station while Linda tried to impose something like order. It turned out, according to someone I took to be her sister that she should have gone to *Tesco* for her Chinese party selection- they'd an offer on. Someone else loudly advocated *Costco* and Linda, sparkling in a top that resembled a glitter ball, forced an expression which was somewhere between a grin and a silent scream. Our lass whispered something to Linda. She poured each of the remaining women a glass of *Cava* and pointed them in the direction of the back garden where their kids were arguing over who got to have a go on the quad bike. Our lass put an apron on, took off her shoes and got on top of directing operations. Which was our lass all over.

14.

In the living room, D impressed a group of his guests with his new home cinema system. He juggled half a dozen remotes and pressed a gaunt young man into having a go. Menus appeared and disappeared like some poorly executed *Powerpoint* presentation as the lad, visibly panicked, tried to make sense of the various options he was presented with. Relieving him of his technical duties, D expounded on his audio visual aspirations,

- What I'm after, ultimately, is turning this room into a full on home entertainment centre: music, TV, DVD, games consoles - the full monty.

He started on about some speakers he was after from my shop and announced my intention to do him a good deal on them, which was news to me. He then went on to intimate that pretty much anyone of his acquaintance was entitled to similarly good deals at my expense. Apparently, it was all about looking after your own and not forgetting where you came from. D was under the impression that he enjoyed privileged status at the shop on account of the fact that he helped me out with the shop fitting when I first opened. Every time he came in, he commented on the sturdiness of the display stands and announced to any hapless customer or salesperson that what he grandly referred to as the whole design concept was down to him. He'd never actually bought anything because he never knew exactly what it was that he was after. Though he considered himself to be very knowledgeable, D's grasp of audio visual technology is tenuous. He's a man, though, and like a lot of men reckons knowing about cars, IT and sound is something that comes with the y chromosome. On the rare occasions that he appeared to be on the verge of buying something, the sale was thwarted at the point at which the matter of payment was raised. He wanted a discount which took account of the longevity of our friendship, a discount for a cash sale, a discount which recognised his sterling work on the fit out and there was no fucking way he was paying VAT. In the end – and it always took a long time to reach this point – he invariably told me that he'd got a mate who could pick him something up at half the price. Which is why his house is full of shit gear.

His presentation sputtered to a halt when a member of the audience asked a searching question about pixels, and D deftly manoeuvred the conversation to the less technologically challenging subject of his leather sofas.

-None of your fucking *World of Leather* cheap shit. These are specially imported for your high-class hotels. Mate of mine works for a firm that fits out all the interiors and he sorted 'em out for me. Got 'em for our lass…Christmas and all that.

He spotted Henry and his wife lurking around the edge of the party. To my mind, they looked like people who wanted to find a suitable moment to leave. Anyway, he plucked them out of the audience and encouraged them to try out the sofas.

- What're you saying about that, mate? Full on luxury or what?

Henry role-played a man who was having the best seated experience of his life while his wife stroked the sofa and declared it very soft and comfy. We were all told that we'd to have a go and for the next few minutes we bobbed up and down dementedly like we'd unexpectedly found ourselves in a game of musical chairs. One guest – another uncomfortable looking neighbour – refused to participate on account of being a vegetarian.

-   I'm not asking you to eat it, love.

We all laughed. The best thing for her to do at this point would have been to let it drop but she was clearly one of your ethical types who was not about to pass up an opportunity to evangelise. She started on about by products of the meat industry and intensive farming methods, points which frankly were lost on her fellow carnivorous guests. I listened, though, because I'd become this shiny new person who was interested in learning new things. I kind of admired her passion and found myself wondering what it might be like to live your life in accordance with some deeply held conviction. She was on a roll and started telling me all about all of her many convictions. She was on about her allotment and third world debt like the two were linked in some way. The words global and local were flipped about and in no time we were on to bias in the media and a war that was being fought (in our names, apparently) in somewhere I'd no interest in. I thought about mentioning my Rwanda experience to her but all that seemed like a long time ago and I'd forgotten whether it was your Tutsis or your Hutus that were the bad guys. It began to feel like she was a woman who didn't get out much and had not properly grasped the etiquette of party small talk. As she got on to complementary therapies and I started to contemplate the relative merits of listening to her or boiling my own head, D rescued me with a characteristically astute intervention,

- If you ask me, all that complementary therapy stuff's a load of bollocks. Saw a programme on it once; there was this woman swore blind that rhythmically tapping your body cleared your trapped energies. Now, don't get me wrong – everyone's entitled to their own daft beliefs - but when you start charging people £50 an hour to have their energies untrapped, that's taking the piss.

The room - with the obvious exception of the vegetarian - nodded, intoned £50 an hour and shook its collective head. Once again, D and Henry established common ground and Henry treated us to a detailed account of his wife's flirtation with acupuncture. His wife stroked the sofa ferociously and reddened as he asked her to specify exactly which bits of her the acupuncturist had punctured.

- She was in tears when she came back. Weren't you, love?

She confirmed that she was in tears and looked close to tears then but that was probably summat to do with Henry broadcasting her water infection to a bunch of strangers. D summarised the key learning points that had been revealed by this touching tale and concluded,

    - See, that's what I'm saying. It's all about preying on the vulnerable.

    He pointed at Henry's wife by way of illustration and then turned to his vegetarian guest as if she was the one who'd stuck pins in her. She looked at me like she thought I might be some sort of ally on account of I'd listened to her sermonising for half an hour.

    I've known all sorts of women over the years but the worst by far are the lonely ones. This woman was leaking loneliness like sweat. Lonely women don't know who to trust. There was this woman – Suzie – who I had a brief entanglement with. It was just after I got the shop and she was a customer. She came in on her own and, on reflection, that should have been a warning. Women rarely come into my shop alone unless they've been given clear written instructions by a man. She was attractive, though, and that must've clouded my judgment. She'd come in late in the afternoon and it would've been rude not to have asked her out for a swift half after she'd knowledgeably completed her transaction. Within a couple of weeks, she reckoned she was in love with me. I think she loved me because she didn't know what love was. She worked and all that; she had routine encounters with colleagues and neighbours and every now and again she'd go out for a drink with her mate (I met her once and, to be honest, she was a classic lonely woman too). But her encounters were fleeting and shallow and, looking back, I don't think she trusted herself to get any closer to people. So, she ended up confusing sex with intimacy and got it into her head that I was a man she could trust. She reframed our arrangement and told herself it was a relationship and she'd carry on if I was late or if I failed to turn up. She started inventing anniversaries and would tell me that this, that or the other was our tune on account of it'd been playing in my car the first time I'd taken her to this, that or the other place. Meanwhile, back at the ranch, our lass was carrying on about where I'd been, what I'd been up to and with whom. I started to get confused about who it was I was accountable to. In the end, I was forced to be John Malkovich in

Dangerous Liaisons: the whole beyond my control thing. Fortunately, a lifetime of low expectations held Suzie in good stead to deal with my rejection of her and once we'd endured the usual whys and hows and tell me what to do to make it betters, she accepted it with what passed for good grace. To be honest, I felt a bit shit about it; if it hadn't been for her sapping loneliness I reckon we could've made it work – within the obvious parameters imposed by my marital status.

Stood in D's living room with his ethical guest looking expectantly at me, I found myself wondering what lasting impact I might have had on Suzie and whether there mightn't be a whole squadron of women who cursed me daily. I promised myself that I was going to stop invading women's lives and settle – or resettle – with our lass where I was no danger to myself or to anyone around me. In the meantime and by way of introduction to this new way of being, I needed to find a way of rescuing this woman.

- Let's not get into a daft argument, D. She's not the one who charges people stupid money for tapping or acupuncture or whatever; it's just summat she believes in.

At which point it turned out she was a full on complementary therapist which went down badly with the audience but better with our lass and Linda into whose kitchen I led her when things started to look like they might turn ugly. I left them discussing some weird therapy called eye movement desensitisation. Apparently, it worked particularly well for people recovering from trauma. Our lass seemed peculiarly absorbed and I was left wondering what trauma she might be recovering from and whether I might have caused it.

15.

    The party continued and once D had stopped entertaining his guests, it began to take care of itself. Clumps of people formed in the living room, the hallway and in the kitchen. A small self selected group of us adjourned to the upstairs bathroom from time to time. Our lass surprised me by joining us on one occasion and when we'd done I took her to one side.

    - You don't have to be like me, Max, for me to care about you.

    She'd had a bit to drink by this time and what with that and the line, she was on a being honest vibe.

    - I know I don't, sweetheart. I'm a grown woman and not every decision I make is based on what I think is gonna make you care about me. There are other things in my life that matter to me.

    I edited out her final sentence because it didn't need to form part of my narrative. And her sweetheart sounded bitter the way she'd said it this time so I took that out too. And since when did she become a grown woman? She wasn't a grown woman when she wanted me to sort out her heating and she wasn't a grown woman when , within weeks of pissing off , she was stood on the doorstep pleading for some sort of reconciliation and I'd had to tell her I knew it was over and I was grateful she'd had the guts to end it before one of us killed the other – which was melodramatic admittedly but she got the point. Waiting inside – and there was no need for her to have known this at the time or since – some woman whose name doesn't matter waited for me to come back upstairs.

So I ignored her grown woman nonsense and I was left with nothing. She smiled and it was the biggest smile in the world.

- Things have got to change between you and me, Si. You need to stop thinking I'm someone who needs looking after. I was just saying to Linda that you and D treat us like we're slightly backward kids that want watching over the whole time in case we run out into the road and hurt ourselves.

I was relieved when she dragged Linda into our predicament because it meant that none of this meant anything. It was just two women carrying on like they do about men. In my experience, if you get two or more women together, chances are the conversation will turn to men and how shit we are and how we're all the same. Our defining characteristics are our inability to communicate, our failure to listen and our belief that we're always right. So when our lass started on about about how rubbish I was and how I treated her like a kid, I just added this to my database of predictable things women say about men.

- All right, babes. I was just voicing my opinion. Obviously it's up to you what you do. Just make sure you can keep on top of it.

She looked at me and frowned. She told me I wasn't taking her seriously, but what was new there. Thankfully, she remembered where we were and clearly decided that it was neither the place nor time to be having a domestic. I performed a bit of a rescue attempt and told her that she was a star and that I loved her. I drew a grin on my face and kissed her on the forehead like you might a child. She told me that she loved me too and that that had never been in dispute. She said it was more about how we loved each other and why but I'd stopped listening by that point because as far as I was concerned the situation had been sorted and there was nothing to be gained from raking over the same ground again. I wanted to feel like I felt when we were driving over there. I whispered something to her about what I'd got planned for her when we left D's and she told me that I was a mucky bugger.

- Max, what do I dress this salad with? I've no olive oil. Will sunflower do?

And she was off back to the kitchen with Linda where she didn't have to worry about the hows and whys of loving me. D joined me at the bottom of the stairs.

- Now then, fella. It's been a rough old coupla days, man, but it looks like it's coming together finally.

I hadn't realised that we'd be needing to start dissecting this thing so soon but this was typical D. In another life, he'd have been some sort of political commentator; he remembers everything and he draws comparisons, considers the lessons that history has taught us and speculates on future developments. There'd be no stopping him once he'd started so I lit a cigarette and waited for his summary.

- You've got to stop fucking up, mate. One of these days, you're gonna drain all the strategies from the strategy bank and you're gonna be fucked: Go to jail, do not pass go and all that. You want to concentrate on the things you can control: your lass, the business and all that, and stop having daft adventures for a while. You want to knock Charlie on the head for a bit too. My guy's under the impression that I'm dealing myself with the amount I'm buying off him. What you're going through is fucking scandalous to be honest. On the positive side, you could be on your way to getting sorted now so you've gotta stop doing shit that stops you thinking about how shit things are in your life. Most of what's been wrong is of your own making, anyway.

This struck me as a somewhat harsh judgment but I wasn't in much of a position to defend myself. He asked me about the business like he thought I might have snorted all the profits and I assured him that everything was sorted in that department. The business was doing well; despite my erratic behaviour over the previous several months, it was summat I'd always kept on top of. It must have been where I'd deposited my pride because, to be honest, I'd fuck all else to be proud of. For the first time, it occurred to me that maybe it was me that was traumatised. Maybe I needed someone to desensitise my eye movements or rhythmically tap bits of my body and pull everything back together again.

When our lass left she took the best bits of me with her. I could pretend that that I'd done my best with the unpromising material she left behind but that wouldn't have been true.

- I've had a proper wake up call, mate. I've stared into the abyss.

Then I told him about this thing I'd read where they said that when a plane loses an engine in mid flight it just glides back to earth and what that means is that as a passenger you've got several minutes to contemplate your demise.

- I'm like a passenger on one of those flights and miraculously I seem to have survived.

I waited for him to nod because it struck me that this was the kind of analogy he'd probably relate to, but his face was all confusion and I became aware that I was maybe not at my most coherent and for the second time that day he looked a bit taken aback like he wasn't really expecting this onslaught of self disclosure. To give him his due, though, he dealt with it reasonably well under the circumstances.

-You want to be talking to your lass about this sort of stuff, mate. They like it, don't they, when you spill. They call it sharing.

Which is where he was wrong because if there was one thing I was convinced of it was that judging by our most recent exchange, our lass was not going to be hugely receptive to my emotional outpourings. It seemed that it was all about her now, what with her being a grown woman all of a sudden. I nodded enthusiastically, anyway, like D had just made a particularly incisive point and hoped that we might be permitted to drop the subject of my ineptitude. Fortunately, one of D's nephews staggered towards the living room mumbling something about wanting to throw up and D, mindful I imagine of the proximity of his sofas, grabbed him and steered him towards the downstairs toilet. The retching sound coming from behind the closed door confirmed the accuracy of the lad's self-diagnosis. D recruited a small army of women to clear up the mess and retreated to the garden to get some fresh air.

I'd no one to talk to but I was glad of the peace. I just observed the women toing and froing with *Vanish* and air fresheners and I listened to the lads' mates taking the piss out of him and going on about his inability to hold his drink. I watched a small clump of girls giggling and whispering to each other behind their hands. Our lass was still directing operations in the kitchen and she'd sent out one of D's kids to clear up the dishes in the living room. Henry and the vegetarian lady seemed to have reconciled and they were sharing stories about the best way to cultivate leeks. The football dads were still stood in the hallway inhaling beer and cursing referees. D's mum had taken advantage of the brief hiatus in proceedings and was encouraging the guests to join her in a rendition of the *Birdie Song*. That done, everyone under 40 left the front room as D's mum tried to figure out how the karaoke machine worked. In the end I went through and as I was leaving she said,

- You've always been good with your hands, Simon, love.

This turned out to be the funniest thing anyone had heard in a long time. When they composed themselves they got on with assassinating Gloria Gaynor and Frank Sinatra. And I was thinking, this is not so bad really, sitting here alone and watching. I didn't have to be in and amongst it the whole time; sometimes it's better to be on the edge where you can do no harm.

I could have sat there all night except it turned out I couldn't.

Part two
1

What happened next was pretty poor but in the grand scheme of things it doesn't matter much anymore. D rejoined me on the stairs and we got on to future plans. The fact that I didn't really have any plans beyond the following day didn't deter me from making a few up.

- I was thinking of maybe taking our lass off somewhere for the weekend. Put all this stuff behind us and all that. Then I was thinking of maybe taking on a couple more staff so that we can get into repairs.

I put the question of how I was going to retain my existing staff when I'd given their bonuses to Maxine on the back burner. D was looking, he said, at acquiring a retail property from which to sell stuff.

- What sort of stuff?
- You know: the sort of stuff I sell just now. I've got a fucking garage full of merchandise that wants shifting. What I need is more space so's I can keep up with demand.
- It's gonna be a bit of a weird shop, mate: sofas, tyres and gazebos?
- *Argos* gets away with it…anyway, obviously I wasn't thinking of selling everything I already sell from here. What I was thinking was that I could look at developing some sort of niche market. Any ideas?

Any ideas I might've been about to have were interrupted by a loud bang on the door. D cursed under his breath and reluctantly got up, mumbling,

- It's a fucking party…why don't they just walk straight in?

He answered the door and immediately put himself into confrontation mode because that's his default position when it comes to coppers. He started on about harassment and demanded to know who'd complained, naming some likely suspects. He speculated scathingly on the overtime rates the coppers were getting and let it be known that this wasn't what he paid his taxes for. He was on about real criminals and all the old ladies they were mugging while Tweedle Dum and Tweedle Fucking Dee were stood on his doorstep embarrassing him and his law abiding guests.

- What happened to community fucking relations?

He also slipped a baggie into Linda's hand as she joined him at the door, which struck me as a deft move. The two coppers at the door struggled to make themselves heard over some old giffer's rendition of *Blue Moon* and D's protests about police intimidation. A lad squeezed past me on his way upstairs and we glanced at each other, smiled and shook our heads. Maxine tapped me on the shoulder on her way back to the kitchen and whispered,

- D'you reckon we should think about making a move?

I told her I'd be with her in a minute; I just wanted to watch the floor show and we'd be off.

- I want your fucking numbers now cause first thing tomorrow morning I'm straight on to West Yorkshire Police Headquarters with a complaint about this. Get us a pen and paper, Lind.

In the background, a handful of his guests murmured their approval of the stance he'd taken whilst others skulked into the kitchen or anywhere else less visible to the coppers. The house stank of skunk and it struck me that unless someone got a grip, the situation could start to get out of hand so I elected myself to the role of mediator because, given the right situation, I've a way with words. I tapped D on the shoulder.

- Shall we discuss this outside?

We accompanied the coppers into the front garden. A couple of lads who seemed to be engaged in some sort of transaction made themselves scarce, and wandered slowly down the road doing a poor impersonation of people with nothing to hide. The coppers verified D's identity and address.

- Isn't it bloody obvious this is where I live?

They pointed at his car and asked him to confirm that it belonged to him.

- It's in my bloody drive, innit?
- The fact that it's in your drive doesn't necessarily mean that it's yours.
- The fact that you've looked up my fucking details on your computer confirms that it's mine. D'you think I was born yesterday?

I suggested to D that he might consider chilling; that this was obviously some sort of routine enquiry. I glanced at the coppers, wanting them to note my calming influence on what had been on the verge of becoming a volatile situation. D's mum poked her head out of the front room window and shouted,

- Simon, love, can you come in and sort out the karaoke machine?

Billy Joel shouted *Uptown Girl* over and over till it sounded like someone crying. Then someone else shouted,

- Will someone turn that fucking thing off?

Billy stopped shouting and Diana told everyone to *Stop in the name of love*. It got to *before you break my heart* and a dozen middle-aged women joined in like this was the eleventh commandment. I was glad I didn't live next door to D. It started to snow and for a moment neither me nor the coppers nor D said anything; we all just looked upwards. There's something about snow at Christmas that works. Faces appeared at the living room window, going ooh and aah. Our lass joined us for a second and asked how long this was all likely to take; there was going to be some sort of champagne toast soon. She smiled at one of the coppers but he didn't smile back. She handed D a pen and paper and he tried taking down the coppers' numbers but the snow speckled the paper and his writing ended up all blurred. Maxine winked at me, tapped her watch and went back inside. The snow was only a temporary reprieve and the coppers clearly had a job to do.

One of them examined the car and said something quietly into his radio. D joined him.

- Listen, I hope for your sake you've not got any daft ideas about giving me a producer cause that would be fucking full on harassment. I swear if...

Then all the air was sucked out of the world and my legs couldn't hold me anymore. D and the copper walked back towards me and they'd stopped talking about D and they'd started talking about someone they referred to as an associate of his, someone known only as Simon. This Simon had visited a young woman in somewhere ending in *ley* that morning and, according to an unnamed witness, had apparently been driven there in D's car. The witness had noted the model and registration number of the vehicle. For a moment, I wondered whether there mightn't be another Simon who'd been in that place with this person stood next to me – the sort of Simon coppers might want to talk to on Boxing Day in the snow. They wanted to talk to Simon about an alleged incident but I couldn't talk because I didn't understand what they were saying and my mouth was full of something that was blocking my airways. There were too many competing sounds and too many disembodied faces staring out of too many windows. I tried to process the word incident to see if it meant the same as accident. Could it be summat you did by mistake and which you needed simply and honestly to apologise for and then everything would be all right? No hard feelings and all that. D's words were a voiceover on a documentary,

- This is scandalous...he's a responsible respected businessman...you can't just pluck a man off the street and start accusing him of all sorts...

The snow distorted my vision and all the edges of the world were like frosted glass. I wanted the snow to be sucked back into the sky and I wanted to be sat on D's stairs. I wanted Maxine to tap me on the shoulder again and say,

- D'you reckon we should think about making a move?

I wanted the answer to be yes and I wanted us to have slipped out the back door and straight to the mythical place I'd told D I was gonna take her to. I wanted a pure and silent moment so I could just get my breath back. There was a whole bunch of people who needed to appreciate how hard this was for me and how much I needed some time to process all this stuff. Instead, our lass and D and all his guests receded and the only people left who mattered were these coppers, Eliz and me. Eliz lived in somewhere ending in *ley* and there had been an incident and this accidental incident which was in the past was suddenly in the present. One of the coppers touched my elbow; he was giving me some sort of instruction which was to involve moving but my legs didn't work properly. D told them to wait just one fucking minute and he ran inside and came back with my jacket and instructions to say nowt until I'd called my brief.

It was warm in the car and from the front I heard them say the things you hear them say on TV when they're trying to put people at their ease; things about a few questions and clarifying matters. They were talking to me but nothing they were saying seemed to apply to me because I'm not the sort of person who sits in police cars. From the back of the police car I noticed a thin woman, running into the road jerkily like a puppet, slipping and sliding and screaming something I couldn't hear. It was Maxine, of course, because no one else would run after me in the snow and in heels with her hair all over the place and her coat flapping behind her like a pair of useless wings. Behind her, a row of people formed a line of specks. One of them broke rank and grabbed her like she was running towards the edge of a cliff. A thought began to form itself and it knitted with other tiny, fragmented sub thoughts and then they all joined together in precisely the right order until they became a scene from a film which was nearly 20 years old:

It's that time in the morning when it's either too late or too early. A man and a woman walk across a frozen park and the grass crunches beneath their feet like they're walking on cornflakes. They pass the swings and slides and they're frozen still. She's in heels and she tells him her feet are like two bags of frozen peas. He tells her that there's a word for that and that he thinks it might be petrified but he's not so sure because it could mean turned to stone. She tells him that he's talking daft and that being petrified is about being terrified. He says that they're maybe one and the same thing: being turned to stone and being frightened and being frozen.

Maxine disappeared into the snow or I did. It doesn't really matter anymore which it was, but when her figure became a dancing stick insect in the rear view mirror, I remembered that the scene I'd recalled was taken from the director's cut of the story I'd been meaning to tell her later on when I'd done to her, or with her, whatever it was that I'd promised to do to or with her (the distinction between the two has become something I'm curiously preoccupied with these days). As the police station appeared and took up all the space in front of us, I knew that I'd be unlikely to get to tell her my story anytime soon and that by the time it got told it would have acquired a different meaning. That was when they stared back at me and started to look worried and embarrassed because I'd started to cry like women cry and I'd become a river that had flooded its banks. There's a word for the sound I made and it's keening; it means lamenting the dead and in the soundtrack to the Rwanda programme I'd listened to the night before that was what the women were doing. It sounded horrible and it marked the point at which – after the professor and his apologies and forgiveness – I'd decided I'd heard enough. My snot glazed my hands and it mixed with my tears and I was the sad sap at the bottom of the stairs and someone had forgotten to collect me and take me home, though it wasn't like home was a concept I was processing anymore. One of the coppers turned to me and he sounded properly worried when he asked me,

- Are you in pain, Mr Williams?

And all I could say was,

- I don't know what hurts anymore.

Because all the bits of me I'd been pulling back together had turned into feathers and they were all over the place. I was road kill on the ground Maxine had trampled as she chased the car and there were bits of me in somewhere ending in *ley* and other bits that D had told me to fix but that'd mean gathering them all together and I didn't know where I'd left them. In some smart office down by the river Joe cursed me then laughed at other bits of me. There were fragments of the rear windscreen that were in the flower beds with the shovel and with all the things I should have said but hadn't and all the things I shouldn't have said that I had. There was Eliz who looked like she was scared of me (on account of being scared of me) and, looking upwards, the sky was her ceiling. There was a wad of money in an A5 envelope and it was scored with love always. All of it snowed in on me and the police station wavered then came into sharp focus then wavered again.

- Would you like to see a doctor, Mr Williams?

And I said to him - sad sap that I was - that I was only lonely. Or I might have said that I was lonely only. It all amounts to the same thing in the end.

2.

And so, for all my frantic searching for who I was and what I'd become, it turned out that it was neither here nor there because suddenly I was – indisputably - a remand prisoner charged with a serious sexual offence. It became the beginning and end of how I was defined and it was just the way it was. I didn't settle well into my new identity because I couldn't quite make it fit with my old one; people like me don't do the sort of thing they reckoned I'd done. My strong ties to the community, prior unblemished character and my status as a successful businessman were all outweighed by the severity of my alleged offence and so my bail application was turned down. I can't imagine that the fact that Maxine was unprepared to offers hers as a bail address did me any favours either. It's not something I'll ever be in any hurry to discuss with her:

- You know, back when I was first charged with raping that girl…well, I was just wondering, why was it that you wouldn't give yours as my bail address?

Any way you look at it, it's not a brilliant conversation opener.

I was brought to Armley and when they'd processed me they asked me a question I didn't understand; the question concerned whether or not I wanted to go on a segregated wing for vulnerable prisoners. That's where they keep the sub species of criminal: the ones that your decent, grafting villains hold in contempt. People like me. I chose to be vulnerable and was surrounded by people whose crimes I couldn't bring myself to imagine. If I'd been in the general prison population, I'd have longed for an opportunity to get my hands on someone like me. I was with the scum, basically, at my own request. I was with the scum because, in the general population, no one would be that bothered about discussing the nuances of my alleged offence. In the pad next to mine, there was a copper. It didn't matter what it was he was charged with on account of any copper's fair game in prison, so he was stuck with us. Every time I glanced at him – because keeping conversation to a minimum was a key priority for me – he looked appalled and shocked. I derived some small but significant comfort from the fact that he was having a harder time than I was and I hoped he didn't get out before me.

There was one remaining thing I had a choice about and that was whether I was guilty or not guilty but I didn't know which I was. I'd never had to make such a stark choice before; there's normally been room for manoeuvre around the edges. I spent some time considering whether it was possible to be guilty in your heart but technically not guilty; or to be technically guilty but not guilty in your heart. The criminal justice system doesn't concern itself with these subtleties and even if it did I still wouldn't have known where to place myself. Because I didn't know, I opted for the default position of not guilty but since my word couldn't be taken as gospel, a jury got to decide.

There's a whole bunch of things I knew I was guilty of and if they'd charged me with those, I'd have put my hands up straight away, no messing.

I was guilty of turning my dad into a small desiccated man whose rheumy eyes stared disbelievingly into mine across the visiting table. When he came to see me on remand he called me son; it was either because he couldn't bring himself to say my name or because he thought I was a kid again. He'd clear his throat and tell me only the smallest, least harmful things. Stuff like how things were as good as could be expected under the (unspecified) circumstances and that he couldn't grumble or how he'd seen our Joanne and she was asking after me. He never mentioned our Sandra because she tends to keep herself to herself; she's reckoned for years that ours is a fucked up family and she'd rather keep her distance. She talks about the sins of the fathers and how she'd rather avoid contaminating her kids with all the shit that went off when we were kids. I told him to tell Joanne not to worry about me and while he was at it, to tell everyone else not to worry about me. I told him that they were all best off pretending I was dead and he examined his nails and made the sort of noises people make when they're trying to hold things together without saying precisely what it is that's tearing them apart. He never said what was on his mind which would be something like, thank God your mother's not here to see this or, is there something I did that made you turn out like this. I suppose I could've taken the opportunity to apologise to him for putting him through all this shit but at the time, the only person I felt sorry for was myself. Or I could've said,

- Well, I've been thinking about my Mum and the way things turned out…

And sparked off a whole different conversation. I wonder, looking back, how much of a difference that might have made.

And I was guilty of forcing D to think he'd to come up to Armley every five minutes to attempt and fail to keep my spirits up. He talked about what we were gonna do when I got out after the ritual of the trial and how he was going to keep tabs on me to keep me from getting into mischief, like all this was just the result of some daft prank that'd gone wrong. Sometimes, he'd stop talking and I could see him struggle to find a way of filling the space between us. If he were anywhere else, he'd have got up and wandered round the place picking things up and putting them down but he couldn't do that there. Every time he visited he told me - like I didn't know - that I wasn't cut out for being somewhere like Armley.

I wrote to Maxine and told her she should only come up if she was feeling up to it. She only felt up to it twice while I was on remand and we each tried to pretend that this was a terrible mistake without once discussing my charge. In the end writing seemed to be a better option. She told me in a letter that I'd be surprised at the number of people who'd wanted to talk to her since what had happened had happened. There were people she'd barely met clamouring around to get a good look at her and tell her how sorry they were for her; how terrible it must be for her knowing what I'd done. There were people she'd not seen for years who'd turn up - sometimes with their screaming brats – carrying on about how they were just passing by and they wouldn't stop long; they just wanted to let her know that their thoughts were with her. It got to the point where she stopped answering the door - not that that helped cause they'd just stuff shitty cards through the letterbox. Fucking flowers piled outside the door like someone had died and random neighbours braying on the door at all times of the day and night. It was like she had a story and they had a right to feature in it. And her story made them feel better about their own shitty lives. She said she could see people thinking, at least I'm not her. At the end of the letter she said she wished she hated me. To be honest, I wished she hated me too because there was nothing I could do with her love in there.

In prison, the world is shrunken and shrivelled and people lie the whole time. As things get progressively worse, they tell you they're getting better. So, while you're on remand they tell you that you'll feel more settled when you've been sentenced and you know what you're looking at. The idea is that everyone on remand is guilty and that not guilty pleas are just a holding strategy while our briefs pick a hole in the prosecution case, but the truth was I didn't know whether I was guilty or not. Then they assure you that once you're sentenced, you just need to get your head down and do your time and that things will start to feel more bearable. Then once you've come to terms with your offending behaviour and you've enhanced your thinking skills and you've completed some sort of programme that tells you you're a nonce but stops you being one in future, there's your first stab at parole to sustain you.

People lie to you in prison because the truth is too fucking shit to contemplate. Lying in my bunk on a night I'd sometimes speculate that at the moment I was found guilty I'd feel a weight lift from my shoulders and everything would begin to feel like something I just had to get through but I was never fully convinced. Finding myself arrested was on a par with being told about my mum's death in terms of shock value. I wanted to tell them that they'd made some daft – but understandable - mistake because there was nothing in me that had been made to process such a bald statement. I wanted to tell them to just hold on one minute and back track and start again and make the ending different this time. Anyway, the arrest experience was surpassed in terms of unimagined horror by the remand experience.

Everything about the first day was a series of shocks. All the words they used for the things they did were wrong; there was reception - which was nothing like any reception I'd ever passed through - then I was processed and allocated my accommodation. My accommodation was nothing like a hotel room despite its TV and kettle. There was a toilet in it and a hatch in the door and a twat on the top bunk who talked shit the whole time. He was a bit like the guy that shows you round on your first day at work and gives you all the ins and outs about who to talk to and who to avoid. He looked like the kind of guy you imagine lurking round school gates offering sweets to kids.

Mostly I noticed the stink because there's no air and too many people in too small a space and the stink lodged in my throat so that it was all I could taste. Then my skin crawled with it and then it burrowed under my skin and my body rattled with it. The noises were the voices of people I didn't know – some of them were laughing like it was possible that something amusing could happen in that place - and I was to live in a place with a door I couldn't open from the inside. Everyone whistled but they all whistled different tunes and I couldn't catch and hold on to a single one of them. The twat on the top bunk did his best to make me feel at home and told me it'd all be fine if I just kept my head down. He actually said,

- You'd be hard pressed to find a better prison than this, mate. I've been all over, me, and this is the best you're gonna get.

I told him I'd take his word for it.

It took a while for me to get my head down. In the meantime, there was a massive sensory overload to cope with and my nerves couldn't handle it. I'm not one for being poorly but I became suddenly very ill and I was put on the hospital wing. They were concerned, they reckoned, about my intrusive suicidal thoughts, which was a bit ironic since I was already as good as dead. D's since told me that that those first few weeks were the worst he's ever seen me which may be true for him but it's not the worst I've actually been on account of at least I've never been crying like a baby in his company or scraping my knuckles down the wall till they bled so that I had some other more familiar pain to deal with. Every night for weeks I dreamt I was falling up a flight of stairs and I'd jolt myself awake and find myself soaked and freezing so I decided not to sleep until not sleeping became worse. I contorted and twisted between these two positions and I found out that not sleeping was shit and that sleeping was also shit so it didn't really matter what I did. That was considered to be progress so they moved me back on to the wing.

One time when D came up to see me, he tried to make me feel better by telling me about some case he'd read about,

- It's fucking scandalous. Did you read that thing in the papers about those parents that starved their fucking kids and they got fucking seven years? Summat about inadequate parenting skills. Don't get me wrong, I'm not saying that what you did – or what they say you did - was right as such, it's just it's all in the interpretation. It's not all cut and dried like they try and make it out to be. It's not like fucking starving innocent kids, is it? There's circumstances they want to be taking account of.

I nodded. And I thought about where he'd be heading to when he left this shit hole. He'd be off home or maybe he'd stop off for a reviving drink. Then I thought about where I'd be off. Which was back to what I'd begun to refer to as my pad.

- Chances are, mate, the beast that starved his kid'll end up being my pad mate when they ship me out to Wakefield or wherever it is they stockpile nonces these days.

He told me that wasn't even funny.

-   Who's fucking laughing, mate?

I'm not convinced that D ever fully grasped the seriousness of my situation; he seemed always to be under the impression that it was just a matter of pulling one or two wily moves and I'd be back on the out like nothing had happened.

Just before he left, he fumbled for summat to say and after he'd gone on about stuff I could obviously no longer have a legitimate interest in – like our mutual mates and his plans for the weekend – he finally came up with,

- You know where I am, Si. I'm not saying I can sort everything out but you know I'm not fucking having people carry on at you or Max or the kids about how you're fucking this and how you're fucking that...I know it sounds like a dodgy charge and I wouldn't normally defend owt like that but...

And his voice petered out finally because maybe he was finding it difficult to defend whatever it was he was defending without naming it. And maybe me and my tears got in the way. He put his hand on my shoulder and kneaded it. I looked into him and said,

- I just can't believe I've done what they've said I've done.
- My point exactly.
- No, that's not what I mean. I know they're gonna find me guilty and maybe that's fair enough. It's just, I can't get my head round understanding that that's who I am now. I'm a prisoner and I'm gonna be a prisoner for fucking years. It just doesn't make any sort of sense but it's also true.

D sniffed and cleared his throat but that didn't stop his voice wavering,

- You're not guilty, mate. You've been fucking stupid but you're not a fucking rapist.

He screwed up the chocolate wrapper on the table and put it in his pocket. I wanted him to go but it's not something you can say when someone's made the effort to come up and see you. If he couldn't help me understand who I'd become, I wanted to be able to talk about the weather – though I didn't get much in the way of weather in there – or the football or summat else that meant nothing. In the end he said,

- It's all about adjustment, mate. It's the same with everything. Once you get your head round it, once you properly understand where you are and that there's nowt you can do about it for the time being, it'll be easier for you.

I nodded sagely and tried to adopt a why didn't I think of that expression. Outside - uncommented upon - the rain fell or the sun shone and Leeds won or lost. Encouraged by the speed at which I appeared to have come to terms with things, D told me things I didn't want to hear about how he and my dad were looking after my wife and kids,

- Your dad's stopping at Maxine's for the next couple of weeks leading up to the trial and all that and our lass'll pass by a couple of evenings a week if he wants to go out or owt. I'll take her up to the *Asda* on a Saturday and I've told her that her and the kids are welcome to come round to ours for their dinner on a Sunday. Your dad's said she can use the caravan at Whitby if she wants to get away for a couple of days. Obviously me and your dad'll be up to see you whenever we can. We're all tryna pull together, mate.

I tried to look like a huge weight had been lifted from my shoulders, like it was all gonna be plain sailing from here on in but Maxine hates the *Asda* and Linda's a poor cook and Whitby's always wet and windy. The prospect of enforced visits from my dad and D for the next several years didn't fill my heart with joy either; I imagined myself growing more and more distant and relying on them and their heavily edited stories to keep me within shouting distance of what was happening in the world of outside. I didn't ask D why he hadn't mentioned Maxine visiting.

While I was on remand, they made a big deal of my problematic substance misuse because a further and - in the scheme of things - frankly inconsequential charge was that I was arrested in possession of a couple of grams. I'd no choice but to plead guilty to that charge. It was in the jacket that D had helpfully handed me on my way to the police car. I tried to explain to my brief and the probation officer that though my coke use – on the face of it – looked a bit excessive at times, it was associated exclusively with my lifestyle choice: drinking, mates, being out and about. Since relocating to prison, I explained, opportunities such as these had diminished and the coke was therefore not going to present me with any immediate problems. If coke was my main worry, I said, I'd be a very happy man. And then, I was talking to my brief one time and he told me that we should be thinking about how my misuse of drugs might, in some way, have led me to put myself in a vulnerable position where an allegation of this nature might be made.

He got me to sign up for an individual drugs assessment followed by some follow up sessions. It wasn't felt to be appropriate – in light of my charge – for me to be in a groupwork scenario. These sessions were – until that point – some of the worst hours of my life. The lad who came in to see me was clearly uncomfortable in my presence. That could have been to do with us failing to hit it off or it could have been to do with my offence (or alleged offence as he politely referred to it). Personally, I favour the latter option; you're not going to come across many people who'd willingly spend time with someone like the person I was supposed to be. With my depleted resources, I did my best to make him less uneasy but from his first enquiry – tell me a bit about yourself – it was pretty bloody obvious that we weren't going to build up much in the way of rapport. In answer to that question I perhaps for a moment forgot who I'd become and for a couple of minutes gave him the usual background details you would in response to such a bland query.

- Well, I've got my own business – specialist audio visual stuff mainly for musos and sound aficionados. I'm married and I've got 4 kids. Stephanie's just turned 18, Ben's 17 and the twins are about to turn 6. There's been one or two problems in the marriage but nothing you wouldn't expect after being together so long.

I could sense his unease as I talked about our lass and the kids and the business. That's when I first properly realised that I was perceived as a threat and that, in his mind, there was probably some sinister motive behind every contact I'd ever had with women and kids. The business was probably a cover for a kiddie porn operation. Anyway, he examined my drug use and concluded that I was a chaotic user who underestimated the impact that cocaine had on both my life and on my lifestyle choices. He told me things I already knew about how coke affects you and some things I didn't know because, frankly, they didn't apply to me. It is not, for example, true that coke served as an escape for me. As I explained to him, I actually did want to sort my life my out and genuinely thought that the Charlie might keep me alert and on top of things. It's also not true that it made me feel unusually gregarious and insightful. I wanted to say to him that if I'd been that bloody insightful I wouldn't be sat there listening to him carry on.

Though he evidently disliked me, I think I was a bit of a trophy villain for him. After a couple of sessions, he started on about how I managed to square my current predicament with my background: degree, house, successful business and all that.

- You don't meet the typical offender profile, Simon. I'm just wondering how you ended up here.

- So am I.

- It seems to me, Simon, that things spiralled out of control and that you lacked the coping strategies to manage your changed circumstances. It's not unusual for substance misuse to accelerate under stressful situations.

I wondered how much he was getting paid for telling me the sorts of things more usually associated with daytime chat shows.

- I suppose you may have a point.

He looked pleased that I'd acknowledged his summary of my predicament. I think they call it a breakthrough or acknowledging personal responsibility.

Finally, he told me that whilst coke can be a factor in all sorts of offending behaviour, it is neither an excuse nor a reason. At which point I reminded him that at this stage we were talking about an alleged offence and that the alleged offence was not part of a pattern of behaviour.

- Yes, but your substance misuse was part of a pattern of behaviour…

- I wouldn't call it a pattern as such…

- … Which was associated with the breakdown of your relationship?

- Yes, but…

- And the alleged offence took place when you were under the influence of a combination of alcohol and cocaine?
- The offence didn't take place. I didn't commit the offence. That's why I'm pleading not guilty.
- But you don't dispute that something took place?
- Yes, something took place. Something that wasn't an offence. I don't know how to talk about something that didn't happen.

The visit was nearing its end and Armley was making all the noises it makes. Soon a screw would come and accompany me to my pad and whatever impression I left with the lad sat opposite me would be the one which would make its way into his report. He looked like a man who would rather be anywhere else.

- Listen, it's hard for me to admit I've got a problem. I'm used to being on top of things but I recognise now that I was using coke to escape from the situation I found myself in. I only wish that I'd addressed this before I put myself in such a vulnerable situation.

That seemed to satisfy him and I was able, for the last couple of minutes, to listen to him tell me that I wasn't alone and that there were plenty of sources of support available. Which was all good except that I was alone.

3.

There was a lad on my wing and he looked like every other lad because we all looked the same. He was stupid and unguarded and he thought he was safe with us because we were all vulnerable prisoners. I was sat in my pad at association because I couldn't quite bring myself to associate with people I'd normally cross the road to avoid. Anyway, his acne – scarred face appeared at the door and he started on about what I was in for which, as a conversational entrée, is pretty shit quite frankly. I shrugged and looked interested in whatever shit it was I was pretending to read but he lurked there like washing that wants fetching in. He told me his problem was the glue and that he'd been on it for years. He said that there'd be an article about him in the *Yorkshire Evening Post* because he'd had his habit that long. He'd got into it when he went into care as a kid. He was in care because his dad had carried on with him. He told me the glue made him do things – like without it he'd have been a model citizen. He'd had his IQ tested, he reckoned, and they'd told him he was unusually intelligent.

- You can't be that fucking intelligent if you're in here.

By way of illustration, he told me about tides and the solar system. Then he saw fit to inform me that he was in on a rape charge and I had to suppress the urge to knock him out. It turned out that he'd been in a park at night sniffing lighter fluid and this lass had appeared and before he knew it…which was when I stopped listening and told him to fuck right off and leave me alone. I told him to fuck off because I don't hold with any of that sort of nonsense.

When he'd gone, I was fuming and I wished I had a mate there like D and that I could say to him,

- You'll never guess what fucking happened…this nonce just bent my ear about raping this kid. Tried to carry on like it was all down to glue and his fucked up childhood…

Anyway, he went and I tried to get back into my book but it was like when you're really tired and you just keep reading the same line over and over and none of it's going in. And a thought kept coming into my head and I kept trying to apply pressure to it like you would an open wound but it was leaking out all over the place. When I was working in procurement, I'd sometimes have to contribute to strategic and business plans and I'd spend hours analysing, creating rationales and well – thought through conclusions based on the evidence. Everyone knew, though, that much of what we wrote was wasted; by the time the report got to the Board, the directors were only ever interested in the executive summary and the bottom line. So, when this lad had gone, all my plotting and graphs and spreadsheets and flowcharts went out of the window and were replaced with one simple bottom line: what separates me from him?

And there were plenty of things: Eliz wasn't a stranger; the offence – the alleged offence - had occurred within the context of a prior (if fleeting) relationship; I'd gone to hers because I'd been invited; my actions had been (if regrettable) completely out of character; I'm a decent, educated man not some poxy twat who sniffs lighter fuel in the park. The word they use for what they said I did is not one I understand when it's applied to me. It's for people like the spotty lad and the guy down the wing who, they reckoned, was in and out the whole time for interfering with kids. In Bosnia, they classified the thing they say I did as a war crime but what I did was not a war crime. They said that she sustained injuries which were consistent with non-consensual sex but I didn't know what that meant. There was a girl I saw a while back and she'd bite and scratch and all sorts. I'd end up looking like I'd slept under a barbed wire duvet.

I knew that in and amongst all the shit that was blocking my neural pathways, there was a small piece of data which would make sense of all this. If I'd have known that this small encounter in somewhere ending in *ley* was going to be so pivotal, I'd have taken notes and got sworn affidavits. I remembered D telling me that I've got to stay on top of the things that I'm in control of so I tried to order my thoughts and to place them neatly in a line so they told a story which was true and which worked. I was in a situation where we had an event that had happened and two different truths which explained it: hers and mine. It all felt a bit mathematical and technical but that should have played to my strengths. To make the story hang together, I needed to consign the awkward bits to the recycling bin but the awkward bits kept coming back and detracting from the narrative. There was the bit where we seemed to be fighting on her bed but it can't have been fighting because people don't fight in bed. And the bit where she reached for something on her bedside table and I had to grab her arm and hold it down. The thing she'd tried to grab was the candlestick and as I'd twisted her arm drops of melted wax hardened onto my wrist. A portable TV flickered in the corner of the bedroom and her wardrobe doors were open. There were stars and planets on her ceiling and my hand was on her mouth. The mattress had too much give in it. And I couldn't remember a word she said that might help me because she didn't say a word.

I didn't sleep properly that night or for several nights afterwards and I knew that if I wasn't sleeping there was something keeping me awake and it was likely to be something I needed to know but didn't want to know. I bumped into this lad and he said,

- It'll be with your trial coming up. It's normal for your sleep to be disturbed.

It was his first time inside as well but I think he'd accepted that he was going down and he was trying to get on top of the things he needed to get on top of before he started his sentence. They said he'd killed his kid on a contact visit and then he'd tried to kill himself but he obviously hadn't tried hard enough. Doubtless, he'd have had some sort of explanation for all this when he got to court but in the meantime he'd figured that his explanation was not gonna be anywhere near good enough for your decent, honest criminals which was why he'd opted to be with us lot. Anyway, his explanation for my sleeplessness didn't cut any ice with me. If I'd been on the out, I'd have been able to do something or go somewhere that'd take me away from this shit and I'd have filed it under things to think about later. But there's no filtration tank in Armley so all the scum just floated to the surface and there was no shifting it because it was part of me and it had been at the top of my to do list for fucking ages. When I was on a time management training course years ago they said this thing that's always stuck with me and it was about how we sometimes bury the things we least want to deal with. The trainer said that often the shit you don't take care of comes up and bites you on the arse because by the time you reluctantly decide to get on top of it, it's gone from being routine to being urgent. And I found myself back on the professor on the radio and the whole did what happen actually happen thing. How does anyone know precisely what happened? At one point I was behind her and I had one hand on her shoulder and the other was over her mouth. That's why she didn't say anything.

I knew that I'd done what they said I'd done. I was guilty.

4.

Knowing you're guilty and pleading guilty are two entirely separate things and it doesn't pay to confuse them. I kept my own verdict to myself. The jury went away to consider its verdict on the Monday just before lunch. My brief told me that he'd given it his best shot and that we'd just have to sit it out and hope for the best. He told me that in the event that they found me guilty I'd be shipped out to an establishment more appropriate to my needs, like that was gonna cheer me up. As we waited I told myself that I was going down then I asked him what he thought,

- It's in the lap of the Gods.

Which made me wonder why we'd bothered conducting a defence when we might just as well have tossed a coin. He shrugged and fiddled about with his cigarettes. He shifted his weight from one foot to the other and looked around him like he hoped someone might walk by that he knew. I asked him whether he'd got any sort of impression from the jury about what their verdict was likely to be.

- It's really difficult to say, Simon. Sometimes you can be absolutely certain that they're on your side and then they come back with a guilty verdict.

He exhaled loudly and shrugged again like this was just one of those quirky things that happens from time to time. What he failed to grasp was that this was happening to me and that it mattered.

- You must have some idea.

- In a case like this where it all rests on consent, there's no saying what they're going to do. Sometimes women can be particularly judgmental about other women's behaviour; and then sometimes they're more inclined to believe the woman. Men often don't seem to know what to believe; on the one hand they don't want to be seen to be condoning Neanderthal behaviour and on the other, they can be naturally inclined to believe that women are asking for it. A substantial age difference between the two parties can also have an influence. The fact that she chose not to appear behind a screen could also – for some – lend credence to her account. It's all speculation in the end, Simon. The fact is, I don't know and you don't know what they're thinking. You've just got to hope that they've done what they've been instructed to do and that they've listened carefully to the evidence and formed an opinion based solely on that and not on any pre conceived notions they might have come into court with.

None of which was remotely helpful to me. I could've told him myself that it was a difficult one to call. I'd kind of hoped that with his years of experience he might be able to be a bit more conclusive. But he was off on one by this point.

- Other times, you can see that the jury's just confused by all the evidence; that's when you need to worry. They stop listening or if they are listening they're only listening to the inconsequential details that they can get their heads round. If it's any help, my gut instinct is that they understood the key issues, which is always helpful. It's just a matter of hoping that we've raised a reasonable doubt.
- And have we?
- Well, I think we have but it's down to the jury to weigh up the evidence. Parts of the Crown's case were probably quite compelling.

That's when I knew for certain that I was going down.

A lad on the wing told me that you could always tell what the verdict was going to be by closely observing the jury; they always give their thoughts away, he said. I ignored his advice and decided instead to try and imagine myself as a member of the jury. I listened to the stories they were being told and tried to work out which I'd be most convinced by. Cross examined by the Crown barrister, Eliz spluttered and sobbed through her account, pausing now and again to take a sip of water. The story she told – for all its pauses – sounded pretty convincing to me; I became this predatory guy who'd basically insinuated himself into her house on the pretext of a chat, plied her with drink, raped her and fucked off. She'd let me in because, on the basis of our previous encounters, she trusted me. She reckoned that at some point in some bar I'd said things which I honestly can't remember saying: considerate things which made me sound like I was a nice and trustworthy guy. It all sounded depressingly like grooming to my mind. She also said,

- The previous morning, he'd made me a cup of tea before he dropped me home.

I wondered what sort of losers she'd been with in the past.

- His behaviour on the night in question, then, must have come as a terrible shock to you?

- It was completely unexpected. I would obviously never have let him into the house if I hadn't trusted him. I'm not the sort of person who invites random strangers into my house in the middle of the night.

The Crown made a fair bit of the disparity in our ages and referred to me on several occasions as being twice her age. He will've been playing to the older members of the jury I expect and, looking at a couple of them, I reckoned that if they could've dispensed with the trial they'd have strung me up there and then. There were minor discrepancies in her story and I scribbled them down and passed them to my solicitor but, to be honest, there wasn't that much for me to go at and as I listened to her story and watched her try to be strong, my own story began to feel weak and unappealing.

At other times, it hadn't felt like things were going so badly; when it was his turn my barrister managed to sow a few seeds of doubt and succeeded in depicting me in unflattering - but, under the circumstances, necessary – terms as a stressed out executive going through some sort of midlife meltdown. Eliz, on the other hand, was a naïve, immature girl fixated on an older man. At one point he said to her,

- So, you are asking the court to believe that at 3 in the morning you let Mr Williams into your house on the understanding that he wanted a chat?

He drew speech marks round the word chat and smirked at the jury. She looked like she was trying her best to stay on top of things but her face reddened and her words caught in her throat as she tried to respond. He asked her to repeat her answer and I think there were tears then though I can't be sure because I found that I needed to look downwards at that point. When I looked up again, D winked at me like it was all going well. She had to tell her truth about what happened and, to be honest, with my man's mock incredulity and requests for clarification, it all began to sound a bit disjointed and unconvincing.

- I suggest that you knew precisely what the purpose of the defendant's visit was.

She shook her head and started to say something but it all came out as a gulping stutter. The judge asked her if she'd like a brief recess while she composed herself. She said that she was ok though she clearly wasn't.

- What were you wearing when the defendant arrived at your door?

She described what she had been wearing. My man let her finish and summarised,
- A negligee, then, if you will?
- It's not what I'd call it.
- And what would you call it?
- It was a sleeveless, satin dress.

The note takers in the jury took their notes.
- So, a man you barely know arrives – invited – at your house in the middle of the night. You consume – by your own admission – several alcoholic drinks. And then you go upstairs with him…
- He dragged me upstairs. I could barely stand…

- If I might be permitted to continue…you go with him into your bedroom. Wouldn't common sense tell you what his expectations were?

I glanced at the jury and a couple of the older women looked like they were mulling on the recklessness of her behaviour. She tried to answer, but frankly my man was tying her up in knots.

- And how much would you say you'd had to drink?
- I don't know exactly. He kept topping up my glass.
- So, it was the quantity of alcohol you had consumed that made you incapable of standing?
- It had contributed but I know that he dragged me upstairs.
- Are you in the habit of drinking to excess?
- No.
- Are you in the habit of going to bed with men you barely know having drunk to excess?
- No I am not.
- And yet your previous meetings with the defendant had been initiated in bars and were characterised by excessive consumption of alcohol?
- Yes, they took place in bars but I wouldn't say that alcohol was what characterised them.
- But by your own admission on each of the previous occasions you had met the defendant you had consumed excessive amounts of alcohol. Is that not the case?
- Yes that is the case, but it's not the way you're making it sound. The first time I met him was at my leaving do where I think it's reasonable to expect that I'd have a drink and the second occasion was Christmas Eve where, again, I don't think it's unreasonable to have a drink.
- And am I right in saying that your first meeting culminated in your returning to the defendant's house?

She nodded.

- And you stayed over?
- Yes.
- Where did you sleep?

- I slept in a spare room.
- Why was that?
- He said he was tired and I was tired too. It was too late to get a taxi back so he told me that I could stay in the spare room.

My man flicked through some papers and cleared his throat.

- So the defendant – a man whom you claim a few days later raped you – offered you his spare room.

She nodded. My man paused. The implication was clear and unstated: if I was a predatory rapist, why hadn't I taken advantage of this earlier opportunity? I had to hand it to him; he knew exactly what he was doing.

- To summarise, then, prior to the night in question you had met with the defendant on two occasions over the course of less than a week. Do you consider that it's possible to know someone well on the basis of a couple of drunken encounters?

She hesitated before answering; she must have known that whatever answer she was going to give would be wrong.

- I don't think you can know someone well but I do think you can form a judgment of what they're like.
- So…a man you admit you did not know well turns up at your door in the middle of the night. Your prior knowledge of him extends to two drunken encounters over the course of a few days – the second of which culminated in your sleeping with him - and yet you claim not to be in the habit of going to bed with men you barely know having drunk to excess.

I glanced at her and I could see in her face that she was trying to process and disentangle what he'd presented her with. I watched her open her mouth then close it and we all waited for her to say something but she didn't say anything. Finally, my man sighed deeply and adjusted his wig before continuing his cross-examination as if this were a tiresome formality we needed to get through before getting down to the serious business of my acquittal.

- Let's move on to the following day. So, after what you've described as the most traumatic event of your life, you were again faced with the alleged perpetrator. And what happened then?

- He came round and said he wanted to apologise but what he was really after was an envelope that he'd left at my house.

She spoke very quietly and I strained to make out what she was saying.

- And what did he say?
- What I've just said.
- Which was?
- He apologised and said that what he'd done was unforgivable. And he asked for the envelope.

My man skirted over the issue of forgiveness - which was just as well - but it hadn't escaped the attention of the scribbling women jurors.

- And you gave him the envelope?
- Yes.

She glanced at me for a second and it was as if she wanted me to confirm what she was saying; like she wanted to establish some common ground because this small detail was indisputable. I found something fascinating to stare at in the middle distance. In the meantime, my man nodded and stroked his chin like he was trying to solve some complicated puzzle.

- So…you endure what, by your own account, was a hugely traumatic experience. A matter of a few hours later, the defendant returns and you have a conversation with him on your doorstep?
- It wasn't a conversation as such. Like I said, he apologised and asked me for the envelope.
- And what were your feelings about this visit?
- I was frightened and angry and humiliated.
- You had not – I understand – contacted the police by this stage?
- No, I hadn't.
- So, it was only after this humiliating visit that that you decided that a crime had been committed and that you should speak to the police?

She walked straight into that one. Someone – I assume it was her mum – wiped her eyes with a tissue and a middle-aged man put his hand on her shoulder. He looked close to tears as well and none of it made me feel particularly good about myself. They were barely older than Maxine and me, and Eliz was barely older than our Stephanie. She wore a cheap black suit which was slightly too long in the arms and when she picked up the glass for a sip of water she had to hitch the sleeve up a bit. Her skin was pale and she looked like she'd had about as much sleep as I had. She looked pathetic and - at a pinch - like a naïve, immature girl fixated on an older man.

When she'd finished giving her evidence there was a recess and my barrister looked at me like he was expecting me to congratulate him on his performance. I couldn't bring myself to do it. I'd kind of hoped that things were going to be a bit less confrontational and a bit more conversational; that there might be some sort of way of reaching an accommodation which satisfied her need for acknowledgement and mine for freedom. Something like truth and reconciliation.

When it came to my turn I said that I'd tell the truth, the whole truth and nothing but the truth the same as she had, but it turned out that her truth and my truth were not the same in this adversarial setting. Maybe it was all to do with the angle of vision or with knowing that confirming her truth was not going to do me any favours. In the story I told it turned out that the drugs had become a major problem (but not quite major enough to mar my judgment on the night in question, an opinion which seemed to be backed up by the report my drugs counsellor had submitted); that I'd found myself relying on coke more and more since my partner of almost 20 years had left me. It was something I deeply regretted and the only positive thing about being banged up was that I was clean and determined never to use coke again. I used words like horrified and hurt a lot and when the Crown barrister harangued me about the specifics of what happened I found that there was a reasonable explanation involving what I referred to as rough – but consensual - sex. My behaviour was described as vicious and merciless and a lot was made of abrasions and bruises and injuries commonly associated with non-consensual sex. According to her evidence, there were things I'd said to her during the act that made me sound like a bit of a sadistic bastard – things to do with wanting to hurt her. The Crown repeated those words verbatim.

- Do you recall saying those things, Mr Williams?
- No I do not.

And the truth was, I genuinely didn't recall saying anything like that; they didn't sound like the sort of words I'd say to someone. Some of the questions he asked demanded more than the truth and some demanded less and now that it's all done and dusted it doesn't really matter what I said or didn't say. What matters is that all the time I was stood in the witness box, I believed every word I said and that made it true to me. It was a bit like a job interview where you embellish and air brush and tidy up all the rough edges. In the public gallery, D nodded and the people I took to be her parents shook their heads. A couple of members of the jury – women – took notes furiously like their lives depended on it. The Crown barrister asked me at one point if I regretted what had happened but I wasn't going to fall for that one.

- Of course I regret what's happened. I've been accused of a terrible crime and I've already had to pay a huge price for that. I've been separated from my wife and my kids and spent months in prison. I regret not going straight home because if I had I wouldn't be in the position of having to defend myself against this terrifying and false allegation.

Then it was my turn to cry because it struck me just how careless I'd been with my life and that all that separated me from an establishment more appropriate to my needs were these 12 people who didn't know me, all of whom had now stopped taking notes and were staring at me like crying was a new and fascinating invention.

I had to say why it was I'd done what I'd done and it was difficult to answer because it's not like I'd clearly thought through my motives at the time; life's just not quite like that. You get an idea into your head and you just follow it through without necessarily knowing what the outcome's going to be. The only true answer would've been because I felt like it but something more complex was required of me, so I talked about needing to talk to someone and to be close to someone following a difficult day.

- You have a somewhat unusual idea of what closeness is, Mr Williams.

And, of course, he then asked me to describe in detail precisely what it was I did to Eliz and what indication she gave of having enjoyed my particular brand of intimacy. It was all a bit tricky and unfortunate because to make the story hang together I had to invent some words that she'd said afterwards.

- She indicated that she'd enjoyed what had happened and asked me if I was going to stay the night. I told her that I couldn't because I had a lot on the next day.

- If it was the case, Mr Williams, that this was an enjoyable experience for both of you why was it that you felt compelled to return the following morning and apologise and ask forgiveness for the events of the previous night?

I'd guessed that this might come up.

- I apologised because I considered that leaving immediately afterwards was a bit ungentlemanly.

I tried to look like the kind of guy who lived by a gentlemanly code of conduct. To be honest, none of it really squared with the behaviour I'd already admitted to. This wasn't lost on the barrister.

- So, Mr Williams, you're asking the court to believe that a man who visits a woman young enough to be his daughter in the middle of the night, plies her with drink, ingests cocaine and finally submits her to what you refer to as rough sex – something which, the evidence will show, is referred to as rape - is the sort of man whose primary concern is with chivalry. I suggest to you, Mr Williams, that you returned in order to recover your property and that the apology you offered was given solely to support you in accomplishing this task.

He'd pretty much nailed it there. There will have been more questions and I will have answered them because it's not like in the real world where you can refuse to answer questions from strangers that you consider to be that bit too personal. I don't know what they were because all I could think about was going down. I remember thinking, stood up in the witness box, that this was the closest I was going to get to outside for a long time. I knew that the maximum sentence for the crime is life and while my mouth was responding to whatever new queries he could dream up, I tried to get my head round being sent away for life. The idea was that if I expected that then anything less would feel like a relief. I'd done my homework; if I got life I'd get what they call a tariff and that would be the minimum I'd serve before being considered for parole.

I used to be one of these that believe life should mean life and that rapists should be castrated. I was in the paper once; I was collecting the twins from school and this journalist was wandering round asking what we thought about a hostel they were thinking of opening down the road amongst whose residents would be sex offenders. I was full of opinions about safety and house prices and the other parents outside the school gates nodded encouragingly. The photograph they took didn't do me justice but Maxine said I looked lovely and for a while we kept the cutting. All that was a long time ago and everything I thought I believed then I don't believe anymore.

5.

If it was down to me, I wouldn't be able to tell anyone what day it was that the jury retired to consider its verdict because everything since has changed so much that the name of the day is unimportant. The reason I know it was the Monday is because Maxine told me afterwards when I was trying to understand and to straighten out what the fuck had happened to my life.

- The reason the Monday stuck in my mind was because it was the first day back after half term and I'd to iron the twins' uniforms on the morning. They were racing round the kitchen in their underwear getting under my feet. You know what they're like.

We took the decision to send them to a private preparatory school and the skirts are like kilts and the shorts have got to have a crease in them so she's to press them properly. Apparently, *Marks's* have got these non-iron school skirts and you just need to put them in the wash, shake them and they're sorted, but these ones you needed to be dry cleaning and pressing between cleans. When she and the kids lived at home, I'd always be on at them to get out of their school clothes as soon as they came in and to put them neatly in their drawers but they don't listen, do they, kids? She's since taken them out of the school. It's not the money, she says; it's the shame.

- On top of the fuss of sorting the kids out and the small matter of your sentencing, I'd a big buffet on for a solicitors' firm in town and the roads are always chocka the first day the kids go back to school so I'd to give myself a good extra half hour which meant getting Stephanie to drop the twins off. Stephanie wasn't happy because she'd to be at college by 9.30 on a Monday and dropping the twins off meant going out of her way. Our Ben's neither use nor ornament so I didn't even bother asking him to do owt. He'd played in a cup match the previous day and he was moaning about his injuries and moaning about having to go into work when he didn't really feel up to it. He wanted me to ring in sick for him but I told him there was no way I was colluding with his nonsense. Stephanie careered round the house saying everyone was in her way and asking me where she'd put her hair wax, her black jacket, her car keys. You know what Stephanie's like: she's always got to blame someone if she misplaces something. Looking back, it was funny really, because there were all these things we each had to get done but at the same time, we all knew that you were getting sentenced that day.

In my response to her I told her that funny was an interesting choice of adjective under the circumstances.

- All the time you were on remand I just ended up taking care of the things I could control like work and the twins and the pressing. I decided not to say anything to the kids about what was going off.

On that at least we were agreed. When I was on remand I spoke to a woman from probation and she was on about how important it is to communicate with kids. She reckoned that if you don't talk to them they imagine instead, and that what they imagine is often worse than the truth. I said to her,

- Believe me, whatever they imagine won't come close to being as bad as the truth.

She had these bog standard answers for every problem you could ever encounter, and they were always about communicating and sharing. It was like a one size fits all solution. She said that there'd been studies done which showed that kids benefit from open and frank communication. I told her that that was all well and good but as far as I knew my kids didn't take part in the study and, in any case, I couldn't bring myself to tell them what it was that happened and what's continuing to happen to our lives. I didn't communicate with the kids when I was on remand and they didn't communicate with me.

Maxine told me in her letters that they were fine and sometimes she'd tell me something I didn't want to know about Ben's football or Stephanie's college or something funny the twins had done or said. She censored everything so it didn't hurt but everything hurt so she was wasting her time.

- So, it was a Monday that the verdict came in. I'd just got a letter from you a couple of days before and in this letter you'd been on about how you were trying to construct a flowchart which would help you understand how it was you'd ended up where you were.

She showed it me. There were squiggles and arrows and dotted lines. I'd put bits of text in boxes and some of them were questions. She was in quite a few of the boxes and there were names and initials she didn't recognise in others. My mum was in a diamond near the middle of the page and there were all sorts of lines leading out from her and arrows pointing towards her. Maxine said she'd looked at it and that it made no sense to her; there was a whole stack of boxes in a column that I'd titled *alternative outcomes* and this was like an appendix to the main flowchart. She told me at the time she'd get back to me with her comments when she'd had a chance to think it all through but she didn't. I wonder sometimes why I wasted my time trying to get my head round things when nobody else gave a toss.

- I'd had your Dad stopping with me for a couple of weeks. I say I'd had him stopping like it was my decision, but it wasn't. The way it worked was that you'd spoken to D and between you you'd decided that I couldn't be left on my own. The idea was that your Dad would help keep my mind off things that would only upset me.

I told her I was only thinking of her and that that was why I'd told her not to attend the trial. To be honest that particular instruction was a bit of a pre-emptive strike because I'd formed the clear impression that she hadn't been intending on coming, anyway. I told her that there were things that she'd hear that she wouldn't want to hear. She said (in a letter naturally on account of her not visiting), that there had always been things about me that she'd heard and wished she hadn't.

I guessed that the verdict was going to get a fair bit of coverage so I wrote and told her to cancel the evening paper and to avoid the news and to advise Ben and Stephanie to do the same. But it didn't stop people ringing on the land, business and mobile lines to ask how she was bearing up.

- Your dad was on the door and he filtered the calls; there was a list of people I'd talk to and if you weren't on the list you weren't getting in. He dropped the twins at school in the morning and cooked for them when he came in from work. When the twins went to bed, we sat in the living room. If we were feeling that way out, we'd watch a DVD. At the end of *All About Eve,* he said, it was funny how you can know someone for so long and not realise how much you've got in common.

She told him that it wasn't that funny, actually; that it was only down to the shit circumstances they found themselves in that they'd discovered that they both liked Bette Davis. Which struck me as a bit ungracious but maybe it was just one of her many ways of having a dig at me.

- By eleven, one or the other of us would say we were tired and I'd fetch the bedding from the airing cupboard so that your Dad could make up the sofa bed in the front room. Sometimes D would come round and we'd sit in the kitchen drinking tea or smoking a spliff and he'd get on to how differently things could have turned out.

D naturally placed himself at the very centre of my catastrophe; apparently he'd go over and over what he'd said to me about sorting my life out and how he'd told me I should be making things right with her, but that by the time he told me all this it was already too late. That was D's take on things. I know now why he felt compelled to explain himself to Maxine and I know now why she felt compelled to explain his explanations to me. It felt at the time – so soon after the verdict - like having someone relate the plot of a film that I was never going to see. Maxine missed out all the nuances and the camera angles and the pauses for reasons which are now obvious.

- So, on the Monday your dad asked how I felt about him attending for the verdict and I told him that I'd only read that word in papers or heard it said on the news and I'd never imagined someone slipping it into a conversation in real life. So, when he asked, I didn't know what to say.

She just got on with her ironing, I suppose, and with planning her trip across town. Maybe she thought that if she didn't think about it, it wouldn't happen; that maybe the jury would forget what it was they were there for and the judge would have an urgent appointment somewhere else and it (the verdict) would be one of those things you mean to sort out but never get round to. And she'd just carry on in this half life she'd invented and then one day she'd come home and I'd be stood in the kitchen saying, fancy a brew? Except I didn't live there and never have and I'd never be stood there saying that. But you get my drift.

- The girls in the kitchen at work knew what was going off and they tiptoed around me like what had happened to me might be contagious. Just after you'd been arrested, I walked in on the back end of a conversation they were having while they prepped the day's salads; they were on about not understanding why I was standing by you and what they'd do if they were me. It was the kids they felt for, apparently. I got a bit sick of people telling me what they'd do if they were me; they're not me and they never will be. But I suppose we're all experts when it comes to other people's lives. Anyway, on the day of the verdict the girls were as nice as they could allow themselves to be under the circumstances. They worked more efficiently than they ever had and told me to get off early - that they'd finish off. Maybe they just didn't want to be in my company.

So, I was encouraged to leave and it was only 4.30 which meant that I'd a good hour to kill before I'd have to go home and face your dad and his verdict. I wanted the hour to last forever. On the way home, I stopped off at the butcher's for a pound of smoked back and some basil and tomato sausages. In front of me, there was a woman and her son waiting to be served. The little boy – he was either small for three or big for two - wore a purple cycling helmet that said *Skid Lid* on it. The woman stared at the poster suggesting *meaty meals with a twist* and her son walked casually out of the shop and towards the road. I tapped the woman on the shoulder, like you do.

The woman turned towards the door with a smile Maxine described as beatific and said John quietly as if she'd been wondering what his name was and it had finally come to her. John – whose big round face was like a mound of rising dough – looked blankly at his mother and continued towards the road. Maxine put her handbag down and went to grab the boy. She said,

- Is it like you don't want him or summat? The woman looked down and the boy looked up. She held out her hand for her change and left the shop. The butcher got on with slicing the smoked back. He reckoned the little lad was a bit backward…you know, special needs. I told him he wasn't as bloody backward as his mother.

Maxine's funny about food; it'll be to do with her profession but sometimes she'll tell you stuff you don't really need to know. She told me that there was blood underneath the butcher's fingernails and round his cuticles and that she tried not to look at it as he weighed the sausages. She's not been back there since; she's found another butcher who does better sausages and whose nails are clean.

She stopped off at *Black List* for a book, though she'd not being doing so well at reading. At one time she could read for England; I was always on at her about the number of books she bought and how I was having to put shelves up the whole time. She looted the bookshelves when she left. All that remained were my DVD's, some manuals and a few books she'd bought me when she was trying to invent for us some shared interest. I remember that on what turned out to be the morning of my arrest, I wiped down the shelves and removed empty fag packets and unopened mail from them. I try to imagine that I felt some regret that all her books were gone but I can't be certain about that. So, she stopped off to buy a book because one of her mates had told her that her inability to read at that time was something to do with stress and her inability to remove herself from the situation she found herself in.

The shop's where the old post office used to be and for several weeks after it opened, people had turned up for stamps and passport forms. According to the guy who owns the place, though people say that an independent bookshop would be a good idea, most would rather go to *Waterstones* or *Borders* with their *3 for 2's*, comfortable seating and over priced coffee. Once you got him on to that subject there was no stopping him according to Maxine.

- The shop was empty but for me and the guy who ran the place; he stood behind the counter and it took me a moment to realise that the stains on his cheeks were tears. He's black is the guy in the shop so he wasn't red and blotchy like white people are when they cry. His face was still and peaceful.

I don't know what it is about her and black men.

- He held an unlit cigarette in one hand and in the other a lighter. It was bright outside and dark inside so no one but me could see this man quietly dripping behind his counter. There was something I needed to do in response to this unexpected situation; there was an intervention that was required which would alter things and make my time in the shop more bearable for both of us

In my mind, I imagine the bookshelves rising like walls. I expect that outside, a small queue formed at the bus stop and that she wished she was queuing for a bus to take her to a place where the matter of verdicts would not be discussed. I can see her crouching behind *Biographies* but finding that there was no one whose life she was interested in. The floor will have been polished wood and her heels will have clicked from *Biographies* to *Fiction: New*. Which is what she tends to read, does Maxine. She's got a notebook and in it she writes down the titles of books she intends to buy. At one time I used to flick through her notebooks and there'd be a title and an author and an extract from a review. More often than not the extracts would concern powerful evocations of love and loss, those apparently being the things that she's into. I imagine her picking up and staring at a book and running her finger down its spine as if it might tell her itself whether it was worth buying.

It was supposed to be a black bookshop but maybe there weren't enough black books or too few people whose tastes were so restricted . Either way, Maxine informed me in one of her many deviations from the point that its stock had expanded to include popular literature, self-help, cookery and the like. She reckoned that this was a good thing because it meant that she didn't have to traipse into town and pay stupid money for parking. Some of her friends felt that the guy behind the counter – who by then had begun sniffing loudly – had sold out. Maxine's friend, Elaine – who's always on about being strong and black and proud - said she felt betrayed by people like him and that she was going to boycott his shop. Maxine had told her that that was fair enough because she couldn't be bothered to argue and if she did she'd only go on at her about how she wouldn't understand. To be honest – and I might as well be given that my honesty or dishonesty doesn't impact much either way anymore – I reckon that life's too short for all that nonsense. Elaine's nice enough, but she's bitter and brittle. Her last relationship ended because of the guy's failure to commit and the one before that ended for the same reason. I said to her once when I was pissed and pissed off with her whining,

- Have you ever thought, Elaine, that you're the common denominator here? Maybe it's not that men don't want to commit; maybe they just don't want to commit to you.

You can imagine how well that went down. Anyway, Elaine reckons she's had enough of men and their fucked up ways and she's happier with a box of *After Eights* and a good film. None of which considerations have stopped her trying it on with D whenever she's been given half a chance and half a gram.

Behind the counter, I can see the guy's face and it's like a building which is being demolished. There's a battle going on between how he feels and how he feels he should appear; how he feels wins and suddenly it's all Maxine's problem.

- I knew that soon he'd have to either decide to carry on crying or pull himself together the way that men do. He made a sound that was like a sob. I turned the *Open for Readers* sign to *Closed* and placed the book on the counter.

And then, she told me, she said something to him which has properly altered my opinion of Maxine. She said,

- Sweetheart.

She said it was because she didn't know his name, but I beg to differ. There are alternatives she could have considered. He whispered I'm sorry or forgive me; she reckoned she didn't remember which.

- The cigarette dropped onto the counter and rolled towards its edge. I expected it to fall on to the floor but it didn't and it felt like a triumph and a sign that things might start to get better. I put my hand out and he gave me the lighter. I placed it neatly next to the cigarette. I handed him £7 to cover the book and told him I didn't need a bag. I put it in with the sausages and bacon, which seemed wrong but unavoidable. I wanted to touch his hand, but that would have been wrong too. He offered me shreds of a story across the counter. It was to do with a woman and the business and they seemed to be connected in some way and he said he shouldn't be there carrying on like a loser in front of a stranger. I wanted him to ask if I was ok so that I could cry like a loser in front of a stranger but he didn't so I just stood there and waited for whatever was coming next.

What came next was that the guy behind the counter continued to leak and to mumble and to apologise and to tell her that he shouldn't be telling her all this. Which begs the question: why the fuck was he, then?

She told me – and frankly I think this was a case of too much information – that she made that sound which is the sound of the sea in a shell, like she used to when the kids were little and she'd rock them till they finally fell asleep, and as the man ran out of words she touched his shoulder and said nothing. I expect that this comforted him. It didn't comfort me.

- A woman tried the door and found it open despite the *Closed* sign. The guy behind the counter dragged his hand down his face and when he'd finished there was a smile there. He thanked me for whatever it was he thought I'd done and I left. I've never been so lonely. Driving home I wondered whether – if you could weigh and measure people's pain – his would be greater than mine. What if I'd said summat like, you think you've got problems... would that have made it better or worse for him? Would I have felt less lonely? Or would he? What would he think of someone blubbing over a rapist?

I struggled for summat to say to that little dig but found that there was nothing.

- Then I pulled into the drive and I stopped thinking about anything.

I, on the other hand, got to that point in the conversation and started thinking about everything.

- When he got back that evening, your dad was like a rough sketch of what he'd been when he left in the morning. There were bits of him missing and his edges were curled like parchment. And he was smaller. He'd made arrangements for the twins to stay with your Joanne, and Ben and Stephanie had known without being told that they should be anywhere else.

I can see him sat at the kitchen table with his six pack from the *Co Op* staring at the cans as if he expects them to open up and pour themselves down his neck. His hands and lips will have shaken as he sucked on his cigarettes. She said,

- His grey or hazel eyes were like the sky before rain.

He will have loosened his tie and opened the top two buttons of his shirt hurriedly like they were blocking his airways.

I know all this because I've seen my dad relay bad news before. When I was 12, I got in from school and my sisters were sat silently at the kitchen table looking at the fruit bowl. One of them – it will have been our Joanne - told me that my dad had something important to say and he'd been waiting for me to get in before he told us. The pots were still in the sink from breakfast time and there was a jug of milk on the table that hadn't been shifted. I asked if I was in trouble for being late and they said that they didn't think so. As it turned out, we were all in serious trouble because he told us a story about my mum and how she'd died that morning.

- I noticed that the hair on your dad's chest was tight and grey and curly and it struck me that that's what yours will look like soon. I picked up the beers and put them in the fridge. I cleared a couple of cups from the kitchen table and placed them in the dishwasher. I wiped down the surfaces with an anti bacterial spray and swept the floor. The air was thick with the smell of cleaning products and cigarette smoke so I opened the window a little and it was all sucked out of the room. The fridge was all over the place so I rearranged it so that the raw meats were on the bottom shelf, the cheeses were individually wrapped and placed in a plastic container and the cooked meats were on the top shelf. Somebody had put half a tin of beans in the fridge without decanting them so they got thrown out. The bacon and sausages, bought from the man with blood under his nails, got binned as well.

She placed some marinated olives in a small bowl and put them on the table, though quite what she thought my Dad was going to do with marinated olives is anyone's guess. I imagine that they were left over from her buffet but she didn't specify their origins. The phone rang and my dad looked at it without moving to answer it.

- You'd best unplug it tonight, love.

She sat at the table with him and brought over a bottle of vodka and two glasses.

- I remember that the headline on the weekly free paper read, *Accident and Emergency is for Emergencies Only*. It said that some people had been using A&E for minor ailments. A consultant was quoted as saying that this was an abuse of a free service and that such behaviour potentially put people's lives at risk. On page 6, three glum children stared out at me; they'd raised money for some picnic tables for their playground and three of them had been stolen. The paper bulged with small crises and I wanted to read about all of them. Your dad just sat there like a spare part and I just wanted him to fuck off. I wanted another few hours of not knowing what'd happened so that I could get my head round things. It's funny because I knew even at the time that I was less concerned about you than I was about me. What sort of woman marries a rapist?

I took this to be a rhetorical question and hoped that she was getting to the end of her story.

- I went into the front room and looked at the world outside the window but where I live whatever happens happens behind closed doors. The neighbour pulled into the drive and I waved at him but I don't think he'd seen me. I thought about ringing Joanne to check on the twins; they're not right keen on school and they sometimes carry on a bit the first day back after a holiday. Your dad must have followed me into the front room because his hand touched mine and then he held it tight. His sovereign ring pressed painfully into my finger before he released his grip and whispered,

- They've give him seven years, love.

And she told me she remembered saying to him,

- It's *given*, Jim, not *give*.

Because it was too big a sentence to get wrong. My dad's chin dropped towards his chest and they went back into the kitchen. He stared into his vodka like there was something important there that just wanted finding. It struck me, as she told me this story, that she seemed curiously pre occupied with touch on the day of the verdict, and from time to time since then I've wondered what that's all about and whether she was trying to tell me something. I didn't know if anyone had touched her since I'd last touched her. I didn't know if I cared but I knew I didn't want to know.

- My phone vibrated. It was D. He said he was outside and was it all right if he came in for a minute. He made his way into the kitchen with four *Marks & Spencer* carrier bags. Your dad said: all right, D, lad? Like it was just another day. And he stood up and shook his hand and placed his arm round D's shoulder. Your dad seemed taller again and younger as they looked at each other and mirrored each other shaking their heads. D rested his head briefly on your dad's shoulder and his hand (the one with the sovereign on its middle finger) skimmed his neck. D's shoulders shook as if something outside himself had grabbed hold of him. He was wearing the suit he'd worn at the twins' christening. D and your dad held on to each other for as long as it's acceptable for men to hold on to each other.

Her story became a bit incoherent at that stage and I felt that if she'd been telling it in another setting she'd have hit me; I suppose it was early days and she was still trying to process everything that had happened but from what I could make out she must have slid to the floor because the next sensible thing she said was that the smell of expensive aftershave approached and D bent over and unfolded her. He whispered something to her as he helped her find her feet but she couldn't make it out. He put his hands on her shoulders and he stared right into her eyes. His eyes, she said, were like sultanas in milk. Which brings me back to this curiously intimate tone of hers. I didn't – and will never – need to know what D's eyes look like and I'm not sure I'm comfortable with him whispering things which she claims she can't remember.

He pointed at things like she had to listen carefully because this was the last thing he was going to tell her and she needed to remember for future reference. Like she was on a mission now. This sounded much more like D.

- Our lass told us to bring this lot round for you. You're not gonna want to be cooking and all that, are you?

He started emptying the bags and placing their contents on the work surfaces. He went on about the ready meals he'd bought and told her that he'd chosen some he thought the twins would like and some that'd just do for one person. Some of them were on a *two for one* but they were quality goods: *Marks's* and all that. She's not really one for ready meals isn't Maxine; one of her company's many unique selling points is that everything she provides in terms of outside catering is freshly prepared so she always feels like she's selling out when she sticks a pizza in the oven. He placed all the boxes in piles according to their size and then he picked them up and put them back down again and stood back and looked at them. Then he looked at his phone like he hoped it might ring. Then he dug into his back pocket and gave her a piece of paper.

- You want to keep that safe, Max. There's Dan's number if you're needing to sort out decorating, and Johnno if you need your electrics sorting and Ed for your plumbing. If any o'them lot start tryna rip you off, you know where I am. In fact, pass every quote through me.

My dad nodded. They like being useful, do D and my dad.

- People carry on alarming, Max, if you let them.

He looked towards D for something like approval. D nodded and prodded produce.

- I've got some of your salad leaves and veg – all full on washed and prepared – and our lass was on about your quilted toilet roll and stuff.

She reckoned she could tell he was embarrassed about the toilet roll. They drank more vodka and D sought my dad's permission before building a spliff. I don't know why she felt the need to let that little one slip; she knows I don't approve of doing drugs in front of kids or oldsters. Maybe it was about showing me that in my absence none of the old rules applied; D had probably had my dad necking E's and snorting coke all the time I was on remand for all I know. At some point she got the calculator out and it turned out that there's about 2455 days in seven years (leap years are funny and she couldn't properly factor them in then there was the remand to take into account) and this first one was almost over. She continued:

- You know when I was calculating your absence, were you thinking of me as I was thinking of you? Were you still wondering what it was – exactly – that led us here? Were you fretting about the kids and had you remembered it was their first day back after the holidays? You don't need to answer, Simon. I know you'll have been thinking about yourself.

When she said that, I found that there was nothing I could say in response because it's not in any way comforting to hear that someone thinks you're that poor a specimen of humanity. I wondered what sort of bastard that would make me. For the record, she was wrong; at about the time she must have been sat drinking vodka I was sat thinking of and knowing nothing but her. I would rather have been Maxine worrying about me than me worrying about her but that's how it goes, I suppose: somewhere else someone else is going through their own private shit. I expect that somewhere ending in *ley,* Eliz was feeling a whole bunch of things. My neighbours and my ex colleagues and the lads who worked in the shop will've been thinking their own thoughts and my kids were thinking all the things that kids are likely to think about situations that nobody will talk to them about. I wanted to sweep up all the chaos I'd caused her and mostly I wanted her to never have met me. I wanted to be 18 again and to see her in that bar opposite the university and to limit my greeting to a wave or a hi. If she walked over to join me I wanted her to be waylaid by some other, better person who wouldn't 20 years down the line cause her so much grief. I'm not the sort of person that people should feel connected to. I disappoint.

Relating her story to me weeks after the verdict, she said,

- They'd decided – 12 people who knew only one thing about you – that you'd done a bad thing and that you needed to pay for this with something they called seven years which was pretty much as long as the twins had been alive. I knew it should pan out at less than seven years but not enough less. There was the time spent on remand which'd be knocked off and then you could do as little as half the sentence and you should definitely do no more than two thirds. But I couldn't work out what two thirds of seven was. And I couldn't work out how I'd ended up married to someone who'd raped some young lass.

I could have worked out what 7 divided by 3 was: it was 2.3 recurring. But I couldn't have worked out – and still can't - why she'd ended up married to someone who'd raped a young lass. So, D helped her put the shopping away and my Dad continued to mumble in the background about all the things they were going to do to make things better for her and the kids. And she just wanted them both to go away so that there would be no noise in the house and in her head. There was a knock on the door – the back door this time – and she told me she remembered jumping. D told her to chill, that everything was going to be OK. My dad got up and he and D exchanged looks which meant something Maxine didn't understand. My dad looked at his watch and nodded. D touched Maxine on the shoulder and said,

- You go answer it, love.

She shook her head.

- You're gonna have to answer the door at some point. You might as well start now.

He insisted, she said, and she felt she had no choice. As she turned the key, D and my dad stood close behind her – like they were protecting her. Linda came in and hugged her though Maxine said she didn't want to be touched, then Linda turned and said,

- Just hold on a second, love. There's summat I've forgotten.

She wouldn't be a minute. And the thing she'd forgotten turned out to be me.

6.

The jury deliberated for just over two hours which, according to my barrister, was either a good thing or a bad thing. There was a frozen moment when it dawned on me that they knew something I didn't know and that whatever it was they knew, there was no going back on it. The judge threatened to have D thrown out of court when the verdict was announced. Anyone would've thought it was both of us that were on trial and maybe we were because I don't know how our friendship would have survived a guilty verdict. I heard a woman scream; it could have been Eliz or her mum. Her dad's face looked like the sort of face that would never smile again. I found that I didn't know how to move and in the end it was a copper that had to tell me what not guilty meant. I walked out of the court and no one was unlocking and locking doors before and after me. My suit stuck to me. I undid the top button of my shirt and loosened my tie.

I got out of the court building and Great George Street was where I'd left it and so was the Civic Hall and the Town Hall. Men in suits who looked – but weren't – just like me took phone calls and slipped into shops and bars for a late lunch or an early drink. D grabbed my elbow and steered me through everyone. He said encouraging things to me and glanced at my Dad for affirmation.

- What did I fucking tell you, mate? It's all about circumstances and context. Your jury's got to take those into account, mate.

My Dad – being shorter than us and older – took up the rear. When I glanced round at him from time to time it felt like he was further away than he was and like he'd never catch up. I said to D,

- Let's slow down a touch, fella. Wait for the old fella to catch up.

And so, for a couple of seconds, we stood still. I watched him as he drew up alongside us and I noticed for the first time that he was wearing his good suit or it was wearing him; his shirt looked a bit big in the collar; and I couldn't properly see his face because he was staring at the ground. In those couple of seconds I wondered what the fuck I'd put him through? Then I thought, no more than he put us through as kids. But it didn't make me feel any better. D had parked where he always parks in town: the *Morrisons* car park where he's been blagging free parking for years and when we got there he bundled me into his car. I told him I just wanted to drive round Leeds. My Dad was small and stunned and he told me that he just needed some time on his own. He looked for a moment like he might want to hug me but he paused for that second too long and whatever chance there might have been was lost. It's one of the many items on my *things I regret* list.

We drove all over and for most of the time we said nothing to each other. I watched Leeds reveal itself to me and found that there was nothing about it I didn't already know. I waited for a sense of euphoria to hit me. In the end, just as we were driving along the outer ring road towards Cookridge, D said – because someone had to say something,

- How does it feel, mate?
- I don't know, D. It's like I can't remember being inside.
- That's your self-preservation mechanisms kicking in, fella. It's like the pain of childbirth; they say women forget that soon as it's over. It'll come back to you every now and again when you're not expecting it.

He wasn't wrong there but I wasn't to know that at the time. He asked me if I wanted to call Maxine and I told him I didn't know what I'd say to her with all I'd put her and the kids through.

- What if she doesn't want to talk to me?

He told me to stop blubbing even though I hadn't started yet.

- Seriously, mate, what if she's thought she wants nothing more to do with me? What if she's thought she can manage without me; that it's no biggy?

He told me I was talking daft and that there's no woman in the world who wouldn't rather her man be on the out. I told him I thought he'd find that Maxine was an exception to that little rule. He said,

- I'll tell you what, mate; we'll put my theory to the test.

At that point, there was a whole load of things I could've said most of which should've started with don't be so fucking stupid. We stopped off for a drink in a pub I didn't know and that's when we hit upon my surprise re appearance. It all got out of hand and it became a sportsman's bet - the type you can't back out of. The story got bigger and bigger and more and more elaborate but D told me not to worry about the details; him and Linda and my dad would stay on top of all that. He phoned his accomplices and it wasn't really like they were in a position to object because D just outlined what the plan was and told them where to be and what to say. All I'd to do was sit it out at his house.

- Will she be up for it?

I laughed because I'd had three pints by this time and each had progressively clouded my already poor judgment. I was imagining the scene and the part I'd get to play. I could see her face like she was sat in front of me though she'd not been sat in front of me for a long time at that point. She'd call me a little bastard and she'd laugh and then she'd cry and I'd get to hold her again. There'd be a line drawn and we'd start again, this time for the last time.

- You won't prolong the agony for too long, will you, D?

He told me not to worry about it; that if things looked like they were coming on top for her they'd come clean. He told me things I wanted to believe about her being a good sport and about how much we'd laugh about all this in years to come. Looking back, I don't know what bit of me thought it was a good idea.

At the bar an old giffer ordered a pint of *Tetley's* and I thought to myself, I could've been that old on my first day out if I'd been found guilty. I got up and went to the bar,

- I'll get that for you, mate.

The old man looked at me like I'd lost it or like I was taking the piss but I wasn't taking no for an answer.

- You celebrating summat?

I told him that he reminded me of someone, which was when he started looking worried and took himself and his bitter to a table where an elderly woman waited. It was time to go, D said; there were places to be and people to see and things to sort out.

It was still light when we got to Maxine's and I felt exposed and out of place in my black suit. We'd picked up Maureen on the way which, frankly, would not have been high on my list of things to do on your first day out of prison but apparently my Dad had insisted that she be there. He didn't want her sat on her own at home. She asked me how I was and I had to stop myself from saying to her,

- How the fuck d'you think I am? I've been banged up for fucking months.

Instead, looking straight ahead, I said,

- Not so bad. Yourself?

I'd kind of hoped she'd take it as a rhetorical question but, being Maureen, she couldn't pass up an opportunity to let me know precisely how she was.

- Well, Simon, love…it's been a funny old time one way and another, what with all this business…your dad's been bearing up but it's been a bit of a strain on him, you know what his nerves are like…we've all pulled together…it's what family's all about…

I hate it when she calls me love and I hate it when she refers to herself as part of my family and I didn't know what his nerves were like. I switched my brain to a different frequency when she got on to what the neighbours were up to and when they were next going to the caravan.

We pulled up outside the house and Maxine's neighbour was putting the cat out. She stared at me like she knew me from somewhere but she couldn't quite place me. Then she remembered me and she started to smile then pulled it back; I waved but she pretended she hadn't noticed and went back in the house. I imagined her putting the chain on and telling her husband who it was she'd just seen going into Maxine's. It was all I could do not to go up to the door and say to her,

    - D'you know what not guilty means?

But I didn't really know what it meant myself.

We walked round the back and under our feet the gravel crunched on Maxine's new path. She'd taken down the twins' swings and in their place was a climbing frame which would have taken some putting up. Somebody – and I hoped it was D or my dad – had obviously given her a hand. I told myself not to ask her and not to get back into all that shit. Linda was an over excited schoolgirl whispering instructions and telling me to stay round the corner while she knocked on the door. There was a pause after Maxine opened the door and then I heard Linda say,

    - How are you holding up, lovie?

I heard Maxine's voice and it was like the first time I'd ever heard it. I've always said she sounds like Lauren Bacall would if she were from Leeds but she didn't sound like that. She sounded like someone who'd just been told her husband had got seven years for rape.

    - Just hold on a second, love. There's summat I've forgotten.

She wouldn't be a minute. She was more than a minute as it goes, because I'd walked back up the gravel path and Maureen was clawing at my arm and telling me I'd to go back and I was telling her that this had fuck all to do with her. My dad said a number of conciliatory things but of these all I remember is one word – son – over and over and over again. I would've said more – and worse – things to Maureen if Linda hadn't grabbed my elbow and told me I'd no fucking choice. I look back and part of me thinks that walking back up Maxine's gravel path and towards her gate is the last sane thing I've done. But then I was back up the path and then I was stood there. And Maxine was stood in the doorway with a face that was older than when I'd last seen it. She'd no make up on which made no sense because she always wears make up and she was wearing a pair of our Stephanie's track bottoms. They were that bit too big for her and they just about managed to attach themselves to what was left of her hips. Her eyes were bluer but maybe that's because her skin was paler. She turned to D and my dad then she looked at Linda and it was like I'd never known her because I couldn't read anything into the expression on her face. Maybe there's a word that's not been invented yet for what it was she was feeling.

- You gonna ask me in then or what?

There was nothing else I knew how to say and sometimes it's as well not to think about these things too much and just to say what comes immediately to mind. It was a luxury I could afford now that I was out and around people who knew me.

- Simon, what the fuck are you doing here?

And this turned out to be the funniest thing anyone had ever said. Over the course of the next few hours one or the other of us would repeat it and we'd laugh again and louder. She shook as I held her and said something over and over which I didn't catch and probably didn't matter. The front of my shirt was slimy when she let go of me and she grabbed some kitchen towel and wiped me down like I was one of the kids.

- You've lost weight, Simon. But your eyes are still the same. What colour would you say they were?

She looked at D like he might know the answer. He shrugged,

- No idea, love. I don't make a habit of looking into my mate's eyes. It's one of those things that's frowned upon in polite society.

She wiped my shirt for too long so it ended up with bits of kitchen towel down the front. I touched her hand and it stiffened then slackened. I asked her where the kids were though I knew where they were. I told her I would've liked to have seen them which wasn't strictly true.

Linda was buzzing round the kitchen like she owned the place, getting glasses and opening champagne. She told Maxine to sit herself down and not to worry about a thing.

- I look a right state, Si.

Maxine pointed at herself and looked at me like she couldn't trust her own opinion of her appearance and needed me to say something. I stroked her arm, and said nothing.

- If you feel uncomfortable, Maxine love, go upstairs and get changed. I'll come with you.

And so Linda and Maxine went upstairs and doubtless talked to each other and tried to make sense of this new and unexpected situation. Maureen followed and they were all up there for a good 15 minutes; in their absence, D and me and my dad clapped each other on the back and paced round the floor. D apologised for the quality of the champagne but it didn't matter to me because it was in a glass and I was drinking it in a room whose unlocked door led outside.

7.

- I knew you'd be all right, son. I knew there was no way you could've done what they said you'd done. You weren't brought up like that.

He'd sat through a fair bit of the trial, had my dad, and he knew that what I'd admitted to doing wasn't so good in anyone's books but that wasn't something we were ever going to talk about so that was all right.

- It's like any young lass with a gripe against a man can cry rape these days. I'll tell you what; it makes me glad I'm past it.

And I knew then that he'd be saying that to anyone who'd listen for the next several days or until he'd convinced himself it was true. He'd always been good at that, had my dad: revising history to suit his own ends. The doorbell rang and it turned out to be a couple of the lads from the shop that D had invited. They looked a bit awkward and out of place and for a few minutes one of them had difficulty meeting my eyes but they settled down with the champagne and the beer. We got talking about technical specifications and a new lighting rig that'd just come on the market and that's when I started to feel normal.

- Some things never change.

Maxine smiled for the first time and it looked like she might mean it. She nodded towards the lad and me.

- Don't you ever get bored of talking about watts and wires and plugs all the time?

D gave her a glass and put his arm round her. She put her arm round his waist and I saw her mouth thankyou at him. Her dress had a deep v-neck and it crossed over at the front and tied at the side. I'd not seen it before. I introduced her to Jake and Andy but she already knew them with going in and doing the books every month. Which was news to me. Jake helped himself to another beer and Linda handed him a glass which he refused.

- So when're you coming back into the shop, Simon? We've all missed you.

This wasn't strictly true on account of D had told me that two lads resigned the day they found out I'd been banged up.

- Tomorrow.

And as soon as I'd said it I regretted it. I wanted to spend more time with Maxine, looking at her and learning what sort of person she'd become since I'd been away. She stepped in at that point, did Maxine, and she said,

- I don't think so, Simon. You want to relax a bit and reacclimatise.

She rubbed my arm as if I'd hurt it and told me to sup up or all the bubbles would go flat. It was good having her take control like that and telling me what I would and wouldn't be doing. It made it look like we were your standard couple that had been together nearly 20 years. Linda laughed,

- That's you told, lad. You need a woman that can take you in hand – show you who's boss.

D glared at her and everyone found something fascinating to do with the stems of their champagne glasses; something which involved not meeting my eyes and being silent for just that half second too long. I laughed and my voice was the only noise in the room until, like them, I realised that what she'd said had been read as insensitive in light of recent events.

- She's always been the boss, has Maxine.

And I squeezed her arm so that for a moment we looked all right and everyone was allowed to relax and get on with their drinking and talking over each other. Maxine beckoned me into the hallway,

- So, you really didn't do it, Si?

And I wondered why she'd made it into a question when it should have been a statement of fact.

- Of course I didn't do it, Max. That's why they found me not guilty. If I'd have done it, I wouldn't be here now, would I?

I tried to smile but it came out wrong.

- Whose idea was that little game?

She gestured toward the kitchen.

- It was D's idea. It was about seeing if you cared or summat.

My voice petered out.

- But you went along with it
- I want us to try and put this behind us, Max.
- What if I don't?
- We'll talk about it later when these lot have fucked off.

She looked at the floor and nodded. I looked at the floor and nodded. It was a bit like praying. I thought about putting my arm around her but it felt like too great a distance to travel so soon. So I said,

- We'd best be getting back. They'll be wondering what's happened to us.

- Will you try and be a bit nicer to Maureen, Si? She's trying her best, you know.

I told her I would but I wasn't. Linda was getting lopsided and her speech was slurred like it always is when she's had a few. Soon she'd be on about how long we'd known each other and how there's nothing more important than having your mates round you when you need them, how you're never alone when you're loved (which is a lie, by the way). Maureen was clinging like a limpet to my Dad and nodding at everything he said like she always does. Maxine was talking to Jake and I overheard him telling her that it was amazing the way she'd coped. He wasn't sure his lass would have been as strong. Maxine added,

- Or as stupid.

And that was then end of that little exchange. Nobody asked me how I'd coped which was just as well because it would've

175

involved more blatant lying about just getting my head down and staying optimistic and knowing that justice would prevail. I preferred things the way they were with my story suddenly being everyone else's story and D cracking jokes about the look on Maxine's face when she saw it was me at the door. The way he told it, it was like it was someone else's face he'd seen because in his version she'd looked shocked and then grinned and said whatever line it was she's supposed to have said. It was a lot funnier in the retelling than it had been at the time, but that was good because I knew that if he repeated this story often enough – and he would – I'd start to believe it and so might Maxine.

D got his camera out – a digital SLR device that does all sorts and was just as good as one twice the price – and arranged me and Maxine at the kitchen table. It turned out that the shop had started stocking these cameras and they were going down a storm.

- We don't stock cameras, D. We do sound and lighting.
- I'll tell you what we do, mate: we do stuff that people want to buy.

I could've said summat then to remind him whose shop it was and who'd built it up from scratch; who'd made the shop an authorised dealership for some of the top brands in the business but I decided to leave it till I got my feet under the table again and got him out of my place and into wherever it was that he was going to start selling his own random merchandise from. He pointed the camera at us and I had to put my arm round Maxine and raise my thumb and she had to lean in towards me with her head on my shoulder. We had to stand like that for several seconds while D located the various function buttons.

- Right then, say free.

So we both said free weakly and D said that'd have to do. Then there were other photographs that had to be taken so that this would be an evening we'd remember for the rest of our lives. There was a cake that Linda had managed to hastily procure from somewhere. Someone had piped *Welcome Home Simon* on the top. Everyone commented on how lovely it was and on how kind it was of

Linda to have sorted it all out. It got photographed like everything else and as I cut into it, they all sang *For he's a jolly good fellow*. It hurt my ears and made me want to be anywhere else. When they'd stopped singing, D demanded a speech, as I knew he would. Obviously I declined and obviously he made me say summat, anyway. I raised my glass,

- Unaccustomed as I am to public speaking...

They all laughed and Jake punched me on the shoulder,

-...I'd like to propose a toast to all of you for standing by me in what's been a tough few months. At times, the only thing that's kept me going has been knowing that there were people on the out who knew that I was innocent. To friendship.

I looked at Maxine and tried to read whatever it was that was happening behind her blue eyes but they were glassy and they were giving nothing away. When we'd stopped clinking glasses, I raised mine again and said,

- To friendship and to love.

Maxine looked a bit taken aback by what I suppose was a public declaration. She didn't look quite as touched as I'd thought she might but then it was late and my delivery was probably not the best. In any case, my acknowledgement of where I'd been for the past few months seemed to release a bit of tension and my guests felt able to tentatively approach the subject of my incarceration. I suppose it was my opportunity to be the conquering hero or the man who's emerged from the belly of the beast but I couldn't quite translate what had happened into a couple of neat anecdotes. I told them it was grim and that it wasn't somewhere I'd be wanting to return to in a hurry. Linda said,

- It must be that much worse knowing that you're innocent and being banged up with proper rapists and child abusers.

She shuddered dramatically like a proper rapist or child abuser had just walked into the kitchen. Somebody else said it didn't bear thinking about but it didn't stop them all speculating on what it must be like to have to share a cell with a dirty bastard that's shafted his own kids. Maxine got on with clearing the table and I got on with appearing interested and engaged in a conversation which left me cold and uncomfortable. As she picked up my glass, Maxine glanced at me and I wanted to say something to her but I didn't know what it was so I winked at her. She looked away and asked nobody in particular if she should put the kettle on. It was a cue for people to leave but no one picked up on it. The champagne and the beer had been done in but there was still vodka and Linda had brought round a good bottle of brandy on account of that being my favourite tipple. By the time my dad and Maureen and the lads from the shop had gone, we were down to half a bottle of Cointreau left over from Christmas. Just after 2, D poured Linda into a taxi, assuring her of his intention to join her in no time. It was pretty obvious to me that he wasn't going anywhere. A few minutes after Linda had gone, Maxine yawned dramatically,

    - I'm off up, lads.

I shifted in my seat and downed my Cointreau in one gulp. She touched me on the shoulder.

    - I'll leave you two to it. I expect you've got a lot of catching up to do.

So that was me told. I told her I'd be up soon and she forced an expression which I could have interpreted as a smile had I not known her so well.

Maxine's table top's glass, which turned out to be convenient. D told me we were celebrating and a couple of lines would be OK just to round things off. I wasn't right bothered about getting into all that again but without it I'd have had nothing to say. He filled me in on what'd been going off since I'd been inside like I'd just missed a few episodes of *Coronation Street*. Everything had been unfeasibly fine in my absence. But for her nerves which were a bit fried for the first few weeks, Maxine had kept her end up and done me proud. She'd spent a fair bit of time round at his house and she'd been out a few times with Elaine and some other lass whose name I didn't recognise. He'd sorted Maxine out with a gravel pathway and replaced the garage door. My dad had not been so good but the verdict had saved him. Then he got on to the shop and how well it was doing with all his new lines and his special clearance offers.

- I'm happy to stop on for a bit while you sort your head out, Si.
- What am I supposed to do for money?
- I was gonna get on to that. Remember, back at Christmas when I was on about opening a retail unit...

Which was when he unveiled his grand plan. There was an empty unit next door and he'd investigated buying it and knocking through. He'd been on to some suppliers and it looked likely that we'd be able to expand our stock to include what he referred to as home entertainment goods. The specialist sound and lighting stuff was all well and good but it didn't attract your normal everyday punter. He'd look after the home entertainment side of things and leave me to get on with the rest. It was a matter of moving with the times or staying ahead of the game or reading the competition or somesuch. If we played our cards right, we could look into expanding into white goods in a couple of years. Then there was the website he was planning which would have a facility for online sales; apparently everyone was at it and we had to keep up to stand a chance of staying in business.

He drew me a plan and filled in the space with squares to represent home entertainment and lavish window displays. Somewhere in the back of the new expanded shop my sound and lighting equipment jostled for space with a home cinema demonstration area.
- How far on are you with these plans, D?
- Well, I've obviously talked to Maxine about it and she's up for it.

He cleared his throat and looked at the white skid marks on the table,
- Thing was, we didn't know what the outcome was gonna be at court so it made sense to be thinking about future possibilities...you know, if things hadn't gone so well.
- Was it a bit inconvenient, then: me getting found not guilty?

That's when he told me to fuck off and grow up. That's when he told me how much money he'd poured into the place to keep it going while I was busy blubbing in jail. The shop had been dead in the water before he'd stepped in; the first week he'd been there some guy from the Inland Revenue had turned up demanding employers' tax and NI. Two suppliers had threatened to withdraw the authorised dealership on account of persistent late payments and there were other things I'd apparently failed to do which he said weren't even worth going into because he'd be there all night.

- What the fuck happened to you, Si?

And he grabbed my arm and stared into my eyes. It felt important to be able to provide him with a reasonable answer but I had trouble processing the question because it was too big a thing to be tackling at 3 in the morning in Maxine's kitchen. He tried prompting me with some possible responses,

- Was it all to do with Maxine going? Or was it before then with the other business going tits up? That was bloody ages ago…you'd think you'd have got over all that by now. I know you've had a hard time, mate…I saw the way you were with Maureen tonight, so there's obviously all that stuff that's still bothering you, but Jesus…

It was none of the above and all of the above and his chipping away at it hadn't made the question any smaller.

- Can't we talk about summat else, D?
- We can talk about anything you want to talk about. I'm not fucking bothered anymore.

I waited for him to smile but he didn't. We had another line and he lightened up a bit but not much. I pretended to see the sense in his business idea because the truth was I didn't have much in the way of a choice. We plotted and planned it and made it feel like this was an opportunity for me to start again. We talked about a relaunch and a new name and I told him I was cool with every half-baked idea he threw at me. It could all be sorted out in the morning, I told him. We'd sit down and go through it all properly; tie up the loose ends and make everything watertight. He reminded me – like it was possible that I could've forgotten – that it'd been a tough day and a difficult few months what with everything that'd gone off. I was bound to be feeling a bit on edge but things would get better.

- We'll sort out the business and you need to get on with sorting out the Maxine situation.

He cleared the debris from the table and paced round the floor for a few seconds. There was something he wanted to say but whatever it was he didn't say it. I felt like I needed to close things off, to draw a line under things, so I said,

- I don't know what the fuck's wrong with me, mate, but once I find out I'll let you know.

I smiled and he smiled back. He called a taxi and we stood together staring out at the street through the slats of the wooden blinds in Maxine's living room. That house was the quietest place I'd been in a long time and I breathed in the silence till it filled me up. And that's when it came to me,

- I don't feel connected to anything, D. I can't remember the last time I felt connected to anything.

8.
    If she had been any closer to the wall she'd have made a dent in it. I slid into the bed and balanced on its outer edge. She breathed like someone who was in a deep sleep but I know when people are pretending to sleep; I've done it that often myself. It felt like if either of us moved, something terrible would happen so I didn't move. The bed smelt of what she smells like but all her cushions and pillows formed a barrier between us. Last time I'd been in her bed I'd leapt out of it at about the time I was getting into it this time. It's funny the way things turn out. I told myself that this sense of unease was to be expected and that things would get better once we got used to each other's company again. It took me a while to get off to sleep because my head was that full of things; I was trying to process all the D stuff and this new business venture which was going to be nothing like the business I'd thought I was coming back to. I remembered – in the way that memories have a habit of creeping up unbidden – that in the months before I'd got banged up I'd adopted an idiosyncratic wages system for myself which mainly involved helping myself to cash from the till when I got short. And all the letters which piled up because I knew none of them were going to tell me anything I wanted to know or was capable of knowing. Once or twice, when things had got tight, I'd slipped through a couple of card sales that had been made on my credit card. Maybe I'd have sorted these things out at some point. On the positive side, I told myself, at least I was contemplating this unexpected business development from the vantage point of Maxine's

bed rather than A Wing in Armley. I wanted to touch her – on her shoulder maybe, and in an overtly non-sexual (and consensual) way – and to tell her how grateful I was to her for letting me in and how humbled I was by her.

  I remembered the story I'd said I was gonna tell her just before what happened had happened: the one about having no money and us being something like content together. It felt like the right time to be saying that sort of stuff to her; like she might be receptive to all that after all this shit. It would place things in context. I tried to adjust my breathing to hers but my breaths were that bit more shallow. It wasn't a problem, though, because I found that the more I thought about reaching out to her the deeper my breaths became. I'd properly throw myself at her mercy and in doing that I'd unlock something in both of us which would enable us to talk honestly about where we had found ourselves, how we'd got there and where we were gonna go from here. There'd be no holds barred but that'd be all good in the end. Maybe I'd get to find out why she'd left me in the first place and maybe I'd get to understand what the fuck it was that had happened to me over the past year or so. They call that sort of thing truth and reconciliation and, lying in her bed that night, it made the world of sense.

  There were maybe 900mm between my left hand and her left shoulder and I plotted the route. They took in places I'd not been to for some time and which I wasn't right comfortable about revisiting but I reckoned that if they were looming up now then they must mean something important and that taking a detour would be a bad and wrong thing to do. There are things that come to you that you push to one side and that you never get on top of; you edit them out. Sometimes, though – and I've seen this with muso lads who come into the shop blubbing over some line they got rid of which they now want to retrieve – you need to go back to the cutting room floor and remind yourself of all the stories you thought you didn't need to tell and all the sounds you thought you didn't need to hear. There was the Eliz thing, of course, but I didn't know quite where to start with that one; the setting seemed inappropriate and, besides, a jury had told me that afternoon that it hadn't happened. Apart from that, though, there were other things we'd never bothered talking about. If you stacked them all up – as I did that night – they were the only things that wanted talking about. But a lot of them couldn't be discussed with her because they'd only do her harm; we didn't, for example, need to be excavating women or my apparent attitude towards the kids or any of the things I'd said over the years in the heat of the moment. There were other things, though, that might shed light on what'd gone off in the past and might help us to plot a new direction.

It's funny the way things come at you when you're least expecting them; I decided I needed to wake her from her feigned sleep and talk to her about my mum because my failure to talk about her had always been a bone of contention between us. Maxine used to say,

- Whenever I bring her up, you back away like you're about to get hit by a bus.

I lay in her overstuffed bed and tried to recover the story.

When I was 12, I got in from school and my sisters were sat round the table looking at the fruit bowl. It contained three bananas and two apples. I wanted a banana but if I did my Mum would tell me off for ruining my tea. My sisters told me to be good and to be quiet and to wait for my dad to tell me something important. They didn't know what the important thing was and none of us speculated on what it might be. There were unwashed pots in the sink. A fly circled them. I looked at my sisters but neither of them looked at me. My Dad came into the kitchen and he looked rough as fuck. His face had set into an expression I'd not seen before. My mum had been in a road accident and suddenly she was dead. I understood what he said at the moment he said it but nobody told me she'd be dead everyday that I woke up after that and nobody highlighted the weaknesses in my dad's story. Everything that had happened before she died had never happened. Things like how she'd disappeared, had my mum, for what must have been getting on for a year. She was with her fancy man; someone she worked with who told her she was wasted on my Dad and that she deserved better. Obviously no one ever told me this; I know it because I heard my dad on the phone carrying on about them. Our Joanne pointed him out to me once; he had black hair that looked as if he'd slicked something through it. Maybe it was dyed; he was at that age when black hair greys. He was sat in a car outside the Co Op waiting – I suppose – for someone who was probably my Mum. We never saw her during that year but sometimes my Auntie Norah would come round and we'd hear him going on at her about how my Mum was an unfit mother who'd abandoned her kids and that she should've thought about wanting to be with her kids before she decided to go fuck the first man who showed any interest in her.

But before then – before she'd left - I remember being sat at the turn in the stairs with my sisters while my dad carried on alarming. Mainly there was just the bass of his voice but sometimes we'd hear my Mum crying or something heavy and human falling. While she was gone – for that year or so – we pretended (me and my sisters) that everything was fine. We never properly talked about what had gone off even between ourselves. Sometimes our Sandra would try to say something but talking about it made it all too real so we'd tell her to stop going on and that would be the end of that. One of the things my Dad used to say to us when we were little was,

- There's nowt worse than a liar. You can trust a thief to steal but you can never trust a liar.

It made no sense then and it makes even less now; we learnt lying off my Dad. Or not telling the truth - it's all much of a muchness in the end. And then she was back suddenly, was my Mum, and from the turn in the stairs we'd hear my dad going on at her about what she'd done and where she'd been and how his mates had told him not to take her back. He told her she was damaged goods and the only reason he was having her back was on account of the kids. He'd be on at her most nights about one thing or another. One night, I was sat there on my own and they were in the hallway. There was a particular spot where you could see and not be seen and that's where I was. He was talking to her quietly and he was holding her arm. She was looking down and he told her to look at him when he was talking to her, like she was a child. When she looked up he spat in her face.

We crept around her nerves. We'd sit rigid in front of *Coronation Street* and my dad would get her to sort out tea and chocolate biscuits during the adverts. None of her friends came to the house and she never went back to work. There was a space between getting home from school and him getting back from work when she was like our mum. We'd sit down and have our tea together and she'd ask us what we'd been up to at school. She'd let us put Radio One on while we ate and sometimes she'd pretend she was a waitress in a posh restaurant and we were her customers. She'd have a tea towel tucked into her skirt and a pencil behind her ear and she'd say,

- Has Sir enjoyed his meal?

And I'd say that it was very nice but there was maybe a little too much salt in the boeuf bourguignon because that was the only posh meal I'd heard of. When we'd eaten one of us would wash, another would dry and another would put the pots away. Then he'd come in and she'd become a quiet, cowering person. Her tablets were in the cupboard above the bathroom sink.

On a Saturday morning, they'd go into town together and sometimes we went with them if we needed clothes or new shoes. We were the quietest family in Leeds. We'd go to the market and to *Debenhams* for a cup of tea and a scone and my mum would ask us quietly if we were having a nice time. We'd say we were though we weren't. Once – it must have been during a school holiday – she told us to get our stuff together because we were off round to Auntie Norah's. She and Auntie Norah told us to go play upstairs while they had a chat. We sat outside the front room door and strained to hear what it was they were talking about. She said,

- I'm not going back, Norah.

Then she started to cry and my Auntie Norah said,

- What's he done this time?

My mum told her what he'd done.

- He just flies off the handle. It can be over owt: if his tea's not on the table; if I've not pressed his shirts how he likes them. He had me up at 4 this morning cleaning the kitchen cause I'd not wiped down the sides properly. There's no talking to him…

Then she started to cry. When she stopped she said other things that were worse but we'd heard enough by then and me and my sisters went upstairs and tried to play like we'd been told to but we were all of us too old for playing. None of us wanted to stop at Auntie Norah's. It turned out we didn't have to because that evening he showed up and we all got in the car and went home. We had a good idea what'd happen when we got in and we each maybe thought that if we were very quiet and if we did exactly as we were told we could stop it happening. So, when we got in Joanne said to my dad,

- Dad, d'you want a cup of tea?

He said yes and me and our Sandra went with her. I told her to make his tea in a good mug and to put it on a saucer with a biscuit.

- And don't spill it when you take it through.

He was sat in his chair when we took it through and my Mum was stood up looking out of place. I got a coaster off the dining table and put it on to the coffee table next to his paper. For ages afterwards I tried to remember if my Mum looked at me and smiled but I couldn't honestly say either way. He blew his tea and told us to get upstairs while him and my mum had a talk. There were sounds from downstairs. It sounded like they were big kids playing tig off ground. There was a knock on the door and it was Mr Scott from next door because we saw him out of our Joanne's bedroom window, but no one answered the door and he walked off shaking his head and looking back at the house. Joanne said we had to go downstairs and I said,

- To do fucking what?

It's the first time I can remember swearing out loud at home. We were both crying and Sandra was just sat on the bed rocking and biting her nails. Three days later my mum had her road accident.

When I went back to school, this lass – Sarah – came up to D and me and told me that her mum had told her that it wasn't a road accident; her mum reckoned that my mum had stepped out in front of a car on purpose. Sarah had long blonde hair pulled back in a ponytail. I pulled her by her long blonde ponytail and thumped her once, hard in the face.

My dad was in bits after my mum died. In the morning sometimes, we'd find him sat in the front room like he'd been there all night. Sometimes he'd take us up to stay at Auntie Norah's on a Friday evening and fetch us on the Sunday. We'd hear her refer to us as those poor kids when she thought we were upstairs.

A couple of years back Joanne tried to bring that time up. She'd had a couple of drinks and she got a bit upset. She wanted to rake it all up and she had this idea that we should confront my dad and tell him what we knew. I told her that there was no point; it wouldn't change anything. She said,

- It would change things, Simon. It'd make it so he knows that we know. It'd make it so that it really happened.

In the end, nothing was said.

Maxine breathed quietly across the bed from me and I found my cheeks damp and warm. It felt like I needed to tell her all this and that if I told her, the words might form some sort of bridge between us. She's always been one for communication and trust and telling her this story might lead to other stories – because she's always reckoned that everything's connected to everything else. I thought that if I started talking I might never stop and I wondered how good or bad that might be. The problem with talking, I've found, is that you can't predict how someone's going to receive your words and once they've been said there's no taking them back. It was better in the end not to say anything and to wait till the morning when we were both straight and fully awake.

9.
When I woke up around 12, there was only space where she'd been which meant that she'd either have had to clamber over me or crawl to the bottom of the bed and make good her escape that way. She'd left me a pile of pressed clothes on a chair in the bathroom, which I took to be a considerate gesture. She was stood in the kitchen when I came downstairs, smoking a cigarette and looking at the back lawn. I walked over to her and rubbed her shoulder. She shrugged my hand away and blew smoke out of the open window. There was something wrong. It could have been anything.

I'd kind of hoped that we'd be like a couple in a cereal advert, sat laughing and chatting in a kitchen bathed in sunlight but the kitchen was north facing and we were more like two strangers thrown together at a hotel breakfast table. It was early days, though, and it'd take time to get back to however it was we were supposed to be.

- You're not working, Max?
- Does it look like I'm fucking working?

I let that one go because there's no point bickering over rubbish. In the months before she'd left me, we'd got into all that: ongoing skirmishes and bitter, spiteful scraps. We'd argue the toss over everything and nothing at all. It kept us on our toes I suppose, looking back, but keeping up that level of match fitness the whole time grinds you down in the end.

- D'you want summat to eat?

- Don't go to any trouble, Max. I'll have whatever you're having.

I smiled. If she smiled back (as felt unlikely), I would not have known, since smiles are rarely discernable on people's backs. So it ended up that I was having a full English, which was not really what I wanted at all. Maxine's not one of these that can just throw together a meal; she's not programmed to prepare anything edible that's less than perfect so I was sat there for ages waiting silently while she fried the smoked bacon and sautéed her field mushrooms and roasted her tomatoes. The juicer whirred as she made up a jug of orange and apple juice. I flicked through *The Mirror* as she cooked. On page 4, D gestured at the camera. Next to him was a man with his suit jacket over his head. He looked grubby and guilty.

- Fucking hell.
- You've seen it, then.

A plate of food materialised in front of me and I felt like gagging. She placed a napkin on her knee and poured some brown sauce on to the corner of her plate.

- Sauce?

I shook my head. Her knife and fork scratched the plate and the sound went right through me. She reached over for the paper.

- They're taking a stance, are *The Mirror*. It seems they're finally outraged at the low conviction rates for rape. Better late than never, I suppose. What do you think? I take it you're not interested in their belated position. I'll read the article aloud, shall I? It's described as illustrative of the scandalous position women reporting rape are placed in.

I said something which meant please don't read it but she didn't hear or didn't care.

- I'll just summarise it, shall I?

She wiped her lips with her napkin and cleared her throat.

- Let's see...well, there's no point going into the background to the case is there, cause I'm sure you're familiar with it...you'll be aware, for example, that the defendant did not dispute that sex had taken place and that the case hung on whether or not the acts committed were consensual or non consensual. I'm sure you also know that Mr Williams' defence successfully argued that the injuries sustained – though mistakenly associated with non-consensual sex – were the result of rough, though consensual, sex. Would you like me to refresh your memory, Simon, on the nature of the acts which took place?

I reached over for the paper then stopped because it would have meant a scrap and I wasn't up to it. I wasn't up to listening to her read out extracts from the story either but I didn't have any choice about that.

- Mr Williams (39) declined to comment as he left court with a friend and an older man believed to be his father. Later, however, Elizabeth Watson (19), waiving her right to anonymity, made a brief statement to the press. Flanked by her parents, she expressed her disappointment with the verdict stating that - quote - Mr Williams and I both know what happened that night. I hope he can live with himself. End quote.

She folded the paper and got on with her breakfast. I cut up my food and chewed it and made it go down. She poured me a cup of tea and placed it next to my glass of juice. The table was full and there was no space to manoeuvre. I buttered a couple of slices of wholegrain toast and they were like sandpaper in my mouth. Maxine held a serving spoon over my plate.

- More mushrooms?

The mushrooms were like slugs and whatever it was she'd done them in coated the scrambled eggs in a brown sludge.

- She's quite pretty, isn't she?

I asked her who she was talking about because for a second I really didn't know. She told me who she was talking about and started on about how she could make more of herself if she just put on a bit of make up and did something with her hair. She looked at me like she was after a second opinion on her suggested remedial work but there was nothing I could say. My mouth was full and I was trying to free up a section of my brain so it could tell me how it was I was supposed to react to all this. I felt like my privacy had been violated; like the line between public and private acts had been breached. I reckon anyone in my situation would've felt that but it wasn't like I was in any position to be getting self righteous about it. My face burnt and then it was cold and clammy; under other circumstances I'd have put it down to the rapid onset of a particularly virulent flu virus. The room needed more air or fewer people and much less food and one less newspaper and all the sides needed clearing of all the stuff that covered them. Everything wanted rewinding and starting again somewhere around 1985.

In 1985, I was at the University doing a course which has been neither use nor ornament in the real world. I stopped in Leeds because, in truth, I lacked the imagination to go anywhere else and because I couldn't imagine what it'd feel like having to make new friends and to leave the ones I had. It turned out to be a bad move because it meant that all the new stuff that everyone was else was experiencing for the first time was stuff I'd been doing for years and, because baiting students was a bit of a pastime amongst my dozy mates, I didn't get much of a chance to do whatever else it is that students are supposed to do. Living in Chapel Allerton when everyone else was in Headingley didn't help much either. I first saw Maxine in the *Ainsley's* opposite the Parkinson Steps. I went there everyday for a sandwich. She told me afterwards that she used to look forward to me coming in. She said I looked like I'd stepped out of a fairy tale in this long black coat I used to wear all the time. She and her mate called me Greyzel on account of my eyes being neither grey nor hazel but something in between. If I'd gone to the health food shop a couple of doors away, chances are I'd have never met her and we'd both have been spared all that came afterwards.

- So, can you live with yourself, Simon? Elizabeth Watson (19) wants to know.

While she waited for my response she spread marmite on a slice of toast. When she'd finished she looked at me and gestured for me to say something. The notion of living with myself wasn't one I'd given any thought to; I'd considered it more of a necessity than a choice.

- I was found not guilty, Maxine. What've I to live with?

As a defence, it was poor and I knew I wasn't going to be allowed to leave it at that. She picked up the paper again and pointed at the photograph. Her hand was shaking.

- I'd been under the impression that when you said you were not guilty, what that meant was that nothing had gone off; that she'd made the whole thing up. I felt badly for you, Simon. What I didn't expect was that you could get up out of my bed and go and fuck some girl young enough to be your daughter. None of that's in dispute is it, Simon? But then I suppose it's not a criminal offence, is it, so it's not like it really matters. I suppose you reckon that being not guilty is the same as being innocent. I suppose that works for you.

She stood at the sink and washed the greasy pots noisily. With her back to me, she told me that when I was first locked up she'd found herself one evening washing glasses in the sink and that she'd broken one of them. The bubbles went pink and she wished she'd opened a vein. Then there was another time driving down Scotthall Road when she'd wished she could lose control of the car and drive into a lamppost. She said that living was like holding her head underwater and waiting to drown. The way she talked, it sounded like plotting her own murder had become a bit of an obsession for a while.

- I was scared shitless, Simon. I couldn't understand how anyone could say those things about you. I got it into my head that this woman was some scheming bitch that you'd knocked back. And it turns out she's a kid you fucked.

Her voice was distorted by this time and it was like her words were coming at me through a faulty PA. She used a word I'd not heard her use before – conflicted – to describe the difficulty of understanding how someone she'd thought she loved could do something so low. She'd thought she was a better judge of character. She said that my crazy diagrams and spreadsheets (they weren't actually spreadsheets, but it didn't seem like the right time to be getting hung up over project management tools) hadn't helped.

- It's always been a matter with you of putting things and people in boxes and drawing little dotted lines and arrows between them. Why d'you think it was I left you in the first place?

I thought it best to treat that as a rhetorical question. I didn't like what I was hearing and it felt like whatever answer I gave to her question would be wrong, which would mean that she'd have to enlighten me and being enlightened would only make me feel worse about myself. I said I was sorry. She spat sorry back at me like it was the worst kind of insult.

- It's not the sort of thing you can apologise for, Simon. You can only apologise for stuff you genuinely regret and I know that the only thing you regret is getting caught. If that girl hadn't had the guts to report you, you wouldn't have given it another thought. Then you come swanning in here like you've just nipped out for a pint of milk and I'm supposed to carry on like nothing's happened. Exactly how long did you think you'd be able to get away with this? Exactly how stupid did you want me to look?

The crockery clattered as she slid it into the draining rack. She was right and she was wrong. If Eliz hadn't called the police, I might have carried on as if nothing had happened but I would have continued to try to make things right with Maxine. Making things right was what I'd been doing before the police showed up. I tried forming my thoughts into words which would make sense to her and would give me a bit of breathing space while I considered how best to dig myself out of the hole I'd dug. Being straight was an option but there was nothing straight about the story. I struggled to remember what she knew and what she didn't know about the events that had led up to what happened. I was pretty certain that she'd not followed the trial; if she had, she'd never have let me in the first place, but *The Mirror* had given what under other – less personal – circumstances would have been a refreshingly accurate summary and there was no explaining that away. The only thing which would sound plausible would be the truth but opening all that up might only give me new things to worry about. Being straight was not an option.

- I am sorry, Maxine. I really am. I know that what I did was wrong. I wasn't thinking straight and I wasn't myself. I would've never carried on like that if I'd have been on top of things. You know me: I'm not the sort of person who does things like that.

- I don't fucking know you. I don't know people who do things like that. Yet it turns out you're precisely the sort of person who does things like that, Simon. It says it here.

And she threw the paper at me. The pages went all over the place and I bent down, picked them up and put them back in some random order. At the end of the article, I noticed a short section headed, *The Mirror says*...I didn't give a fuck what *The Mirror* said.

- This is not all there is to me, Maxine. You can't read some fucking sensationalised story and decide that's all there is to me.

I was stood in front of her by this time and I was shaking the paper in her face like if she just looked at it and then looked at me, she'd see they weren't one and the same thing. The paper tore and there were bits of it in each of my hands.

I've always said to the lads in the shop that when you're selling a product the first thing you've got to do is to convince the customer that you're convinced by the product. Once you betray a lack of confidence the sale's fucked. Another thing you can do, sales wise, is to make a connection with the customer. You appear interested in and engaged with them; you create a connection and you establish common ground so it begins to feel to the customer less like a sales pitch and more like a joint endeavour. I'm good at sales and I've had lads nodding and taking notes when I've delivered my sales training. But all the words I said to Maxine were lame and they weren't holding me up. If what I was trying to sell her was my integrity, my lack of faith was showing and jeopardising the sale.

I tried to think about what it was she might want from me and what there was that I could give. It's what you might think of as a problem solving approach; what I needed to do was to neatly line up the immediate issues and to allocate resources with which to address them. It was likely to involve open and frank communication and there would maybe be an element of conflict resolution. What we needed to work towards was some notion of a mutually satisfactory outcome which was not going to be likely for as long as she buzzed round the kitchen like a caricature of a 1950's housewife and I stood shaking a paper like some crazy man. She picked up my plate and wiped the space where it had been with an anti bacterial spray. She scraped the plates into the bin. Next to the bin, all the bottles from the previous night stood like skittles; I thought about asking if I should put them in a bag and take them to the bottle bank and just as the thought was about to turn into words she started loading them into a bag. I said,

- I was about to do that, love.

I suppose it's always possible that she didn't hear me. For a good 15 minutes, she carried on with her cleaning while I just sat there like a guest who'd outstayed his welcome. On the fridge, there were bills and some of them looked to me to require pretty urgent attention. All the bills were in her name – she'd ditched the Mrs for Ms in my absence - and they made me feel bad and irresponsible. I wondered whether I actually had access to money anymore and if I did whether she'd accept it. By my age, most people have sorted out some sort of stash: rainy day money or whatever. I haven't. There was the house and there was money in that but I suspected (rightly as it turned out) that I'd be needing to liquidise my assets to fund the new business venture. I'd never worried about money which – on reflection – is worrying. I thought about D sorting out her gravel path and how it should've been me doing all that sort of stuff. In the back garden flowers she knew the names of were blooming in pots and flower beds. I'd almost tripped over the twins' toys on my way to the shower because I'd mistaken their room for the bathroom and the toys I'd nearly broken my neck over weren't toys I'd bought them or given her the money for. She'd accommodated my absence. She'd got older also - not so's you'd notice if you didn't know her as well as I did – but there was something that had hardened in her or frozen or petrified. The plates and the cups and the knives and the forks banged one against the other and it was beginning to do my box in because I was trying to think and the noises her implements made were stopping me concentrating.

Finally she stopped. She picked up the paper I'd dropped on the floor and held it over the bin.

- Are you wanting to keep this? No, I thought not.

She told me it was getting late and that she'd have to go fetch the twins soon. Ben and Stephanie would be back at some point, she said, on account of this being their home.

- I don't think they'd be overjoyed to see you, Simon.

Which was a relief in a way because I'd no idea what I was going to say to them.

- How d'you think we should handle that, Maxine? Talking to the kids and all that?
- I don't see that that's my problem, Simon. Maybe you should draw them a fucking diagram.

Which was not what I was expecting at all on account of the fact that the kids are something she's always been on top of. I didn't flinch, though, because I'd gathered by this point that whatever control I'd thought I had over events was slipping and that I could either struggle or relax. The outcome would be the same either way. She sat down and sighed and for a second I thought she might've got all the bile out of her system.

- What are your plans, Simon?

I didn't have any anymore.

- You know that you can't stop here, don't you?
- I wasn't planning on stopping here. It's not where I live.

My head was pounding and my throat was dry. I asked her where the *Alka Seltzer* was and watched it fizz in its glass.

- So, what did you think was gonna happen?
- I thought we'd see how the land lies and work at sorting things out between us like we'd started doing before all this shit came on top.

She laughed. I told her I'd had a lot of time to think and that I'd realised we needed to talk more. I told her that I'd kept a lot from her over the years.

197

- You don't say.

She had plans, it seemed, and they involved me in a supporting role. She talked about personal growth and adversity and I got the distinct impression that she'd been spending a lot of time with Elaine in my absence. There were things she'd meant to do with her life but had never got round to on account of spending all her adult life waiting for me to become this person she wanted me to be. Reading *The Mirror* that morning had given her a wake up call because it told her something about me that she'd not allowed herself to contemplate: that I was a bastard whose every decision was motivated by self interest. I would've defended myself but there were things she was saying – indisputable facts – taken straight from *The Mirror* that would never stand close inspection. I wondered when D might be up for a swift half so I could maybe get some expert counsel on this whole thing. But there was no time for any of that as it turned out.

For the next half an hour or so I sat and listened while she told me about the plans she'd made for my future. There were things I needed to do. They seemed cataclysmic to me but she pointed out that in fact they were the least I could do. She said that two months should give me more than enough time to sort everything out. When she'd finished she asked me for my thoughts. I made a sound which was like someone else in another room laughing.

10.

While I'd been away, Maxine and D between themselves had tidied up my accounts to make it look like a sane man had been at the helm of the business. Under different circumstances their diligence would have impressed me. It impressed the bank, though, and it seemed that I was precisely the sort of entrepreneur they would be happy to support in expanding his business empire. When we left the bank I was both £30000 richer and £30000 poorer. Maxine had insisted on coming with me because, left to my own devices, I couldn't be trusted not to fuck things up. Afterwards, I managed to persuade her to join me for a swift half by way of grim celebration. We went to a place I'd never been to because it was only a couple of weeks since I'd got out and I was trying to avoid places where I might bump into people I knew. A couple of days after my release I'd suggested to D a session in a bar close to my house – it was something to do with getting back in the saddle and facing down fucking arseholes. It hadn't gone that well; I'd see someone I knew and watch as they struggled for something non contentious to say to me. One guy I'd known quite well at one time smiled at me then mouthed fucking cunt at me. Others saw me and pretended not to so that by the end of the evening I'd managed to create a pretty unpleasant atmosphere for everyone.

It was after five and the bar was filling up with suits. They carried on like getting out of work on a Tuesday evening was the cause for some major celebration. I expect Maxine and I looked like we'd called in on our way from a funeral or like one of those couples you hope you never become: the ones who, after too many years together, sit on opposite sides of a pub table staring into their drinks or at their watches. In the absence of anything else with conversational potential, I offered,

- That seemed to go well, Maxine.
- Well, it worked.

She looked at her glass and at her nails. There was a blue catering plaster on one of her fingers. She's always cutting herself; it's a hazard of the job.

- So, they'll be releasing the money in a fortnight. When do we want the builders in?

She looked at me like I'd asked a stupid question which was understandable given that we'd discussed just that subject in a terse telephone conversation the previous night. Then she said,

- I suppose we need to be looking at getting some quotes but it's hard to find builders that aren't gonna cost an arm and a leg in Leeds.

Which gave me a moment to shine and to be on top of things,

- There's a couple of builders I know of, Maxine, that helped me out with the original refurbishment. Maybe I could get on to them for a quote.

She looked for a moment like she might be taking my suggestion seriously, then she said,

- If I've a decision to make, Simon, I've learnt that the first thing to do is to think about what you'd do in my position. If what I'm considering matches what you'd do, I rule it out immediately. So, thanks but no thanks, Si.

It seemed sensible at that point to let the subject lie and for want of something to fill the silence, I said I was off for a slash.

- To powder your nose, I assume?

She'd decided I'm some sort of junkie, had Maxine; it was her little joke. I wished it was true; it might have made it all a bit more bearable. The truth was that since I'd got out I'd not been right bothered about any of that stuff. There were fewer opportunities for

200

going out and getting hammered and even when they arose I preferred to stay on top of things. It all made for pretty dull nights out but I'd rather that than find myself in anything approaching a situation which could end up with me getting locked up again. The truth was, I didn't really trust myself. D reckoned I was getting old and that I'd lost my touch. He said that sorting things out with Maxine shouldn't deter me from extra curriculars. If he'd known what sorting things out with Maxine meant in practice, I reckon he'd have revised that little bit of advice.

I got back to the table and she'd bumped into someone she knew who'd knocked years off her and had turned her into the sort of gregarious woman you'd look at across a bar and think, I wouldn't mind a bit of that. I hovered at the edge of her conversation with two glasses in my hand waiting to be introduced. She pointed at me and took a glass.

- Johnnie, this is Simon. Simon – Johnnie.

We shook hands and he studied my face like he thought he might know me from somewhere and was trying to place me. I wondered if I looked like the guy pictured on page 4 of *The Mirror* leaving court with a jacket over his head. It turned out I was the double of a colleague of his; it was uncanny, he said. He pointed over at my doppelganger, a gaunt dark haired guy who looked like he had a lot on his mind.

- Can't see it myself, mate.

But he wasn't listening. He pointed at a pack of suits and kissed Maxine on each cheek before going back to join them. Before he left, he made that stupid gesture which indicates that a phone call's in order sometime soon. After he'd gone she must have forgotten for a moment that we weren't supposed to be natural in each other's company.

- Bloody hell. I haven't seen him in months. He's a partner at that accountant's that I do lunches for. He's so funny.

So funny, it seemed, that they'd need to be calling each other to arrange a meal at some place that had just opened which –

according to those in the know – was on its way to getting a Michelin Star.

- He's more money than sense, has Johnnie, but he's just so funny.

I wondered whether she'd shagged or was planning to shag this amusing, over fed accountant with the beginnings of a bald patch in his over gelled hair but I wasn't in much of a position to be interrogating her about any of that. She was at least talking to me and I was beginning to look to all the world like someone she didn't hate. She got on to the other partners in the firm and how most of them were a bunch of inadequate arseholes. You found that in accountancy firms, she reckoned: it was always the scum that rose to the top. And then she was on about sexism in the professions and how badly women were treated. She got quite passionate about it and it felt like a good idea to go along with what she was saying. She said that the relative success she'd achieved with her business was a double-edged sword because on the one hand it meant she'd managed to gain some respect and on the other it was within the confines of a traditionally female sector.

- That's what makes expanding into electrical retail so exciting. It means that I'll be breaking into a sector which is more usually associated with men.

I couldn't share her enthusiasm, what with this exciting new venture requiring £30000 of my money and the relegation of my status to that of a sleeping partner.

She managed to sustain her sexual inequality theme and to hold her end up when we were persuaded to join her new best mate at his table. They'd managed to negotiate table service and we worked our way through a few bottles of what I was told was half decent Cabernet Sauvignon before ordering tapas which Maxine dismissed as a pile of fucking shite. Some guy who looked like he'd last seen active combat sometime in the early 90's commented,

- I love a woman who talks dirty.

And I didn't smack him.

We got on to what I did for a living and it turned out that nobody was much interested. What they were interested in, however, was boring me rigid with the tech specs of their *Bang and Olufsen's*. Just as I was slipping in to a catatonic coma, Maxine rescued me.

- Is there a particular reason why men can only talk about the things they own and what they cost? Do you think things only matter if you own them?

Which surprised me a bit because for one thing it seemed like a bit of a generalisation and for another I'd never really known her to be that combative in male company. She carried it off, though, and the bulbous accountants listened and nodded respectfully as if they'd never before been in the presence of such a razor sharp intellect.

- Is what you own who you are?

We mulled and murmured and processed her query till one of us said,

- That's a good point, Maxine. Owning things can sometimes be a substitute for being. If you can point at the stuff you've got, it's kind of reassuring because it convinces you that you exist and that you've made some sort of impact on the world. People are unreliable and they have minds of their own. Things have a limited shelf life but you know that from the outset so the idea of replacing them is factored in.

The table nodded in my direction because it was me that had made this contribution. Maxine was lost for words for a moment but she recovered and soon she'd veered the conversation onto the relative merits of two restaurants which had recently acquired new chefs. Since I'd not been in much of a position to dine out recently, my contribution was limited to nods and oohs and aahs. One of the party told me that I really must take Maxine to this place which between themselves they'd decided was the better of the two restaurants. He directed me to a website which reviewed restaurants and told me that he thought I'd find that his views were shared by reviewers across the country and beyond. He gestured expansively – to indicate the world I suppose. There was not a cat in hell's chance of Maxine and me going there together but we both nodded as if it was a splendid idea and one

203

we'd be taking him up on. Cigars and brandy were procured to round off the evening. Someone suggested a *Southern Comfort* for the lady and Maxine told him to fuck off before leaning over and kissing him on the lips. As she bent forward her bra was visible and I wanted to get up and pull her off his face. According to one of our slurring throng, that was the point at which I was supposed to challenge him to a dual. I didn't.

We made our way to the taxi rank after they'd chucked us out. She was leaning into me because she wasn't too steady on her feet. She was on about what fun she'd had and how funny and entertaining everyone had been. I agreed that it had been fun. I told her it was great to see her so happy and so on top of things even if it wasn't me that was making her happy. If she'd had less to drink she'd have said something cutting in response to that one but in her altered state she seemed prepared to let it go. We approached her house and I inwardly rehearsed the sense of gloom I was about to feel.

- It's just here on the left.

She gave me a fiver and got out. I gave the driver my address.

- I thought your luck was in there for a minute, mate.

This turned out to be a really funny thing to say to someone whose luck was clearly not in. I wished I lived closer to Maxine's. That way I wouldn't have had to listen to him repeat his acute observation three times before I was finally allowed to get out of the taxi.

11.

In the fortnight since I'd been out I'd had to spend a fair bit of time sorting the house out. Though Maxine and D had dealt with an avalanche of bills, they'd not got round to dealing with the other things that happen to a place when its occupant's away for a while. My most pressing concern was the graffiti that told my neighbours and me that I was a nonce, paedo scum and an evil bastard that wanted hanging. Call me naïve, but I'd not thought that people in my neighbourhood did things like that. Strictly speaking, I suppose, I could've called the police but I didn't fancy having to explain why these particular terms of abuse had been chosen. Since I hadn't called the police I couldn't make a claim on the insurance so it all ended up being quite a pricey job. Predictably, D had a mate who could sort it all out for me and who had clearly been instructed not to ask any questions. It was gone in no time but it didn't mean it hadn't been there and it didn't mean that wasn't what people thought of me.

To give him his due, Tony from next door called round one evening when his missus was out and asked how things were going. He stood on the doorstep looking awkward for a moment. I shuffled him into the living room and he relaxed a touch.

- Glad to see you back, mate.

I thought that was probably putting it a bit strongly but he meant well. I fetched him a beer from the fridge and he seemed relieved to have something other than me to talk about. We managed to invent a conversation about different brands of beer and the offers

205

they had on at the off licence down the road. Then there were other things in the room that he looked at and was able to comment on; things with wires and plugs mainly but that was OK.

- You want to ignore this lot round here, mate. They're just after summat to talk about. They've short memories so they'll soon find summat else to grab their attention. There's talk of a mobile mast going up round the corner so I expect that'll occupy them for a while.

It was mildly encouraging to learn that a harmless aerial was likely to steal my thunder. It made things feel less bad and irreparable. That was all he said about my recent unpleasantness and for the rest of the hour or so he was there, we talked about football and roadworks both of which proved to be surprisingly engaging subjects. He's something in Highways so roadworks are a bit of a specialist subject for him. It turned out that the reason roadworks seem to take so long is because of all the co ordination involved with utilities companies. This gave me the opportunity to discuss my spell in procurement. In short, the conversation actually flowed. I think that under different circumstances he might have suggested that we nip out for a drink sometime. When he heard his wife's car pull into the drive he leapt up, thanked me for the beer and fled. Other than D and Maxine he's been my only visitor. I hoped that once the mobile mast started frying my neighbours' brains, people might start talking to me again.

As well as the graffiti, there were other things to get on top of; the bed was as I'd left it so it was like someone had just got out of it that morning. I'd not sorted out the uncleaning up adventure I'd had when I was looking for the envelope so the place looked like it was in the process of being burgled. On the living room floor there was a TV guide turned to 27 December 2003 and I seemed to have gone to the trouble of underlining some stand up show that I must have been planning to watch. In my diary there were appointments I hadn't kept and, underlined in red and in Maxine's writing, a reminder about the twins' birthday in February. The to do list I'd started to write remained on the table; though I'd cut back on the drugs I hadn't managed to see more of the kids. I picked up a lot of stuff and took it to the tip. The clothes in the laundry basket didn't seem any dirtier than they had been when they'd been thrown there but I went into town and bought new bedding and clothes. I knew that the coppers had been in and collected whatever it was they'd needed to collect to substantiate the case against me. I felt them in every room and I wondered what they'd touched, what they'd picked up and what they'd said about me as they combed my house. The neighbours would've seen them going in and coming out and someone – probably Mr or Mrs neighbourhood Watch – would've asked them what was going off and they'd have refused to comment. I wondered if they'd gone through the box where I kept daft stuff that Maxine had given me back when she cared enough to write me notes and cards. I threw it out, anyway, without looking at its contents.

There was the odd bit of residue left over from the kids that Maxine had missed when she left. When I'd come across it in the days after she'd gone I'd decided to keep it in a carrier bag on top of the wardrobe on the off chance that she and the kids might come back and might once again need that bit of lego, the headless Barbie and one of the twins' babygros that we'd cut up and used as dusters. I imagined the coppers muttering about what sort of sick bastard collects stuff like that – they would have referred to them as mementos.

Since coming home meant the beginning or the end of something, I also changed my landline and mobile numbers. *Carphone Warehouse* commented on the downturn in activity on my account and asked if I'd been away, a question to which I was able to confidently answer yes.

- Anywhere nice?
- No, not really.

I tried to cancel my cable TV subscription but found that the cable company had helpfully done this for me, what with the bill not having been paid for months. D and Maxine had obviously done some sort of prioritisation exercise in respect of my outgoings and had decided that cable TV services and broadband were luxuries I could ill afford. So, technologically speaking, I found myself back in the late 90's for a while. The leased car had also gone. D had explained (almost gleefully, I thought, but I let it go) that,

- There didn't seem a right lot of point shelling out 300 and odd quid a month for a car that wasn't gonna get driven – a drain on the business resources and all that.

His recently acquired financial prudence hadn't stopped him upgrading to a Z3. He passed his souped up *3 Series* on to me, without the expensive wheel trims, which he told me he'd sold for a good price.

I prolonged the tidying up of my life for longer than was strictly necessary in order to avoid having to go back to the shop. On the night I got back from my impromptu excursion with Maxine, I came in to a call from D checking that I was going to be in the following morning as promised. Five minutes later, the beep of a car horn announced his arrival.

- Looking a bit minimalist in here, mate.

He pointed at the rectangles in the walls which indicated where my prints and photographs had been. That was another thing I'd done while I'd been tidying up: I'd found that I wasn't much interested in being stared at by people – like my estranged wife and kids - who could barely bring themselves to talk to me. I told him I was thinking about decorating. He told me he'd get me someone in.

Basically, he was there because he wanted to know how it'd gone at the bank. I told him the good news and for as long as it took me to tell him I almost convinced myself that this signalled the beginning of a new adventure.

- So, you coming in tomorrow to tell the lads? New dawn and all that…phoenix rising from the ashes. Didn't I tell you, you just had to hold tight and everything'd be all right.

I confirmed that he was correct and that I'd be in the following day. He asked a question about how things were going with Maxine and I gave him an untrue answer I don't want to recall in light of everything that's happened since. He told me he'd been planning a full on celebration for what he referred to as our merger but refused to give away any details other than the necessity for me to be free the following evening from 8ish onwards. He'd already told Maxine, he said, and she was up for it. He went on for a while about how much he was looking forward to being a full on bona fide businessman and how all them lot out there would finally have to show him some respect. It became difficult to listen to him.

- Listen, mate, I need to get my head down if I'm gonna be in early doors tomorrow.

He agreed and apologised for going on before going on again,

- I think you'll approve of what we've done to the shop. It's not finished yet obviously, but we decided to change the façade a bit…make it a bit less intimidating to the casual browser.

D is not the sort of man to use terms such as 'façade'. I walked him to the front door and I noticed that his eyes really were like sultanas in milk. I went straight up to bed but I couldn't get off to sleep. Eliz swirled around my head for hours. From time to time – in what became intermissions – my mum and Maxine would make an entrance. I turned on the radio and someone with a strange accent told me that President Bush had spent more than 40% of his presidency holed up in one of his retreats. The Democrats were up in arms about it and reckoned he wasn't taking his job seriously. I tried to tune my brain in to the radio and to engage with what was happening in the rest of the world but the bad things I'd done and the good things I'd failed to do came at me one after the other. Maybe it was something to do with guilt or with self-pity.

12.
    I arrived at what was still officially my shop at about nine thirty. D winked at me and then got back to encouraging an uncomfortable looking sales lad to demonstrate the various functions of a karaoke machine. He had him singing *Fly me to the Moon* for the benefit of a middle aged woman who was considering a karaoke themed party for her husband's 50th. Her husband looked unconvinced and muttered,
    - What's wrong with a bloody meal and a couple of drinks?
    D raised his voice above the lad's,
    - This is a gift that keeps on giving, sir. You can use it for all sorts of family events and celebrations.
    He gestured towards Linda who was stood looking out of place behind the till and made it clear that her presence was required to complete the sale. Together, they stood and described the memorable times they'd had with family and friends, all facilitated by the very karaoke machine that the couple were thinking about buying. And it all seemed genuine; within no time the two of them were off on one about who'd sung what when and the time when so and so did such and such. The last time I'd seen it in action was at their Boxing Day do but they didn't mention that particular occasion. The couple laughed and joked about what it'd be like if they got someone with the unlikely name of Wolfgang in front of the mic. Looking at D and Linda and the couple, you'd think they'd known each other for years.

My office wasn't my office anymore. My desk had been shoved into a corner and it buckled under the weight of boxes stuffed with the sort of cheap electronic fancy goods you'd buy from the back of the market. A photo of the kids – which, in fairness had only ever been there for form's sake – was propped up against a jumbo pack of toilet rolls. The stationery cupboard had a handwritten label across the front saying *Damaged Goods* and inside it were shelves of items that punters had poked and prodded into submission. From somewhere near the desk, a phone rang. I ignored it.

I pretty much ignored everything and everybody that first day back at work. I managed to free up a small space in my store cupboard and spent several hours going through suppliers' catalogues, looking at new gear which I knew I wasn't going to be purchasing. Every now and again, D or one of the lads would appear at the door and check in on me. Once – and this represented the high point of the day – Linda appeared at the door looking frazzled wanting to know how to void a credit card sale. On my rare excursions onto the sales floor, I made a point of avoiding punters and tried to get my head round what exactly it was we specialised in these days: everything was what we specialised in. There was a new section called *Price Cruncher* which was basically a jumble sale; you'd have to have been a complete numb nut to be seduced by any of the dubious offers on display. But then, the whole shop had become a refuge for numb nuts and care in the community candidates who'd be turned away at the door of a reputable retailer. These were, I assumed, the sort of casual browsers D and my estranged wife thought we should be attracting. The odd discerning customer who came in looking for the sort of stuff we used to specialise in was pounced upon and led to safety by the lads who worked on what was now called the *Sound and Vision: Professional* section. Pretty much all the sales were cash but that would've been on account of the fact that most of the punters were the sorts of people who probably didn't trust banks - or whom banks didn't trust - and who kept their stash in a box under the bed. On the positive side, there was so little there of any value it was unlikely that shoplifting was going to be much of a concern.

I'd thought that going back was going to be hard; that it'd remind me too much of when I thought I was on top of things but pretty much every trace of me had been obliterated and none of it felt like mine anymore. I think that D knew that too, and as much as he'd carry on in his rare spare moments about how bloody marvellous everything was and how much better it was going to get for us, I saw in him a tinge of embarrassment at having to spin me a line. For my part, I grinned like a full on happy person and told him what a difference he'd made and how good it felt to be in and amongst it again. As shit as the shop was, D was in his element there and he was doing an excellent job of selling people the rubbish they thought they wanted. For the first time since I'd got out I felt good about myself. I was doing something that Maxine said I was incapable of, which was to put someone else's needs above my own. I made a mental note to tell her - at some point when she'd stopped hating me - that I wasn't a complete bastard. In the meantime, she was called upon to pretend she loved me while we endured the celebration D had planned.

I picked her up in a taxi and waited while she came out. Naturally, I wasn't allowed in to collect her so I phoned as we approached the house and she rushed out, waving to my unseen kids. She looked like someone you'd describe as beautiful if you were the sort who went for thin, blonde women in heels. I wasn't sure whether it was all right to say she looked lovely so I didn't. How she looked was none of my business anymore. She slid into the taxi and gave the driver the address of a new restaurant somewhere near Park Row. Everywhere was new since I'd got out. She told me I looked nice or, to be more accurate, she told me she was glad I'd made an effort for a change. It turned out, as it always does when Maxine has confidently given directions to somewhere she's never been to, that she was wrong and that the place was nowhere near Park Row. If the rules of engagement had been different I'd have gone through to directory enquiries on my mobile and found out where it was we were supposed to be going. Instead, we drove round town until finally Maxine was forced to ask me to phone D and find out where the fuck this fucking place was supposed to be.

The ideal location for this fucking place would have been somewhere a long way from Leeds to which neither D nor Linda had access. In fact, it was on Boar Lane. Walking in and finding it populated by people who could obviously afford to eat there, D went instinctively into class war mode. Demanding *Cristal* and dismissing the menu as crap is never going to go down well at such an establishment. By the end of the evening, I think the waiters were pretty clear about the fact that his money was as good as anyone else's but I left feeling that the food we'd been served was probably not as good as everyone else's on account of if I'd been a waiter I'd have gobbed into it before bringing it to the table. Maxine did a passable job of pretending to be at a table light years away from the one D and the rest of us occupied and talked knowledgeably and then desperately to the waiter about the various courses. What I could see she wanted to say was that she wasn't with D and Linda. But she was and she will be for some considerable time. I expect she felt conflicted about the whole thing.

Anyway, we got to leave and the maitre d' got to clock our faces so's he'd know never to let us darken his door again. The night being young, we then went to a scrutty bar at the top end of town. It played soft rock anthems and other shit suited to its 30+ clientele. The hotel next door spewed its expense account guests in through its doors and they got to carry on like middle aged teenagers who remembered all the words from the first time round. Maybe that's what we looked like too, with D and his champagne and Maxine and Linda giggling and pointing at whatever it is women giggle and point at. In any case, it was a better place for pretending that everything was bloody marvellous.

D and I drifted into that over excitedness that grasps men when they start going to and emerging from toilet cubicles together. Linda and Maxine wiggled by their chairs with champagne glasses in their hands laughing at a couple of other women wiggling by their chairs. At some point it became necessary to propose a toast to shared futures and wealth and prosperity. I looked at Maxine and she looked at me and I like to think that we shared a moment where we silently acknowledged how difficult and sad everything had become between us. There was a time, years ago, when that look would have meant summat different – like, let's get the fuck out of here - and we'd have made our excuses and left and laughed in the taxi on the way home about the fucking madness of it all and how glad we were to be so different from, and better than, all that.

13.

There was no negotiating with Maxine over the things I had to do and when I had to do them by. Sometimes I'd detect what seemed to be a softening in her attitude and I'd broach the idea of maybe thinking things through a bit and looking at other alternatives but she'd say something like,

- Just because I'm being civil it doesn't mean I've changed my mind.

Then she'd be off on one about how she felt contaminated by what I'd done and she'd repeat the thing that Eliz had said about living with myself and whether I could or not. Whatever answers I gave her were either wrong or inadequate but that didn't stop her digging and prodding at me. She never full on asked me what exactly had gone off the night I'd left hers; I suppose it would've been humiliating for both of us to have to listen to that little story.

She put her house on the market as planned. I was with her when they came to value it and was called upon to pretend to be someone who gave a toss about likely market values. She said it was important I was there because it was about time I knew what it was like to have to pretend to the world that everything was fine; that that was what she'd been doing for years. All of which came as news to me but I suppose in extremis there's all sorts of things that come out of the woodwork. She hadn't yet told me I was crap in bed but I expected that'd come soon enough. The digs were just one element of her punishment regime and they felt no better and no worse than anything else she did: sometimes she'd do this thing where it seemed like she was on the verge of forgiving me, then she'd say something cold and cutting; other times she'd ask my opinion about some particularly horrific story in the papers to do with women and the bastards they found themselves with, then she'd stop herself and say something like,

- Soz, Si. I suppose you're not in the best position to offer an unbiased opinion about these things. It's all about getting off, isn't it?

In the end, the best thing to do was to say nothing. If she'd have read the sorts of books I'd started reading about crime and criminology she'd have known that prolonged punishment stops working after a while; it becomes predictable and bearable. We adapt.

The estate agent told us the house would go in no time but that we'd be well advised to sort out the twins' bedroom in order to maximise the purchase price. I told her just to give it a lick of magnolia but she reckoned that if it was going to get done it should be done properly. We spent an afternoon in *Homebase* discussing and disagreeing about colours as if they mattered.

Everyone agreed that the sale made a lot of sense. My dad was relieved that things were finally getting back to normal.

- There's no point paying two mortgages, is there? And what with the money you get from Maxine's you can see to your roof and look at extending into the loft.

It'd be better for the kids, he said, coming back to somewhere bigger and familiar where they weren't falling over themselves. Space and privacy, he reckoned, were very important in a family. I've no idea what he meant by that. He told me all this the final time I saw him. It was a Sunday afternoon and he'd said he'd cook us a proper dinner. He let me in through the back door; he never uses the front door – it's like he's saving it for best. He made a pot of tea in his narrow kitchen and I sat on a bar stool facing the wall as the kettle boiled. In the corner by the door, his washer juddered through its spin cycle. He washed two cups then washed his hands carefully like a surgeon might.

- Strong and white…that's how you take it, isn't it?

I followed him into the front room while we waited for the beef and Yorkshires. My cup was too full but I was careful not to let it drip because my dad's always been fastidious about drips and spills. Above the mantelpiece, a large framed photograph announced *The World's Best Grandpa*. Beneath the swirly script, my dad beamed. In each of the alcoves to the sides of the chimney breast there were gilt framed photographs of all the grand kids. My four were in a huge frame; our Ben and our Stephanie each held one of the twins on their knees. I placed my cup and saucer on a coaster illustrated with a map of Tenerife. That was the destination of choice for my Dad and Maureen on their annual October break. You're guaranteed year round sunshine, apparently. The sun came through the vertical blinds in wide stripes. There was a small, framed photograph on the drinks cabinet I'd not noticed before. It showed two teenagers in wide collared shirts and wide ties, arms around each other, laughing. The darker haired of the two was olive skinned with almond shaped, dark brown eyes. He was clasping the other's shoulder, tightly it seemed. We looked, the pair of us, like a 70's *Coke* ad.

- I've not seen that one before, dad. When will that've been taken?

- You'll have been 14 or 15 I reckon. I think I took it at our Joanne's engagement do.

He smiled.

- I was just clearing stuff out and I came across it so I thought I'd stick it in a frame. It makes you wonder where the time went.

We exchanged pleasantries about time, where it might have gone and how much and how little things change over the years. The oven timer tinged and he brought the food in. It was plated because he likes to avoid any potential for mess, does my dad. By way of condiments we had salt, pepper and brown sauce because, according to my dad, there's nothing that can't be improved with a dash of *HP*. I'm not so keen myself and neither's our Joanne. I don't know what our Sandra's tastes are in condiments these days. I told him he looked like he'd lost weight and asked him if he'd been working out. It was meant to be a funny, throwaway comment but you can never be sure how my Dad's gonna take things. I could've put a less positive spin on things and told him that he looked like shit; like someone had drained his face and filled it in with something the colour of alabaster. But then, he'd looked pretty down for months so it was a bit late in the day to be commenting on something that had been apparent for so long. He filled me in on work; the dry cleaner's he managed had just been taken over by another firm and there were all sorts of changes in terms and conditions. He wasn't sure he was happy about it and he was considering finding summat else. I didn't tell him that no one was likely to take him on at his age.

- How's Maureen doing, Dad? I've not seen her for a while.

Last time I'd seen her was when I'd failed to talk to her the day I got out. Her photograph stared at me from the top of the drinks cabinet. Her face looked like someone was urging it to smile. It turned out she was not so bad. Her chest was playing her up but she couldn't complain. I asked a few supplementary questions framed to give the impression that the state of her chest was something that kept me awake nights. The truth is I'm not right keen on Maureen and I'm pretty certain she doesn't like me either. They've been together twenty odd years and the idea is that everyone's happy that he rebuilt his life so quickly and efficiently after my mum died. Sometimes, when she's had a few, she'll get all maudlin about how hard it was at the beginning, walking into what she calls a ready made family, and how concerned she was that we'd not warm to her. She's no kids of her own, hasn't Maureen. It's not a conversation that ever picks up much speed and as her voice peters out, my Dad or Joanne – speaking on behalf of us all, apparently - will say something which indicates our gratitude for her selflessness. Joanne sends her Mother's Day's cards and on my Dad's mantelpiece there's a photograph of her kids entitled *To Nana with love.* I've made sure my kids call her Maureen. Once, after Christmas dinner a couple of years ago, we were left alone together in the kitchen and she started a conversation with me which began,

- Why is it you're always so cold towards me, Simon?

I gave her question some thought and started to frame a response but then somebody walked in and that was the end of that little exchange.

They worked together, Maureen and my Dad. She was mainly on the till but, between mouthfuls of Yorkshires and beef, my Dad announced she'd recently completed a course in specialist stain removal which made her job that bit more interesting. It was in Barnsley was the course, so he'd had to drop her off and pick her up. Which is Maureen all over: getting my dad to drive halfway across the country just so's she can learn the best way to deal with stubborn stains.

- She's not too happy about this takeover because it means they'll reduce her hours and we'll not be working the same shifts anymore. She reckons she'll leave if I leave. I've told them it's not right messing her about like that with all the years she's put into that place but apparently it's all about business priorities and rationalising. I was talking to someone at the Morley branch and he reckons it's only a matter of time before they start shutting shops down.

- But they've not said they're shutting down your branch, have they?

- No, but that's not the point. They say one thing and, before you know it…

In a nutshell, then, a new boss was taking over from the old boss. His job was safe and, but for the gossipmonger in Morley, no one had indicated that his job was on the line. To hear my Dad talk, though, you'd think this was some major life – changing event but then he's always been one for worrying about small things, has my Dad. He picked at some specks on the table and put them on the edge of his placemat. I wondered whether he treated Maureen the same way he treated my mum and if not, why not.

- Where is Maureen, by the way?

- She's just next door. She's watching the kids while they nip out for a couple of hours. She'll be back in no time. I think they've gone to *B&Q*; they've a sale on garden furniture by all accounts.

219

He looked at the clock. Our Joanne had got it him one birthday. Its face had a picture of her two girls on it. I thought it was grotesque the way the hands moved round and sliced Gemma and Louise. The food was good. He'd done the Yorkshires himself with the dripping from the beef and along with the potatoes he'd roasted shallots and courgettes. He'd learnt that off Maxine. He'd tried something adventurous with the stuffing which didn't really come off and he looked disappointed that I refused his offer of more. We drank wine with the meal from his heavy crystal glasses like it was a proper occasion. It was white and I only really drink red but I made an exception for him. I watched him brace himself to say something.

- I'm glad all that carry on's over, Simon. It means you can get on with your life…make a fresh start and put it all behind you, concentrate on sorting things out with Maxine. She'd a hard time when you were away. I think she was lonely.

I nodded and imagined a snowplough clearing up my life and putting it all behind me. It wasn't a comforting image.

- D'you think that's what you did, Dad, after Mum passed away? Put everything behind you like it'd never happened.

I stared at my potatoes like they might provide me with the answer. It took him a while to say anything and I wondered whether I'd imagined asking the question.

- It's what everyone has to do. It was hard with me working and three kids to bring up but you've no choice. You can't live in the past.

He wiped the table pointlessly with a piece of kitchen towel and cleared his throat.

- You've no photos of her, Dad?
- They're all up here.

He pointed at his head.

- I don't need photos of her. And it would only've upset you and your sisters having photos of her all over the place.

I've three photographs of her. I got them off our Joanne and she got them off Auntie Norah. Joanne says I take after her but I can't see it. In all of them she's younger than I am now and it doesn't make any sort of sense. They're in a box somewhere and I've not looked at them in years. I said to him,

- You never talked about her after she'd gone, Dad.

And I was probably as surprised as him to be bringing all this stuff into the open. Maybe it was to do with knowing there was fuck all to lose. He stood up to clear the table and the conversation.

- I never talked? After she'd passed, Simon, you barely said a word for weeks. We were worried about you for a while…thought you'd never talk again. I think you took it worse than the girls – it must be that mother son thing.

With the benefit of hindsight, maybe I should've left it there but at the time I was dissatisfied with his neat summation and since I knew I probably wouldn't be seeing him again for a while it felt like a good time to be getting stuff off my chest. I suppose he's like all of us and he's got his own particular brand of truth to which he's entitled. In my world, the truth is that I did talk; I just didn't talk to him. When I'd given him my version of the truth, he went into the kitchen. I heard him washing up. He always washes up as soon as he's eaten then he dries everything and puts everything away. I could hear him whistling and it was a tune I recognised but I couldn't put my finger on what it was. I followed him into the kitchen and put the kettle on. I promised myself that by the time it had boiled I'd have asked him something important.

- But why didn't you talk about her, Dad?

He turned round from his washing up and his hands were covered in suds which dripped onto the floor. He was nearly 60 then, though you'd never have known it; I get my eyes from him and the dimple in my chin. When I looked at him I could see myself in 20 years.

- I'm not one for talking about that sort of thing. What's that thing they say? Words are like nails; you can pull them out but they leave holes. I know they say you should talk but sometimes it's easier not to. Whatever you say's never gonna make anything better and you just end up remembering things you don't want to and regretting things you can't change. You draw a line under things.

- It's hard to draw a line under your Mum, Dad.

And that's when I said things that, on reflection, didn't want saying. I didn't say much and everything I said was true. For the record, I didn't mention the bogus road accident; I knew that would've done him in. I watched the back of him while he washed up and it gave nothing away. After a couple of minutes, he wiped his hands on a tea towel and turned round, which was when I started to run out of things to say. At the point when he started looking a bit shaky I told him that it was all in the past and there was no changing anything. I told him I wasn't angry with him but that was a lie and maybe, looking back, he knew it was.

- Have you no idea, Simon, what it was like to have to listen to them lot in court talking about what you'd done? I thought I'd break. I wanted to get up and tell them you weren't like that but it turns out I don't know what you're like.

I don't know what it was made him bring me into the story. Maybe it was your classic evasion strategy or maybe he was drawing some sort of twisted parallel. It wasn't something I was keen to explore. I told him that if it was any help, I didn't know what I was like either. I told him I was sorry for putting him through all that, and if we'd been the sort of family you see on TV, I suppose at that point that we'd have hugged and forgiven each other for whatever harm we'd caused. Maybe it was a case of there being too much water under the bridge for all that or life just being nothing like what you see on TV because in the event, he wiped the suds up with a piece of kitchen towel then wiped his hands on a tea towel again. He turned his back on me and I imagine he stared at the pots in the sink and thought he'd best get on with finishing them off. It sounded like he had something stuck in his throat when he said,

- The problem with talking, Simon, is that you don't know what you're gonna hear. I'd let it lie if I were you.
- What if it just won't lie down?
- Then you make it.

It would've taken an archaeologist to get any deeper into that one so I left it. I watched him wash and rinse and dry the pots. I watched him put them away and I knew that I'd ruined for him what was supposed to be a pleasant afternoon where we picked up the pieces and carried on from where we'd left off before all this happened. Before I left, we went into the back room and watched a bit of football on *Sky Sports*. He asked me how our Ben was doing with his football and I gave him a plausible sounding lie because I'd no idea what the truth was. The twins, in my story, were adapting well to being back in a state school and were making friends and influencing people. Then he asked after our Stephanie. All I knew about Stephanie was that last time I'd bumped into her when I was collecting Maxine for a solicitor's appointment, she'd told me to fuck off. She'd said that she couldn't wait to leave home and go somewhere where no one knew she was the daughter of Simon Fucking Williams. I told her that Simon Fucking Williams was still her fucking father. She said she'd change her name to whatever the opposite of Williams was. I didn't faithfully recount that little conversation. I told him Stephanie was fine which was what he wanted to hear, anyway. When I'd finished with my story, I realised that I didn't know a right lot about my kids and that I probably never had; I'd made these people and they could be anybody's.

    We scraped the conversational barrel for crumbs and found that we both urgently needed to talk about his decorating plans for the hall and stairs. The ceiling was Artexed and it'd prove a job getting rid of it. I told him to get someone in and that D was bound to know someone that could sort it out for him for a good price; I'd have a word with him. Then there was the wallpaper to strip and the woodwork to prepare. Maureen'd give him a hand, but still it was a big job. He obviously wanted me to offer a hand but, being my dad, he couldn't bring himself to ask. I didn't offer. It was a relief when his decorating mate came back – on time as always – and we could finally abandon the task of not talking about what we should have been talking about. Maureen heated up her dinner in the microwave and ate it off a tray on her lap. She said it was lovely and asked me if I'd enjoyed mine. She told me my Dad had been carrying on about the dinner all week and how much he'd been looking forward to it. Sat in his armchair, staring at the TV, my dad didn't look like someone who was looking forward to anything. Maureen asked me the same questions my Dad had already asked about the kids, together with some more challenging follow ups about how Maxine was which required new, improved lies. It was all a bit awkward and unsatisfactory until my dad stepped in and rescued me,

- Can't you see the lad's trying to watch the football?

He glared at her then turned back to the TV. She smiled weakly at me and raised her eyebrows like she was trying to tell me something about what he was like but whatever it was I wasn't receptive. The match ended and we both agreed that it'd been a disappointment. Maureen looked disappointed too. They both went into the kitchen because apparently it takes two to make a pot of tea these days, and from the back room I could hear him,

- How long've I been on at you about interfering? If he wanted to tell you how everyone's doing he'd tell you. You've no bloody idea what he's been through the past few months.

Her answer was too quiet for me to make out but it obviously didn't satisfy him.

- If it's not one thing its another with you.

I wondered what these things were and whether they were going to be brought up later when I'd gone. For all my dad goes on about letting things lie, he rarely does with Maureen. He'll bicker over owt with her. Their domestics are so domestic, it's embarrassing. I remember one time, Joanne and I had gone round and found them in the middle of a barney about when the houseplants had last been watered. He piled on all the other things she'd forgotten to do so that by the end of it, Maureen didn't know if she was coming or going. After we'd been there a good half hour, he told her that they'd talk about it later and she went off to sort out the tea.

This particular Sunday afternoon, they managed to frame themselves before they came back in with tea and biscuits. My dad's got a mate that works at *Foxes* so whenever anyone goes round they're treated to the luxury assortment. We were permitted for the final hour of my visit to talk about the caravan at Whitby. I accepted

224

an offer I didn't intend to take up to join them there in a few weekends' time. For my part, I invented some plans for the summer involving Greece or Turkey depending on which the kids fancied. On my way out he asked me when I'd next see him and I told him I wasn't sure, but it'd be soon.

He and Maureen stood at the gate and waved as I drove off. From the rear view mirror I watched her walk slowly round the house towards the back door. He stayed put and I wondered what they'd say to each other when he went back in.

It turned out, I didn't have to wonder for long on account of our Joanne phoning me later that night and telling me that my Dad had told Maureen to sling her hook. Maureen was beside herself according to Joanne and was staying with her for a couple of days until all this sorted itself out. She wanted to know if I could shed some light on what the fuck had gone off, what with me being the last person to see them together. I told her something which wasn't entirely untrue about him appearing to be his usual self. Our Joanne said she'd tried him on his landline and his mobile and they'd both gone straight to voicemail. She asked me – like I'd know – if he might've done summat daft. I told her that going 2 days over on his car tax was about as daft as my dad ever got.

- Well, Maureen says he's been in a funny mood for months and it was like you coming round tipped him over the edge.

She paused as she inhaled on her cigarette and took a sip of something – wine in all likelihood being our Joanne. I imagined Maureen stood next to her with her arms crossed, a snotty tissue clutched in her hand.

- Maybe Maureen should look closer to home. Maybe living with her for fuck knows how long has finally tipped him over the edge.

- Are you not bothered about any of this, Simon?

Which was a good question that got me thinking: maybe if I hadn't so much other stuff to be bothered about, this would have been of some concern to me. My Dad turfs his missus out and then he goes AWOL; it's the sort of thing that should have mattered. I wonder now –

because I've plenty of time to ruminate on these things - when and why I became so cold; what it is that's in me that made this possible. I look at myself and I shiver.

- Well, Simon? What are we gonna do? I can't have her stopping here forever. She's already doing my box in and she's only been here a couple of hours.

Presumably, Maureen had sloped off to another room by this time. I provided Joanne with the only précis of the situation that made any kind of sense to me.

- Listen, Joanne, he obviously doesn't want her anymore. It happens. People stop wanting people; they hold it down for a while and then finally it all comes on top. You decide you don't want to try and make it better; you just want it to stop. I don't know why he doesn't want her but presumably he'll tell her in his own good time. He'll say summat about growing apart – though to be honest I don't know how that'd hold any water in this case with them practically being joined at the hip – then life'll move on. She'll put it all behind her and start again.

- And in the meantime?

It was pretty bloody obvious what would have to happen in the meantime.

- In the meantime, you keep hold of her. Try and scrape her off the walls once she starts climbing them and I'll go find my Dad.

It wasn't difficult to find him on account of him not having gone anywhere.

14.

I don't know what it is that makes people do the things they do. If you were to ask Maxine, I reckon she'd talk about learned behaviour and socialisation and coping mechanisms. But it's not the sort of question I'm ever likely to ask Maxine so it's all speculation on my part. A lad I bumped into in Armley said that the past is gone and what you've to do is look forward and change your future. He'd done Enhanced Thinking Skills on a previous sentence and that was what had stuck with him; maybe he wasn't paying attention when they did the bit about strategies to avoid reoffending. D, when I asked him a while back why it is that people do apparently inexplicable things, said,

- Listen, mate, if I spent all my time thinking about why other people do what they do, I'd never get round to doing what I'm supposed to be doing.

Nine times out of ten, I think you'll find that when it comes to the things that really matter, people act on instinct and it's a matter of luck as to whether those instincts turn out to be trustworthy or not. Generally speaking, by the time you've realised summat's a bad idea it's too late to do anything about it and – if you're lucky – you get to spend the next however long patching up the chaos you've caused. It's a matter of dealing with the consequences of your actions but much of that's about fixing – or trying to cover up – what's gone before and trying to convince other people that they need to collaborate with you in this endeavour even if it's not in their best interests. If you're not so lucky, you find that your mistakes can't be rectified, forgotten or forgiven. One thing I do know is that you can plan as much as you like and things – people mainly – can still mess things up. That's my take on things, anyway.

Take Maxine, for example: what with one thing and another, her meticulous plans for my future went a bit awry. The idea – the one she'd unveiled to me the morning after my release - had been that she'd sell up and move into mine with the kids. I'd put her name back on the mortgage and then I'd get the hell out of there and leave them to get on with their lives (or rebuild their tattered lives as Maxine put it when she was in a particularly melodramatic frame of mind). She assured me that – being a sub standard father – the kids wouldn't miss me. For the record, I think she wrong on that one; kids miss their parents whether they're sub standard or not, but it's all academic now. In the meantime I was to keep all this to myself and carry on as if we were sorting out our differences. If we were in a film, it'd be called heightening the dramatic tension. I'd continue to draw some sort of income from the shop but to all intents and purposes I'd be transformed into a social pariah who'd fucked off and left a woman who'd stood by him through thick and thin. She'd get to be vindicated and I'd get to be punished. That was basically the nuts and bolts of the plan. I don't know how good she felt about it but once she'd hatched it the question of feeling good about anything was not one that overly concerned her. For my part, I was past caring. By the time she'd put her house on the market, I was just wanting it all to be over so that I could be somewhere I could cause no harm to anyone.

For a while I'd no idea where I was going to end up but I knew that wherever I went would be where I was supposed to be. Then, a couple of days before I'd been to see my dad I'd looked at a few rental properties in a grubby, insular hamlet which hangs off the edge of Leeds. There's a lad at work who's from there – though, tellingly, he doesn't live there anymore - and he's harmless enough. Also, I associated it with the airport and driving up there on a Sunday with my Mum and Dad when I was a kid. When I was little, the closest we got to air travel was looking at planes taking off and imagining what it might be like to be on one of them. We'd bags the planes – me and our

Joanne and our Sandra – and the first to take off was the winner. I got it into my head that if the worst came to the worst, living there I'd only be an hour or so from Amsterdam. I began to fancy myself as the kind of jet setting guy who'd pack an overnight bag and nip over to Amsterdam or Barcelona or Prague or Budapest on a whim and on my own. I'd come back on the Monday and people would say,

- What did you get up to over the weekend?

And I'd say I'd been here, there or wherever.

The first place I looked at was a Yorkshire stone terrace. The owners had done their best to make it look all right but to be honest it was pretty poor. There was a fully equipped kitchen I'd never use and the sort of living room our Joanne would aspire to with its oak floors and pale furniture. There was room in one of the alcoves for a TV and DVD player and my hifi would fit in the other. The lad who showed me round the place did his best to sell its location,

- You've a *Morrisons* on the High Street and there's a market on a Saturday. There's the odd do on at the Town Hall and then there's the leisure centre and the park. And, of course you're only a ten-minute drive into Leeds.

Its proximity to Leeds seemed to me to be the only positive thing you could say about the place but I tried to look like the sort of man who might be availing himself of its numerous other attractions. He must've been taught on his induction that you need to be making some sort of connection with customers so he asked,

- Why is it you're thinking of relocating here, Simon?
- I fancy a change.
- A slower pace of life?

I pretended I hadn't heard him and looked out of the window at what passed for a view. It was about 4ish so there was a clump of kids walking past. I heard one of them – a girl – say, don't fucking start. Then she swung her bag over her shoulder and walked ahead with another girl. The lad she'd sworn at turned to his mate and laughed, then the pair of them ran to catch up with the girls. I don't know what happened when they caught up with them because they were out of my sight by then. The lad who was tasked with flogging me this prime property joined me at the window like if we both looked hard enough we'd find something worth seeing. When we went back to his office to sort out the paperwork, he told me to wait a minute while he brought up the local website. He told me that it contained everything I'd need to know about the place. I fiddled about with it while he printed off contracts and credit check forms. It turned out that everything he'd told me earlier was all there was to say about the place. The site was full of online forums – local news, clubs and societies, events and the like - containing no postings. I closed the site and told him it looked very interesting. When we'd finished, I wandered round the high street where I felt like a new fangled idea that'd never catch on. I couldn't imagine ever feeling any connection to the place at all, which was when I knew that it'd be ideal for me.

To be honest, it was a relief for it to be all over. I thought about all the terse and angry conversations Maxine'd no longer have to have with me, and the idea of never having to see her sad and disbelieving face again felt a bit like peace. It wasn't like I didn't already know that I'd failed her pretty badly and that for too long she'd done what a lot of people do which is to keep on trying beyond the point when trying's going to make the slightest bit of difference. The thing they made out I'd done – which, the jury reckoned, I hadn't – was what stopped her trying in the end, so I suppose in that respect I did her a favour. I suspect that Eliz might disagree. The thing is, I know that Maxine knows that I did what they said I did. She wasn't like D and my dad and our Joanne and random acquaintances I bump into who might as well put their hands over their ears and say, I'm not listening. She decided – and there's bits of me that admire her for her stance – that it compromised her integrity to be involved with someone who could do what I did.

I'd been thinking about all this stuff and getting my head round being someone who lived in a shitty house in some backwater when our Joanne had rung, flapping about my Dad and Maureen. It was all just about beginning to hang together and to look something like a life that wouldn't kill me. I was pissed off by the time I got to my Dad's. Having sorted my life out, I'd been planning on spending the evening doing what I'd been doing for the past God knows how long, which was nothing mainly. I brayed on the door but there was no answer. The woman from next door popped her head out,

- I'm sure he's in, love. Maureen went out a couple of hours ago but she was on her own.

I could've told her that but I nodded like it was all news to me. Her husband came out to join her on the doorstep, like someone knocking on a door and not getting an immediate answer was the most exciting thing that had happened on his street for months.

- He sometimes goes to the club on a Sunday evening.
- Yeah, but they'd normally go together.

Basically, they managed to establish that he was either in or he was out which was something I could probably just about have worked out on my own. I thanked them for their help and they went back inside. I knew he was in the back room because I could make out the light of the TV through the blinds. In all likelihood, he'd have got himself rat arsed and sat himself down in front of whatever crap was on. It wasn't like it was the first time he'd gone off on one and sent Maureen packing. By the morning everything'd be sorted, she'd be back and we'd all be able to get on with pretending everything that'd happened hadn't happened. I liked to think that these minor explosions were summat to do with their obvious incompatibility but until this evening I'd always kept that little theory to myself. I let myself in because we've all got keys in case of unspecified emergencies. The pots from the tea he and Maureen had made were unwashed so I washed them and put them away and while I was at it I tried to work out what it was that I'd say to him when I went through into the back room. I called out to him but there was no answer. I hoped he'd be too out of it to have a sensible conversation and it'd just be a matter of persuading him to go up to bed and phoning our Joanne to let her know everything was sorted. It will have taken 5 minutes or so to sort out his kitchen. He wasn't in the room so he'd have gone off to bed.

And then he was there, looking terrible and nothing like me. I was out of myself then because I couldn't lift him and cut him down at the same time. I'm at next door's and I'm telling the lad he's to come round now so I pull him out from his beer and his DVD and his missus and I lift and he cuts. There's some memories from a First Aid course that come back to me and I can feel this lad I've never spoken to till tonight shivering behind me. He's looking scared and like he might throw up. He's saying fucking hell over and over again till I say to him,

- Will you fucking shut the fuck up?

He's still got the knife in his hand when the police and ambulance arrive. I've called the police and ambulance because it's an emergency which doesn't involve fire. My Dad's there on the floor and nothing like I remembered him because people don't look good when they've done that thing they've done to themselves. He's quite obviously beyond help but I'm on at the paramedics to do the things they do on the TV programmes. I can hear the woman from next door running up the stairs but maybe that was earlier because she'd followed us in straight away. My dad's on the floor and his trousers have slipped so I can see the top of his boxers and I never knew he wore boxers. They're from *Gap* and I'm wondering if he's got a mate who works in the *Gap* warehouse because he'd never spend that sort of money on underwear. There's grey curly hair above his waistband. And the world is as still as a photograph suddenly. They tell me things about him not being alive and what I need to do next; there are procedures to be followed and questions the coppers have to ask. The body – because that's what my Dad is called now – will need to be taken away and then a coroner will need to determine the cause of death. They seem themselves embarrassed. There's tea to be drunk and there's no hurry but the coppers and the ambulance crew seem to want to be out of there. Maybe they're wanting to be somewhere they can make a difference. The woman from next door – who turns out to be called Angela – tells her ashen husband to get next door and see to the kids while she does whatever else wants doing. The stairs are still and stable and I can sit there without falling but she walks me into the back room and sits me down in my Dad's chair. The TV news tells me the score of the match I'd watched earlier with him.

- Who d'you want me to ring, Simon, love?

The way she says my name it's like it doesn't belong to me and it takes me a moment to twig that this is a question only I have the answer to. I tell her that there's a phone book on the little table in the hall. You press the button with the initial letter of whoever it is you're wanting to phone and the book springs opens straight to that page. He's had it years and there's hardly any numbers in it. Next to the phone there's a wooden box with a picture of a telephone on it and the idea is that you put 20p in when you make a call. That way, the bill's pretty much paid by the time the bill arrives. And it's our Joanne she wants to be ringing. I spell out Joanne's name like there's half a dozen different ways of spelling her name but I struggle with her second name because she was married at one time and I don't know if she's kept that arsehole's name or reverted back to ours. My heart's like a bone that's broken except there's no fixing it.

It seems Joanne called D and Maxine and our Sandra. Angela waited with me while they arrived. She stood behind me and rubbed my shoulders like she knew me well. She said nothing at all. I lit a cigarette and watched it burn down without once touching my lips. Upstairs my Dad's body was doing whatever it is bodies do when they stop breathing. My face felt like it'd been out in the rain.

When D came in, he looked at the TV for a moment then he said,

- Can't someone turn that fucking thing off?

Angela turned it off and then she and D walked together to the back door; I imagine he must've been getting the low down on what had gone off because it took a while for him to come back into the room and when he did his face had set into an expression I'd not seen before. They reckon I was beside myself when they arrived and that me and Maureen did something they called holding on to each other. I'm not sure I'm having that. What I do know is that it felt a bit like a homecoming. It felt a bit like how when I came out of prison should have felt – without the stupid seven years sentence nonsense and putting Maxine on the spot the way we did. It felt authentic. If you were to ask Maxine, she'd tell you it gave her a glimpse into the bit of me that might be human because that's the way she talks about things. They'd tell you – the people that were there – that we sat in the back room till morning and that we cracked open a bottle of good whisky my dad had been saving for best and necked it. When we'd done that in, D phoned out for some more booze from some delivery service.

- He liked a drink, did your dad. This is what he'd have wanted.

I've no idea when D got to be such an authority on what my Dad wanted. They'd tell you that D was in bits and that he went on about how when he was being tret like shit at school – on account of being one of the few Asian lads there – it was my dad that stood up for him and helped him keep it all together. It turned out, he'd gone down to the school a couple of times and had a go at the teachers; told them he was gonna get on to the Education Authority unless they sorted it out. They'd tell you that when D's mum was on nights, my Dad'd make sure he had a proper tea and how he'd let D stop over most weekends. They'd tell you that Maureen was like a second mother to him.

I didn't say much because some situations just speak for themselves and there's nothing more to add that's going to illuminate anything. I had a tissue in my hand that got smaller and smaller as I tore strips off it. On the coffee table next to the chair where I was sat, there was the *Sunday Mirror* and it looked like he'd been halfway through it. He was funny, was my Dad. He had this ritual with the Sunday paper: he'd walk up to the newsagent and buy it on the morning but he wouldn't start reading it till late afternoon after he'd done all the things that wanted doing during the day. Sometimes, you'd ring him and Maureen would answer and she'd say,

- Your dad can't come to the phone. He's reading his paper.

He'd have read the sports pages first and then slowly and meticulously worked through from the front page. On this particular evening, he'd got to page 8 and then what? He folded it, put it on the coffee table and went upstairs to do that thing he'd been putting off? Fuck knows. My stomach felt like it was too full or too empty and when they'd been and taken the body away, I rushed past where he'd been and into the bathroom. I threw up everything I'd eaten and drunk. When I came back downstairs, I heard Linda whisper to Maxine,

- He's white as a sheet. It'll be the shock.

I remember our Sandra saying that she'd forgiven my dad years ago for the way he carried on when we were kids and how she wished she'd told him instead of just distancing herself and getting on with trying to make things better for herself and her kids. Her kids smiled at us from the chimney breast. She said that there was no point in holding on to bitterness; that it corrodes you and your relationships. I remember wondering where all of Sandra's words had come from; they flowed so easily that it was like she'd been storing them up for just such an occasion. Joanne's face was still and calm and it was only the tears she wiped away as if they were distracting her, that gave her away. As for Maureen, I mainly remember her looking stunned and useless.

Between then and the funeral, all the talk was of why he'd done what he'd done when he'd everything to live for. We were round at Maxine's one afternoon planning catering and hymns and our Joanne tried to convince us that it might have been a cry for help gone wrong but that didn't hold much water given his chosen method of self obliteration.

- Maybe if you'd gone straight upstairs, Simon, instead of seeing to the dishes…

- So, d'you think that was the cause of death, Joanne? Me washing the pots?

- I'm just saying…would the time you spent in the kitchen've made any difference?

- D'you want to test that little theory, Jo? Why don't I go into the kitchen and you nip upstairs?

That was tasteless, apparently. Somebody – it must've been Maxine – said that the pair of us should fucking grow up. Maureen picked at the samples Maxine had prepared and said the chicken was very nice but she wasn't so sure the crispy duck would go down that well. Joanne – who by now had grown up as instructed - said that last time she'd seen our dad, he'd promised to come up and see to her guttering on account of her chap's a waste of space when it comes to that sort of thing. Maureen said he'd been a bit down over the past few months what with one thing and another, but that he'd seemed to be pulling himself together. He'd been on tablets for his nerves apparently, which came as news to me but not to Maxine and Joanne.

- We'd been planning to go to Whitby. We'd booked extra days off each side of the bank holiday.

Nobody mentioned my Mum and the fact that our Joanne, our Sandra and me now had two parents who'd decided that we weren't worth living for. But then Maxine didn't know about all that and I was pretty certain my Dad wouldn't have told Maureen. I sat and listened and nodded and shrugged at their speculations. They all clearly wanted me to provide them with some answers; it was like I was some sort of expert witness on account of my proximity to events and I was supposed to verify or dismiss their various explanations. I finally said, because I thought it wanted saying, that we were none of us ever going to know why he did it and that we could pull ourselves apart trying but it wouldn't get us anywhere. I'd probably made my point by then, but it didn't stop me saying,

- The only person who's responsible for what he's done is himself.

It wanted saying out loud because the endless what ifs and whys were doing my box in. There was the note, of course, but the way I see it, it's inconclusive and it only raises more questions that'd keep people awake nights.

I've thought it through over and over and I know that to do what he did he can't have been thinking straight so whatever explanation he gave needs to be interpreted in that light. I've read up on the tablets he was taking and some people reckon they can make things worse rather than better. There's been times when they've all been beside themselves proposing this, that and the other explanation like they're suddenly full on forensic psychologists, and I've questioned whether I was right to keep the note to myself but it's too late now to be turning round to people and saying,

- I knew there was summat I forgot. There's this note he left.

I thought, with reading it just the once, that it might become a small inconsequential detail that I'd soon forget. It was short and he said the sorts of things you'd expect people to say under those circumstances: we weren't to blame ourselves; he was sorry for all the wrong things he'd done; and he'd ask us to forgive him but he couldn't forgive himself. He didn't specify what the wrong things were. They seemed to me to be thin words that hid more than they revealed, like he was making his life into some sort of mystery that we had to solve. But then, he never was one for talking, wasn't my Dad. You'd have thought that, at the end when there's nobody watching and what you have to say is gonna be the last thing you ever say, you'd maybe take the opportunity to rise above the limits you've placed on yourself; that you'd maybe think: well, this is my final act so I might as well tell it like it is. My dad was evasive to the end. Reading the note, no one but me would've known what it was that made him do what he did: that I'd dragged something out of him that wanted leaving where it was.

When we were kids and he'd had to write us a letter for school, he'd get one of us to check it over before he put it an envelope and when we'd said it was fine, he'd say,

- Not bad for a lad that left school at 14, eh?

His final letter was written on the proper writing paper he kept for the rare occasions when a formal letter was in order. He'd included a salutation – *To Whom it May Concern* – and signed it *Yours Truly, James*. Everyone called him Jim but I suppose he must have thought that with this being an official letter he should use his proper name. The *truly* was odd and out of character and it still bugs me; I know that he will've considered and rejected *faithfully* and *sincerely* and decided that for this, his final communication, truth was preferable to faith and sincerity. He'd used a fountain pen and the upward strokes were finer than the downward strokes, which is exactly as it should be. He'd written it in his usual neat, precise handwriting and he'd put the date at the top like we were ever likely to forget it. Beneath his swirly signature, he'd printed his name. His grammar was a bit out in places and he'd missed out the first *e* in forgiveness. I felt embarrassed for him. Each paragraph – there were only two – was indented. I imagine him, sat at what he called his bureau, composing it carefully and making sure it conformed to the etiquette associated with written correspondence. Then he'll have read it through a couple of times; he'll have assured himself that it was ok; that it didn't read like a letter written by a lad who'd left school with fuck all. Then he'll have folded it neatly and placed it in its matching envelope. The whole exercise will have taken some time because, being my Dad, he'll have drafted it first on a sheet of rough paper so's not to waste the good paper. I reckon he probably struggled over what to put on the envelope; in the end he decided on *To my family*, printed in red and underlined. And it's all that – the pointless fastidiousness of his penultimate act – that breaks me.

Maureen lives there now on her own and all of us and all of our kids make a pilgrimage on a weekend because everything's changed and we've all had to adapt. The house is exactly as he left it though I'm told she got the neighbours to clear out the loft and take his clothes to a charity shop. She's not got round to seeing to the hall and stairs and I've not mentioned it. The place is so neat and precise, it's like he's still there and like he was never there. Maureen's still at the dry cleaner's and it turns out the new owners are not as bad as she'd expected. They sent a wreath for the funeral which everyone agreed was a nice gesture considering it wasn't like they really knew him. She's kept the same shifts and there's some sort of productivity scheme in place which means she gets the odd bonus every now and again. Linda went in not long after Maureen went back to work because they had a 3 for 2 on and she said it was weird not having a little chat with my Dad. Maureen's toying with the idea of going to Tunisia with her cousin over Christmas and we've all told her it's a good idea; D's mum goes for a month every year and she reckons that even with the cost of flights and accommodation it's cheaper being there than being at home. The neighbours – the ones whose evening I ruined – have been a tower of strength apparently; always inviting her round for a cup of tea and popping round a couple of evenings a week

just to check on how she's doing. Sometimes, when there's no more trivia to talk about, she'll try and say summat which begins,
- It's a pity you lot weren't round so much when Jim was here. He would've liked it.
But there's no point dwelling on the past. It's gone and there's no changing it.

15.
   The shop's been expanded and relaunched. At our grand opening, we had an *Unbelievable Giveaway Offer*: the first 20 customers got a piece of tat that looked like it might do what it was supposed to do for a while; the first 50 got 25% off anything over £50; and the first 100 got a 15% off voucher redeemable against future purchases. In the end, it was an *Unfathomable Giveaway Offer* because no one was on top of the counting. One of the first customers collared a salesman and claimed to have been ripped off,
   - I want 25% off my TV / DVD unit.
   - But it was free.
   - That's not the point. You lot reckon it's got a retail value of £129.99 so that's £32.50 you owe me. Thankyou.
   He put his hand out and turned round to beam at his crew who stood smirking behind him.
   - It's 25% off a purchase over £50. You never purchased it; you were given it.
   That tells you as much as you need to know about the calibre of customers we attract. D and I walked over to calm the situation down. D relieved the lad of his free gift, threatened to twat him and told him to fuck off. We'd no trouble after that.
   The shop's got a new name which is so tasteless I can't bring myself to commit it to paper. Our biggest seller coming up to Christmas has been DVD players which should break down just after

their 12 month warranty expires. D's put up a sign above them. It says,
- *Cheap DVD's!!*

I wince whenever I walk past it. Most of my sales are online these days. Maxine's done some half - baked analysis on profit per square foot and, surprisingly, I've turned out to be the least profitable part of the business. It does all right, does the website, but to be honest it's a bit dispiriting dispatching orders to people I've never met. People can order owt and I don't get to have a say in whether it's the right solution for their audio and visual needs. Our Stephanie's finished college and she's reluctantly agreed to work at the shop provided she can be called Marketing and Promotions Manager. She gets to sit in what used to be my office and compose quarter page ads and advertorials for the YEP. She goes to networking events; it's important – she reckons – to make links with other businesses in order to encourage inter trading. She asked if she could have a company car and D told her that'd be fine provided the company logo featured prominently. She declined. A couple of months ago she got us to do a charity fundraiser for some helpline that sorts out depressed people. There was a raffle and collection tins by the till. The idea was that we'd double whatever our customers donated. Our customers are so tight that we had to way more than double their paltry donations to make it up to a respectable amount. Above the tills, there's a framed article from the YEP. I'm stood looking suitably grave holding a giant cheque for £2000. D's stood to one side of me shaking hands with a local councillor. Maxine and Stephanie stare blankly into the camera. Maureen wanted to be in the photo but each time we posed she broke down. The accompanying article's headlined, *Out of Personal Tragedy Comes Charitable Windfall*. In the article Stephanie talks about the importance of corporate social responsibility – which I suppose must be a term she learnt at one of her networking events - and she assures the YEP's readership that the charity fundraiser will be an annual event. She urged readers to nominate a charity; you'd be surprised at the number of deadbeat causes that have managed to acquire for themselves charitable status.

I think for Maxine it's been a case of be careful what you wish for when it comes to the shop. I reckon she envisaged something a bit more upmarket: something which would enable her to expand and enhance her business portfolio. She imagined that as a partner she'd have some sort of say in what it is we stock, but she didn't bank on D and his impulse purchases. She tried to set up regular Directors' meetings but D's not one for meetings. I could've told her all this had she thought my opinion was worth listening to. But the place is making good money and I suppose that should take the edge off things for her.

All the things that had to be done before my Dad died still needed doing afterwards. The estate agent started having a go at Maxine, saying that viewers' feedback had been less than positive.

- It's not that they don't like the house; it's just that you don't appear particularly enthusiastic or committed to the sale. Viewers detect that and they find it off putting.

She told me that she wanted me there when people came round to view the house; she reckoned it'd look better. If any of the potential buyers noticed a stilted atmosphere they were too polite to mention it. It was my job to answer the door while Maxine arranged herself with a book or a newspaper in the kitchen. As we walked round, Maxine invented anecdotes about when we decorated this or that room and I'd spin a line about how happy we'd been there and that if it wasn't for needing more room we wouldn't have been thinking of leaving. After a couple of gos we settled into our roles and I began to look forward to going round to hers and looking like the sort of husband she might've wanted years ago.

The purchasers were a couple with two girls. We were required for a few minutes to compare and contrast kids. Maxine pointed out a photo of the twins and the husband said,

- I bet they're a handful.

He did one of those jobs whose title could mean anything – Project Manager or Development Co ordinator – and she was a sports physiotherapist. When she'd said what she did she paused for a moment as if she was expecting one or the other of us to say something like that sounds interesting. She asked me about fixtures and fittings and he asked Maxine about schools and nurseries. They both took notes.

    - The girls'll be arguing about who gets this bedroom.

They were talking about the newly decorated twins' room with its lemon walls and candy-striped curtains. The duvet covers matched and they had the nerve to ask if Maxine was leaving them. When they'd gone, I said to her,

- You can tell them to fuck right off. Who do they think they are, hovering around the place like scavengers?

Maxine laughed. And it's the last time I can remember making her laugh.

The final time they visited before moving in, the wife told me I looked familiar and we had to go through that fruitless exercise where you name friends and acquaintances before finally inventing somewhere – in this case a gym we'd both briefly been members of – that we might possibly have come across each other before. He stood there with his arms crossed and when we'd finished he smiled and said,

    - Is there anyone you don't know, Sam?

When they'd gone Maxine said they seemed a nice couple. I said I'd give them 5 years before one or the other of them was consulting a divorce lawyer.

My drama's been put on the back burner to make way for the new drama my dad's left us and sometimes it feels like everything I've done I haven't done at all. People want you to be one thing or the other I find: either I'm the sick bastard accused of raping some girl young enough to be my daughter or I'm this poor guy who's found his dead Dad hanging from the top banister. For most people, it's like my Dad's final dramatic act has wiped out all that preceded it. They keep telling me how awful it must have been for me and that if there's anything they can do I've only to ask. Leaving me the fuck alone would be a start. Even Mr and Mrs Neighbourhood Watch crept round to the house under cover of darkness and posted a card through the letterbox.

Tony's poisonous missus accompanied him when he came round with his cans and condolences. There was a mildly embarrassing moment when it became apparent that I didn't know her name. She grinned and introduced herself,

- I'm Sally hyphen Anne with an e.

Like I might be needing to write her name down sometime soon. She was particularly interested in the gruesome details of my plight.

- So, there was no pulse then, nothing?

She helpfully indicated where I might have checked for a pulse and shook her head grimly,

- I just can't begin to imagine what it must have felt like for you, Simon.

Which, I assume, is where I could've described to her precisely what it felt like. Instead I put on a face which said, I'm still overcome by it all, and shook my head.

- We met your Dad once, didn't we, Tony? He was seeing to your hedge a couple of summers ago. He seemed like a lovely man. You'd never think, would you? At least you've got support. You're not alone.

She smiled sadly. By support she was referring to Maxine who, as we spoke, was refilling cups and offering them something stronger if they fancied it. Tony pointed at his cans and his hyphenated wife sipped a glass of very good bourbon. She sighed and placed her hand on mine.

- If it's any comfort, Simon, you have our heartfelt sympathy.

It wasn't any comfort but I told her it was. Truth is, if there was anyone they should've been sympathising with, it was Maxine because what all this had meant for her was that she found herself in a position where, if she'd have gone through with turfing me out of the house, she'd have been the one that ended up looking cold and heartless. I suppose that once the funeral was over and once I'd started firing on all cylinders again I could've taken things into my own hands and left, anyway. I could've told Maxine that all this had got me thinking and I'd decided I needed to be on my own for a while to sort my head out. I could've told her that I hadn't forgotten what I'd put her and the kids through and that I still felt bad about it. I think that's what she hoped I'd do.

So, she and the kids are back here with me. Everything had gathered its own momentum by the time the house was sold and it wasn't like she had a choice. She put all the photographs back on the walls I'd removed them from and gave the place a good going over. She said the house looked like a squat and that there was no way she was having her kids living in squalor. She got Linda in to give her a hand. She loved it, did Linda, tutting round the house being efficient and superior,

- I don't know – bloody men. They can't be left alone for five minutes. What's that James Brown song, Max, about how shit men are without women?

She remembered it and started singing it. They were at it the whole weekend before they were satisfied the place was fit for human habitation.

On the Saturday night, D and me went out on the lash. It was his son's annual football dinner and D had agreed that we'd sponsor the club's strip for the following season.

- D'you reckon, Simon, that seeing as how we're major sponsors that'll give us a say in tactics and all that?

Other than a sentimental and instinctive devotion to Leeds United, D knows nothing about football. I told him I reckoned it was down to the manager to look after the day-to-day operations.

- But what about starting line ups and all that? Our Damian's not started for the past three games. What's all that about?

What it turned out to be all about – according to the manager – was Damian's poor disciplinary record. D let it be known that as far as he was concerned football's a man's game and that instead of turning the team into a bunch of shrinking violets he should be encouraging aggression and determination. Damian sloped off to join his mates at a far corner of the room.

The bar at the social club was poorly stocked but that didn't matter too much since we'd taken the precaution of travelling with hip flasks. We've been doing that since we were teenagers when it was a matter of stretching cash. It's a matter of principle now. A mate of ours – Lardy – was there; he's the assistant manager of the club which basically means he gets to be a linesman most Sundays. He's big built, is Lardy, and the odd time I've seen him plodding up and down the line he's not looked so comfortable.

- Now then, Lardy. Long time no see, man.

There was a millisecond's hesitation before he extended his hand. It's summat I'm used to these days and it's a matter of guessing whether it's to do with the charge or my Dad. Normally, people pretend it's neither and we end up having a short and awkward conversation about trivia. To give him his due, Lardy was straight in there,

- Good to see you, Si. You've had a rough old time, I hear.
- I've had better years, fella.
- I was sorry to hear about that business a few months back – and then your Dad.

He exhaled, stuck his hands in his jacket pockets and leant to one side. I think he was maybe trying to indicate what it's like to be knocked sideways by unexpected events.

- You know what it's like, Lardy. We've all got our crosses to bear. You've got to take the rough with the smooth…roll with the punches and all that.

D stood on alert to my side, ready to go into combat mode if Lardy started pushing his luck. Lardy leant in towards me,

- You know that lass they said you…

He struggled for the appropriate word like it was on the tip of his tongue but it'd eluded him for a moment. D stepped in.

- Now then, mate. We don't need to be getting into all that.
- Just let me talk my talk, D.

He looked like a man who was going to say what he had to say – and he's a big lad is Lardy. He was cock of the school right the way through high school and though that's 20 years ago now it still counts for summat. Last time I'd seen him at a match he'd been sent off after 20 minutes for running across the pitch and squaring up to the referee over a dubious free kick. It's unusual for a linesman to be sent off. I quickly ran through all the worst things he could say and concluded that it couldn't be any worse than what anyone else'd already said to or about me. I reminded myself that I was not guilty.

- What it is, right, our lass used to work with her...
- And what? Is it like open season on Si all of a sudden? It's like suddenly people forget about your fundamental judicial concepts like due process and double jeopardy. The man's fucking not guilty. You can tell your ...

I sensed that D might be working up to saying something Lardy might find it hard to forgive – something to do with his missus, perhaps. I interjected,

- What is it, Lardy?
- Like I said, our lass used to work with her. Not the same department, like. I think that Elizabeth was summat in Business Development and our lass has always been on admin with Human Resources or whatever the fuck they call it. She was only on a temporary contract was this Elizabeth; apparently she was saving up to go travelling. It's what they all do these days: bloody travelling and gap years and all that...

D was like a dog straining on a tight leash,

- We're not after her CV, Lardy. Are you gonna come out and say what it is you're gonna say or fucking what?

- Are you gonna shut the fuck up and let me continue or fucking what?

For a moment it was like I wasn't there because we were pursuing a different agenda now which was to do with posturing and backing down or not backing down. D's daft but he's not stupid.

- All right, man. I was just saying...
- Well, the due process in conversations is to let a man say what he's got to say. Have you got a problem with that? Mate.

I had a serious problem with trying to work out where this was all going to end up.

- Listen, Lardy, just say what you've gotta say. I know exactly what went off that night and I also know that I'm not guilty, so there's nothing you or anyone else can say that can change that.

I reached into my pocket for a cigarette. I offered Lardy one, the idea being that the few seconds it took for him to light up might serve to defuse the situation. He took one,

- Cheers. Where was I? That's right; what I was gonna say was that our lass was sat reading *The Mirror* – you know the day after the verdict when she'd give that press conference or whatever – and she just put down the paper and said, poor fucking bastard; he had a lucky escape. She said, your mate should've steered clear of a girl like that cause you never know when they're gonna turn and start making wild accusations.

Neither D nor I had been expecting this so we fixed our faces and looked interested and expectant.

- Our lass reckons that Elizabeth one's a right slapper. You know, they go on these work dos? Well, she always ends the night sucking the face of some guy. There's hardly a lad in her department that's not had her according to our lass. Vermin, that's what our lass called her. Vermin.

It seemed D and Lardy were back on the same side. It seemed that Lardy was entitled to a finger of brandy from D's flask. They shook hands gravely,

- Now, if you'd made that clear from the outset Lardy, man, we could've avoided all that unpleasantness. It's just most fucking twats you come across are wanting to have a pop, so that's why I might've appeared a bit less than civil about the whole thing. You know what people are like: they know fuck all about a situation but they think they're entitled to stick their oar in like suddenly the verdict of a jury of your peers isn't good enough for them. So what I've done in this situation is I've thought that you…

He pointed at Lardy to make it clear whom he was referring to,

-…are gonna go off on one. It's like your Pavlov's dogs scenario…

I was pretty certain that Lardy didn't know much about Pavlov's dogs and the summary D gave was not the best,

- Anyway, the point I'm making is that I misjudged you on the basis of my prior experience. And for that I apologise. Unreservedly.

There followed a prolonged period of male bonding. There were old times that wanted reliving; some legendary fight between our fifth form and the fifth form at a neighbouring school was of particular significance in illustrating the importance of loyalty. Then there were women and how you had to be on your guard constantly, and the value of friendships; you can have precious little contact with someone for fucking years but there's still that bond. It was my job to nod and say, yeah you're too right, from time to time. Then it was my job to go the bar and buy the pair of them treble brandies just so's it was clear how much I valued their support.

Truth is, I felt sickened and compromised by the whole thing. What Lardy or his missus had said might not be untrue but it wasn't the truth either. I know what went off that night and thinking about it turns my stomach.

Once Linda and Maxine had finished with their cleaning the kids slotted back into their rooms like they'd never left them. Stephanie wants a corner of her room turning into a shower room, which is fine by me. She's already got a microwave, TV and hi fi up there so, chances are, once a shower's installed we'll see next to nothing of her. She's highly strung, is Stephanie, and she's got a habit of throwing the house into chaos with her carrying on about everything and nothing at all. Our Ben's wired into his MP3 player the whole time so there's not much in the way of communication with him. He's sorted out broadband again and he's set up a wireless network which connects us all to each other. The twins have started at the school up the road and from what I can gather, they seem to be doing fine. The house has become a noisy place where people other than me leave things lying around all over the place and everyday someone loses something. Whenever something's lost it's someone else's fault and the house quivers with low level bickering the whole

time. Maxine says the sort of things you only say when you share a house with a bunch of kids; things like,
- If I've told you once I've told you a thousand times…

16.

So she was sat there, was Maxine, with her head still in her book, licking her finger as she turned a page. My phone was vibrating again and I knew I really needed to be getting off this time. I was about to say goodbye when she looked at me and smirked.

- Someone waiting, Simon?

I picked my jacket up off the back of the kitchen chair and started to put it on. This was clearly one of those things I was just going to have to rise above.

- How old is she – this one? You want to be careful.

She sniggered and held my eyes coldly. I felt disarmed and uncomfortable. I had thought that with the passage of time and with the inevitability of our new situation, she'd given up on these little digs. She'd probably forgotten that I can give as good as I get.

- I imagine she'll be about the same age Joe was when you were fucking him.

She was utterly still for a moment and I took the opportunity to pick up my nutritionally balanced meal and throw it – and its plate - into the bin. She closed her book, folding over the edge of her page first so she wouldn't lose her thread. I can't count the number of times over the years that I've told her to get a bookmark but she's never been interested. Books, she reckons, are for reading not preserving.

- You can always be relied upon for the grand gesture, can't you, Simon?

I'd tired of all this by now and I zipped up my jacket. As I approached the back door, she said,

- You were wrong, by the way, about Joe.

I didn't even bother turning round because the last thing I needed to do was to get into a barney about what did or didn't happen years ago.

- It was Devdas.

For a moment I had no idea what she was on about. It felt like a name she'd made up. I look back on the pause before I repeated his name like it was the last fresh, clean second in the world and I wish I could live in it forever.

- Devdas?

Nobody but his missus calls him by that name. At school there was a brief phase – when he was trying to fit in or to pretend that he wasn't who or what he was – when he demanded that we call him Dave but by the time we were 13 or so he'd become D and that's who he's been ever since.

My mobile continued to vibrate with texts and entreaties and I wanted to throw it against the wall so I did. It left a chip in the tiling which'll want fixing but won't get fixed.

- It started back when you were running *Something Tech* so I suppose your timescales were right. But back then it was nothing, really, just something to do to relieve the tedium.

- Tedium? We were fucking loaded. How can that be tedious? And even if it was, how does it explain anything?

I maybe wasn't as coherent as that but it's what I meant to say. I was crying like they said I did after that business with my dad and maybe a bit like those women in Rwanda.

- It was tedious, Simon. We didn't really deserve anything that we had so it all seemed a bit unreal. Like it was going to disappear at any moment – which it did, didn't it? So it was like anything that happened during that time didn't really matter. And because we could do anything we fancied everything became dull. You know, I've clothes I bought back then that I've never worn.

She got a cloth from beside the sink and wiped the bin where some of my dinner had splattered. She sprayed the cloth with an anti bacterial spray, rinsed it and draped it over the taps. Then she washed her own hands and dried them with kitchen towel. There was a bottle of sparkling Pinot Grigio in the fridge (I'd bought it from the list she'd given me) and she opened it carefully and poured herself a glass. She didn't hand me a glass which was just as well because I would've been doing something other than drinking from it.

- He was never gonna tell you, was he? He made it my secret. I left you in the end because I didn't feel like I could live with you and keep it any longer. If it's any consolation, I don't think he struggled with it and I don't think it meant a whole lot to him. I think it worked for him because I was someone he could always come back to when which ever of his squeezes was putting the squeeze on him.

She actually laughed at this point.

- For all your pie charts and graphs, Si, you could learn a lot from D. He's a very logical, rational man and he's absolutely focused on getting what it is he wants. He puts people into boxes and he keeps all his boxes separate. There's no leakage. So he never mentioned you once while it was all going off. Even when it kicked off again – when you were banged up – and it was obvious that the only reason it was happening again was because you weren't here and because he saw an opportunity to muscle in on the business, he never once mentioned you or your absence. In fairness, I didn't either. Except obliquely when he suggested the shop expansion – which he referred to as an insurance policy just in case things went tits up (his phrase, naturally) - it was like you didn't exist.

It was *The Great Gatsby* that she was reading. I know for a fact that she's read it a dozen times before and I've asked her why it is she needs to go on re reading it. It's not like the ending's ever going to change. She says that there are nuances that you miss or rediscover and I suppose that explains why it's full of underlined text. Maybe if she put together all those nuances and bound them, it'd tell her all it is she needs to know.

- I've known D longer than I've known anyone.

- Your Dad knew. He never said anything but I knew he knew. Once – we were at the kitchen table – and I leant over to pick a bit of fluff off D's jacket and your Dad just looked at me and he knew then. It's these small things which give the game away, Simon.

She picked up the bits of my mobile and placed them in a neat pile next to her book. The screen was cracked.

  - I knew he wouldn't say a word because he'd so much to hide himself. He was a closed man, your Dad. D worshipped him, you know, and your Dad had a lot of time for D. So maybe he was torn…divided loyalties, I suppose. It was a scary and confusing time.

When someone's talking and talking at you there are only so many things you can do: you can shut them up; you can hot tail it to that girl's house and hide yourself in her; or you can just wait till whoever's talking (Maxine in this case) has finished talking and see how it feels then. See if it kills you.

I've not known D longer than I've known anyone; I've known my sisters longer and my Dad. But I've talked to him pretty much everyday for nearly 30 years. When I bump into mutual acquaintances they always ask after him and I'll say summat like you know what D's like or he's safe or I'll tell him you asked after him. And then next time I see him I'll tell him who it is I've bumped into and nine times out of ten he'll say he's a fucking arsehole, that one – you want to watch out for him. Like he did about Joe at about the time he was fucking Maxine.

My mobile had stopped vibrating by this time for obvious reasons and there was nothing to distract me from Maxine's voice.

- I didn't know how I'd feel about the verdict but on the day – a Monday it was, the kids were back at school – I suddenly knew that I wanted you back. It was like a new planet I'd discovered. And that's what I told D. I told him that whatever happened at court it was all over and done between us. I suppose that's why he concocted that elaborate scene. Seven years. Just to see where my head was at and if I meant what I'd said. It wasn't like I hadn't said it before. To be honest, I don't think he was that concerned about losing me – not really. He just didn't like the idea of not being the one in control. And it'll be why *The Mirror* turned up on the doormat the following morning. There'd been this pact – between your Dad and D – that I'd be spared all the news coverage and it worked for me because it meant that I had permission to pretend it wasn't happening, that you hadn't done what they said you did. That if all those months on remand were a punishment they were my punishment for what happened with D. Somehow that made some sort of sense to me.

And it was her turn to cry then. Soundlessly. Just tears striping her face and no attempt to stop them.

- But you did do it, Si, didn't you? And now I don't know where the truth lies. I used to think I had some sort of moral compass. I used to think that I would know what the right thing was to do. But I didn't count on you raping someone.

- And I didn't count on you fucking D.

I got up from the table again but – standing up – I found that I had nowhere to go. The CD had stuck and there were just the same couple of bars playing over and over again. I pulled the plug out from the wall.

- What you did and what I did are not morally equivalent, Simon.

There was nothing I could say in response and there was still nowhere to go. I needed to feel a more familiar pain. She grabbed my arm and said,

- What the fuck?

There was blood smeared on the chipped tile where I'd banged my head against it. But at least the blood was my blood.

She dampened a piece of kitchen towel and handed it to me. She could – I suppose – have dabbed my forehead herself but it's those small things that give the game away.